An Impossible Promise

A WWII Survival Novel

A

T. Lynne Jackson Novel

Reecer Creek Publishing
Ellensburg, Washington

ISBN: 978-0-9660761-9-6

www.reecercreekpublishing.com

DEDICATION

To music teachers.

ACKNOWLEDGMENTS

An Impossible Promise is a work of fiction. Names, characters, places, and incidents are products of the author's imagination. Any resemblance to actual events, locales, organizations, or persons, living or dead, is entirely coincidental.

Special thankyous to:
Jim and Diane at Reecer Creek Publishing
Editor Dori Harrell
Violinist and teacher Barbara Riley
Gretchin Kingston and Zander Kingston for their support
of this book

CHAPTER 1

Even the teacher has it in for me, Jodi's inner voice grumbled. She peered over her music stand, from the back row of the second violin section, at Mr. Johnston's hardened face and glaring eyes.

"Jodi, this is the third time you've missed the B-flat in this phrase," the haggard conductor barked, his squeaky conductor's stool echoing his displeasure. "Please practice it tonight so that you get it right tomorrow. And stay on top of the beat. You're dragging."

Ignoring Kristen's and Julie's snickers in the front row, the stooped, graying conductor, donned in his trademark brown sweater vest and wire-rimmed spectacles, tapped the conductor's stand with his baton, and sighed. "Okay, orchestra, let's start again from letter B."

After faking her way through the remainder of the rehearsal, Jodi packed her scuffed-up violin into the battered case, thankful that it was her last class and she could escape the rowdy students and overbearing teachers who crowded the drab hallways of Sage Grove Junior High School. How she longed for the summer break, which

1

although only a week away, seemed light years into the future.

She gathered her homework from her dented hallway locker, gave the combination lock a spin, and bolted out the side door and down the half dozen steps toward her shortcut through the faculty parking lot, where she almost ran into Kristen, who, as the most popular girl in school, had attracted a large crowd. "B-flat, B-flat, Jodi," Kristen chanted to an improvised tune. "Jodi can't play a simple B-flat. Oh!" She raised a hand to her cheek in feigned astonishment. "I guess that's because she *is* flat. Ha-ha-ha."

The leers of the other chuckling kids migrated to Jodi's undeveloped chest. Her cheeks burned, and her lower lip trembled as she stifled the tears that threatened to spew from her dampening eyes. Behind the teasing students, Mr. Johnston hobbled down the steps, grinning as he hustled to his car, pretending not to notice the taunt.

Jodi spun and darted through the parking lot in the opposite direction of her normal walk home. Backpack slung over her shoulder and violin case swinging at her side, she ran, gasping for fresh oxygen to propel her as far from her nemesis as possible.

With searing lungs and pudding legs unable to carry her farther, she crumbled to the curb of the potholed street in the tired working-class neighborhood. She wrapped her arms around her shins and stared at her frayed Converse sneakers, barely aware of the menacing clouds over the high desert of the Southern Idaho Snake River Plain. "One more week," she muttered. "How am I going to make it through one more week?"

As she wiped an escaped tear with the back of her hand, she heard music drifting from behind her. She sat in the stillness, absorbing the sweet sound of a violin. She rose and pivoted and stared at the small house. A tender melody floated from behind the peeling siding, a flicker of beauty sifting through the tangled web of humiliation and despair that strangled her soul. Her hand inched toward the gate of the warped picket fence that surrounded the overgrown yard. Her rational inner voice warned her away, but an invisible current lured her through the creaky gate toward the music. She stood just feet from the porch, mesmerized by the enchanting melody.

Then the tune stopped mid-phase. "Who's out there?" a grizzled voice shouted as the door flung open.

Jodi wanted to run, but her feet felt wedged to the crumbling walkway.

"Quit bothering me, or I'll call the . . ." The old man stopped midsentence as he squinted at Jodi as she stood with slumped shoulders and eyes wide with fear.

"I . . . I . . . I'm sorry. I just heard the music and . . . I'm sorry." As she backed away, her heel caught on the jagged walkway, and she tumbled to the pavement.

The frail man wobbled down the step and held out a hand to her.

Jodi grasped his hand and scrambled to her feet, then brushed the dust from her faded jeans. "I'm sorry. I didn't mean to bother you." She retrieved the violin from the sidewalk.

"You play the violin?" He eyed the battered case in her hand.

"Not really."

"You just carry one around?"

"Well, no. I play at school, but I'm really terrible."

CRACK! The ominous thundercloud that darkened the midafternoon sky let out a frightening roar. Wind gusts thrashed the trees, flinging leaves and twigs through the dusty air. Icy, marbled hail pounded the ground.

"Quick, get inside," the man shouted. "Hurry!"

Jodi rushed after the shuffling old man to the safety of the weary house, where he shut out the storm behind the creaky door.

Unlike the neglected yard, the cozy living room was well kept. The furniture, though well used, was arranged to form a tight rectangle, with a brick fireplace as the centerpiece. Bookshelves lined the far wall, and a thin light slithered through a gap in the faded curtains.

Never enter a stranger's house! Her mother's warning loomed in the back of her mind. But nothing about the fragile, elderly man appeared threatening.

"I was just going to make some coffee. Might help ward off the chill from the storm," he said as he shuffled toward the kitchen, his frayed slippers sliding along the oak floor. Jodi hovered by the front door.

"Well, come on. I'm not going to bite."

She followed him through the living room and stopped at the archway to the kitchen. A few appliances, including a Mr. Coffee drip coffeemaker that the old man hovered over, rested on yellow countertops. Chips and stains speckled the checkered linoleum floor, and faded, flowered curtains fluttered over the open window above the sink. She leaned against the doorframe, her palm gripped around the handle of her violin case and eyed the small oak dinette table and three matching chairs. She wondered what happened to the fourth chair. She decided not to sit.

"What is your name, young lady?" he asked while dumping the stale coffee grinds into a trash can under the sink.

"Jodi."

"Pleased to make your acquaintance, Jodi. My name is Michael Kaszubinski."

"It's nice to meet you, Mr., uh, Kasz . . . uh."

"Call me Michael."

"Okay, ah, Michael." Jodi tried to place the faint accent that colored his graveled voice.

"So you are a fledgling violin player." He reached into a cabinet and grabbed a red can of Folgers.

"I moved here to Idaho after school started last fall and got stuck in the orchestra since all the other elective classes were full. And this crappy violin"—she raised the beat-up case—"was the only school instrument available."

His hand quivered as he tilted a pitcher of water over the coffeemaker. "But you like Brahms."

"Who?"

"Brahms. Johannes Brahms. I was playing Brahms's 'First Violin Sonata.'" He shook his head. "Young people. Don't know good music."

"It was very nice. That's why I stopped, to listen. Will you play some more? I've just never heard anything like it before."

"Dear Lord! Come and listen to one of the greatest violin sonatas ever written."

She followed him back to the living room, where he retrieved his violin from the coffee table. "Please have a seat." He nodded to the overstuffed chair facing the fireplace and then nestled the instrument under his chin.

Jodi was mesmerized by the beautiful melody, amazed that the frail man with the shaky hands could be so nimble and steady on the strings. His mop of white hair shook with the rhythm of the stroking bow. The warm vibrato, the soaring high notes, the dexterity of his wrinkled fingers as they massaged the strings. She had never heard of *Brahms*. The soulful tone the old man coaxed from the violin warmed her from the inside, like a steaming cup of hot chocolate on a frigid winter morning. Her favorite.

She leaned her head back, folded her arms over her chest, and closed her eyes, the roaring thunder and hammering hail, along with Kristen's degrading taunts, a mere murmur in the background. A whiff of brewing coffee drifted from the kitchen.

"That was beautiful," she said when he stopped playing.

"You must hear it with the piano. Let me play you the phonograph while I pour the coffee." He hobbled to the corner and placed a vinyl record on an old-fashioned turntable and lowered the needle. "Isaac Stern, one of the best recordings of the Brahms, in my humble opinion."

The old man shuffled back to the kitchen as Jodi listened to the scratchy record. Her eyes wandered to the photographs decorating the mantel.

"I suppose you're too young to drink coffee," he shouted from the kitchen. "How about a cup of warm milk?"

"I drink coffee," she replied.

The old man returned from the kitchen with two cups of steaming coffee. "I hope you like it with milk and sugar." He handed a cup to Jodi.

She pointed to a photograph on the mantel with her other hand. "Is this your wife?"

"Yes. That is my lovely bride and lifelong companion. She passed last fall after a long illness." He sighed, set down his mug, and lifted the frame from the mantel and brushed her image with his wrinkled finger. "My soul died with her, and I grieve for her every moment."

Like the aromatic coffee, Jodi could almost sense his sadness filter through the tiny house. "I'm sorry. She was very beautiful."

"Yes, she was the most beautiful woman I've ever laid eyes on. My whole reason for being, and I wouldn't be here today if it weren't for her."

"How'd you meet her?"

"It's a long story. We were young. I had just turned fourteen."

"I'm almost fourteen," Jodi interrupted, wishing she hadn't. But she could tell his mind, as if hypnotized, was drifting to another realm.

He replaced the photograph and eased onto the sofa and began his story . . .

CHAPTER 2

It was spring 1943. A blustery day. I was home from boarding school for Easter break. It was also my birthday, so I was expecting a special day. My father owned a steel factory in Warsaw, Poland, but the Nazis commandeered it after they invaded the city in thirty-nine. They recommissioned the factory to make chassis for their jeeps and tanks, rails for the miles of track they were laying to transport their massive armies, and siding for the numerous boxcars they were adding to their rail fleet. Because a trickle of German blood ran through my father's veins, his mother was part German, he was permitted to join the party and, as an incentive for his patriotism, allowed to run the factory. Of course, the Nazis would never admit that they needed his expertise to keep the facility operating at peak capacity. All the Jews in the region, including the many who worked in the plant, were relocated to the ghetto, the slums of the city, and marched at gunpoint each day to work long, grueling hours as slave labor for the German war effort.

That Easter Sunday afternoon I accompanied my father to the factory, where he had to take care of some tasks. He hovered over a flutter of papers that cluttered his metal desk. A contrail of smoke drifted from the nub of a cigarette smoldering in an ashtray near his hand. I sat on the floor in the windowless office, leaning against a gray file cabinet, struggling to solve a math equation. I often felt guilty doing schoolwork. The Nazis had closed all the secondary schools and either executed or deported most of the teachers, as they did not want the Polish people to have an education. However, the previous year my boarding school reopened clandestinely, and my father insisted I return to continue my engineering studies.

A soft tap on the door drew me away from the equation. The knock signified that it was not one of the German "supervisors," as they just barged in and barked their orders as if they owned the place, which of course, they now did.

"Come in," my father said without lifting his eyes from his papers.

The door creaked open, and a stooped, bearded man shuffled in, holding the hand of a frail dark-haired girl. Both wore the mandatory armband depicting the Star of David, which identified them as Jews. I was shocked when I realized this shriveled man was my father's assistant, Mr. Bujak. His shabby clothes dangled from his emaciated frame. His long beard was mostly gray and looked like it might drift from his sunken cheeks at the slightest breeze. The girl didn't fare any better. Her clothes were tattered and ill fitting, her matted, lice-infested hair hung uncombed at her shoulders, and her puffy lips were chapped and peeling. But I was spellbound by those chocolate-colored eyes. Guilt ridden because of my privileged position, I cast my gaze to the floor. I knew the Nazis had slashed the daily calorie allotment for Jews far more than other Poles, but I was sickened to see this captivating girl in such a state.

I couldn't stop myself though—my eyes rebounded to the gaunt girl.

"What can I do for you, Mr. Bujak?" my father asked, still studying his papers.

I presumed that my father did not want to acknowledge his assistant's condition.

"I am sorry, sir," Mr. Bujak responded. "I won't take much of your time."

"What is it then?" My father finally raised his head. "You look troubled."

The girl noticed me watching her and lowered her eyes. Then she looked at me again and blushed. It was rude to stare, but I couldn't help it. I was smitten.

"I am sorry, sir, but I must tender my resignation," the assistant responded. "All exemptions for Jews to work have been revoked by the Germans, and we must be ready for resettlement by next week."

"What! You have an important job. The Germans rely on our production to support their war effort. They permitted you to stay because of your expertise. How am I going to get by without you?"

"I am sorry, sir. We have no choice. I expect that all the Jewish workers received a similar notice. You will have to find another assistant until we are allowed to return."

The girl glanced at me one last time as my father moved from behind his desk and shook his assistant's hand and wished him well. Then they were gone.

That evening at supper, my mother, father, and I were seated at the formal dining table, waiting for my older brother, Jakub, to arrive. The cook and maid stood at attention, waiting to serve the soup. My father raised his hand, about to order the staff to remove the empty place setting, when my pompous sibling, dressed in the brown shirt of the Nazi Youth Organization, hustled in and slid into his seat across from me.

"Go and change your clothes," my mother demanded.

"Why?" my snide brother responded. "We are all Germans now. The führer will expect that we show our support for the party."

"Go put on a proper jacket and tie for dinner," my irritated father demanded. "We can be Nazis outside the house, but inside we will act and dress like civilized gentlemen."

I could tell my father was careful in his choice of words, as the risk of reprisals could be severe if any of the household staff suspected that any one of us were not loyal to the party.

When my brother returned to the table, his Nazi shirt concealed beneath a dinner blazer and tie, the maid and the cook served the soup. I tried to muster the nerve to ask my father about the girl. I bit my lip as I watched him pick up the proper spoon, dip it into his bowl, lift it to his lips, and blow a cooling breath on what he expected to be hot soup.

"Johnas," he shouted, and the cook scurried from the kitchen. "The soup is cold. Please warm it straight away."

"Yes, sir. I am so sorry, sir." The cook, head bowed, scooped up my father's bowl. "I will warm yours as well, ma'am." He scrambled to the other end of the table and reached for my mother's bowl.

"My soup is fine, Johnas." My mother held up a polite hand and waved the cook off.

The maid reached over my shoulder to take my soup, but I covered my bowl with my hand. "My soup is fine also. Excellent in fact." I took another sip of the watery bisque. The soup had been much thinner since the Germans invaded Poland and rationed the citizens' food, even though my father's position afforded us higher allotments than most Polish families.

"My soup is cold too," snipped my brother. "Take it back as well." Jakub hadn't even tried his. He always emulated my father.

After the soup dishes were cleared and we indulged on the main course of roast goose and potatoes, a special treat for the holiday, I washed down a bite with a gulp of water and blurted, "Was that Mr. Bujak's daughter this afternoon? What's her name?"

"Oh, was Mr. Bujak working today?" my mother asked. "You didn't make him work on Easter, did you, dear?"

"Jews don't celebrate Easter, darling. And I no longer dictate work schedules. The Nazis work the laborers seven days a week, fourteen, sometimes sixteen hours a day. Another one collapsed today just as the shift was ending," My father shook his head. "Mr. Bujak stopped by the office to inform me that he has received resettlement orders from the Nazis and that I am going to have to find another assistant." He returned his gaze to his plate. "And I do not know her name." He skewered a bite of fowl with his fork.

I thought it odd that my father did not know the name of his assistant's daughter.

"Michal's got a crush on a Jew girl," Jakub teased. My brother's teasing was relentless.

Heat seeped into my pale cheeks. "How can I have a crush on someone I haven't even met properly, dodo. I was just asking her name."

"Be nice to your brother, Jakub." My mother was always the peacemaker. "So what are you going to do, Wiktor, about Mr. Bujak? Can't you help him? After everything he's done for you? How are you going to get along without him?"

"There is nothing I can do. I will have to find another assistant. I have many workers, and I'm sure I can find one who can do the job. Although with the Nazis resettling all the Jews and conscripting the young Aryan men for military service, the pool is rather limited."

"Your Jew girlfriend is headed for the death camps," my brother taunted.

"Shut up, you dope," I fired back.

"Quiet, boys," my peacemaker mother said again. "There are no death camps."

"Yes, there are," my brother said. "Everyone at school is talking about them."

My mother looked at my father. "Wiktor, tell the boys that there are no death camps. It's just a horrible rumor spread by imaginative children."

"There are no death camps," my father stated while concentrating on his plate.

After my father washed his last bite down with a sip of wine, he asked, "How are the courses at the academy, boys? Jakub, I assume your business studies are going well so that you can take over the factory one day. And Michal, I expect to see better grades in math so that you can concentrate on engineering next year. I need some good engineers, especially now that the Nazis have seized my best ones."

My mother smiled. "The headmaster let me know that Michal's music studies are progressing marvelously. If his progress continues, he may be good enough for the Warsaw Symphony someday. That is, after the war. And the symphony gets reinstated," she added with a frown.

The Germans had disallowed all forms of entertainment, including music, theater, and the arts. However, I studied in secret with a local prominent violinist.

"Michal is not going to play the violin for a living," my father growled. "His music lessons are to round out his studies in mathematics and engineering."

I knew better than to say anything, but I was far better suited for a career as a violinist than an engineer. I had no interest in my father's business, and I hated math.

As the maid cleared the dishes and the cook brought out a cake with fourteen candles on it, my mother sang "Sto lat"—"One Hundred Years"—the traditional Polish song expressing good wishes, good health, and long life. It would have been beneath my father and brother to sing along, but the maid and cook joined in.

My mother and the maid applauded as I blew out the candles. "I've been waiting all week for this." My mother clasped her hands. "We have an extra-special gift for you this year."

The maid returned to the room and handed my mother a violin.

"Happy birthday, Michal." My mother's face beamed with pride as she presented it to me. "I had your uncle ship this from Italy. It's from the latest Italian master violin maker. Play it for us. He says it has a beautiful tone."

I cradled this beautiful instrument, stood from my seat at the table, and played the opening of the Brahms's "G Major Violin Sonata," which I was just learning. My mother listened, eyes gleaming, while my brother dug into his cake and my father sipped his coffee.

***

The clock on the mantel chimed five times. The old man jolted, as if waking from a trance. Tick-tock, tick-tock pierced the stillness of the dim room. Outside, drips from the eaves slapped into a puddle under the window.

Jodi sprang to her feet and reached for her backpack and violin. "It's five o'clock. I have to go. My mother will kill me if I'm not home when she gets there. Thank you for the coffee."

"Thank you for brightening my afternoon, young Jodi." The old man stood and moved to the door.

Jodi's hand rested on the knob. "It was nice to meet you Mich . . . er, ah, Mr. K." She opened the door, hesitated, and then stepped onto the cracked porch.

"I will make a bargain with you," the old man said as she started down the walkway.

She turned and squinted at his frail figure framed in the doorway. "What kind of bargain?"

"I have been unwell this spring and behind on my garden. You come by whenever you like and help me with my garden, and I will teach you to play Brahms."

Jodi smiled. "You're on, Mr. K." *How hard can that be?* She dashed down the walkway and hustled home, frantic, as she made up a plausible excuse to explain her absence if her mother beat her home.

CHAPTER 3

Jodi spied her mother's dented older-model gray Honda Civic as she rounded the corner and entered the parking area of her apartment complex. "She's going to kill me," she mumbled as she opened the door to the smoke-stained hallway and trudged up the creaky stairs to apartment 203. Although her mother was home, she used her key to unlock the deadbolt, a habit carried over from years of residing in a rough metro neighborhood.

Jodi stepped into the entryway and peered through the living room into the adjoining kitchen. Her mother was hunched over the sink.

"Where have you been?" her mother cried without turning from the carrots she was scrubbing. "You had me worried. I didn't know whether to call the police or the school or . . . I just don't know. Where have you been?"

Jodi glanced at the digital clock on the stove—5:26. It was unusual for her mother to be home before 5:30, as she usually lingered at work and gossiped with coworkers after her shift. "I'm sorry, Mom. I was at the library. The storm. I, ah, I went into the library to get out of the storm and started doing my homework. I guess I lost track of time." She hated lying, but she knew her mother would not approve of the old man with the violin, especially the detail about her going into a stranger's house. "If I had a phone, I could have texted to let you know where I was."

"There we go with the phone again. You know they're too expensive. I thought we hashed that topic to death."

Jodi clammed up. Nothing she would say would change her mother's mind. Another cell phone was a luxury Mom claimed they just couldn't afford, although her mother always had hers close at hand. It wasn't as if Jodi had anyone to call or text or friend on Facebook anyway.

"Go wash your hands and help with dinner."

Yippee! Diet tuna salad again, Jodi grumbled under her breath as she sat across the table from her mother. She studied her plate, swirling salad greens and tuna chucks with her fork, her stomach too tied up in knots to eat. She hoped her mother was too consumed with the game show that blared from the TV in the living room to notice Jodi's lack of appetite. The TV audience applauded, and the announcer cut out to a commercial break.

As if a cue for conversation, her mother asked, "So how was school today?"

"Fine." Jodi focused on her plate. She didn't dare to bring up the humiliating episode in the parking lot. Too embarrassing to tell anyone, especially her mother.

"The other kids weren't hard on you again today, were they?"

Here we go again. Jodi lowered her eyes. Of course they harassed her today. Why would this day be any different?

"I just don't understand, Jodi. You need to learn to stick up for yourself."

"I don't want to talk about it, okay?"

"I just don't understand why you let those kids get to you. Now when I was your age, I had lots of friends and. . ."

"I know. I know, Mom. You were the most popular girl in school and head cheerleader." *And no doubt the Kristen in your class.* The wrench in her gut clenched another notch tighter each time her mother bragged about her teenage social status. She would never understand the pain and loneliness of being the class outcast. Jodi bottled up her hurt, sometimes feeling like a bubbling can of shaken soda about to explode.

"Is your homework done?"

"Almost. I have a little more to do. And I need to practice the violin."

"I don't see why you want to play that silly thing anyway. All that scratchy noise. It's hard to hear the TV when you practice."

"Not my choice, Mom. You know that I didn't have another elective option."

"Well, only one more week and you can put it up for the summer. Maybe next year when you get to high school you can take a different elective."

Jodi rolled her eyes. "Don't you remember, Mom? Junior high goes through ninth grade here, so it's another whole year before I go to high school."

"Oh, yeah. I guess I did forget that. Well, maybe something else will open up."

"Yeah, maybe."

"I met a nice gentleman at the café this morning." Her mother changed the subject. "He was *sooo* sweet. He asked me out on a date tomorrow night, so we're going to see a movie. Don't wait up if I get home late."

"Okay." Jodi used to pepper her mother with questions about her suitors. But not anymore. There was seldom a second date, so why bother.

After dinner, Jodi shut herself in her bedroom and breezed through her homework. A boring task she trudged through each weekday evening. She rarely learned anything new from the repetitive exercises in the textbooks since the information had already been covered in class.

She scribbled the answer to the last math question, slipped the answer sheet into her textbook, and snapped it shut. She snatched her basketball to shoot hoops in the parking lot, then turned to the closet to grab a sweatshirt. As she headed for the bedroom door, she spied the violin case on the bed, where she had tossed it earlier. She threw the ball onto a pile of laundry in the closet, sat on the edge of the bed, and picked up the violin. She opened the music folder to the Mozart *Minuet.* The sweet tones of Mr. K's violin echoed in her mind as she positioned the instrument under her chin. But the scratchy noise that reverberated from her bow stroke sounded more like a sick cat. She put the instrument down in despair. "I'm never going to be able to play this stupid thing."

***

The next morning Jodi hustled to get to school ahead of the tardy bell. She dashed through the town center, with its skinny streets framed by chipped and faded double-stacked brick buildings, many displaying FOR SALE OR LEASE signs in the boarded-up windows. A left at the gas station. A right at the library. Past the coffee shop—where she froze. Kristen and her entourage streamed out of the Java Grove, each with a specialty drink clutched in one hand and a smartphone in the other.

Kristen, of course, led the pack, her followers hanging on to her every word. "Hey, here comes B-flat," she shouted. "Stopping in for a mocha, B-flat? Oh wait. You probably can't even afford that cheap black goop they serve at the greasy spoon where your slutty mama works."

Jodi willed herself not to cry as she darted past the laughing bullies.

Ten minutes later she sat in the back row of math, a horrible class to start the day with, when Kristen waltzed in with her iced mocha. Julie and a few others trailed behind. Kristen sneered at Jodi, flicked her perfectly styled, bleached-blond hair with the back of her hand, and plopped down at the workstation two rows in front of Jodi. Julie imitated the act, although with less drama. Clique etiquette, as far as Jodi could tell, forbade any act that upstaged or even equaled the clique queen.

The teacher waddled in carrying a pile of papers. "Good morning, class."

"Good morning, Ms. Cavendish," the students replied in unison, an exaggerated mocking of the teacher's nasally voice. Jodi stayed silent as she eyed the stack of papers—likely the prior week's graded quizzes—Ms. Cavendish clutched between her flabby arms and droopy bosom.

Jodi watched the teacher, who looked as if she had time traveled from the1970s in her flowered muumuu and Birkenstocks, as she squeezed through the narrow rows of desks, forcing students to veer away from her abundant midsection. Reaching Kristen's workstation, she frowned at the class prima donna, who held a smirk on her face. "Well, Kristen, still not studying, as usual. I trust that you'll be ready for the final exam next week."

"Of course, Ms. Cavendish," Kristen replied with her best phony sincerity.

"And Julie"—the teacher handed Julie her graded quiz—"I'm sure it's just a coincidence that you missed the same questions as Kristen."

"Ah, just a coincidence." Julie diverted her eyes to her desktop.

"And Miss Evans . . ."

Jodi stared at her open math book as the plump instructor glared down at her.

"A ninety-eight again. I just don't understand how you always miss the easiest question on the test."

"Uh"—Jodi reached for her paper – "just lucky on the hard ones, I guess." She made a mental note to miss a harder question on the upcoming final exam.

CHAPTER 4

Finally, the first morning of summer break. Jodi had thought the glorious day would never arrive. She lounged in bed and tossed her basketball toward the ceiling and caught it just above her nose. Free from the tricks and barbs of Kristen and her cronies who made her days unbearable. She lobbed the ball again. Free from having to grit her teeth and sit on her hands when she was the only one in class who knew the answer to a difficult question. Another toss. Free from having to fake ignorance on easy test questions so as not to be branded a brainiac. She caught the ball and hugged it against her chest.

Her thoughts drifted to the frail old man with the violin. The sweet sound that Mr. K. coaxed out of his instrument haunted her in a way she couldn't explain. It was as if the Brahms's melody wrapped around her like a wool blanket and warmed her soul and smothered Kristen from her consciousness, at least until the music stopped. If she could play like that, would she earn the respect of the other orchestra kids? Mr. Johnston? Definitely not Kristen. She thought it odd that the old man would be willing to teach her, especially since he barely knew her. And why help with a garden? The yard was such a mess, she couldn't imagine how he could possibly tame it enough to grow a garden. But then again, she had never had a garden. Never even had a yard to host a garden. There couldn't be much to it. Toss some seeds on the ground. Give them a little water. Jodi wasn't sure if she was trying to convince herself to take him up on this offer or talk herself out of it.

The baby in the adjacent apartment let out a screeching wail, and Jodi bolted upright. "Oh crap. Just do it," she mumbled, playing on the slogan of her favorite sporting goods company. She didn't have anything else to do today anyway, so might as well wander over there and see what happened.

She dragged herself out of bed, took a quick shower, slipped into a pair of cutoff shorts and a T-shirt, and wrapped a hair band around her shoulder-length auburn hair. She glanced in the mirror and frowned at the hazel eyes and misshapen face that peered back at her—the splotchy freckles that dotted her cheeks, the mole on her chin, the pencil-thin lips hiding a crooked front tooth that was chipped at the corner—a casualty of a pickup ball game – and the narrow nose that curved up like the tail end of a playground slide.

She made her way to the kitchen and poured herself a glass of milk and fixed her favorite breakfast of a peanut butter and banana sandwich. She then slipped her frayed backpack onto her shoulders, the violin case protruding from the top.

Instead of taking the most direct route to the old man's house, she traversed a more circular course among the back roads and alleys. She figured her classmates wouldn't be hanging around the Java Grove on the first morning of summer break, but she wouldn't take any chances. Nothing would spoil her first official day of freedom.

Upon arriving at the old house with the wobbly picket fence, she paused before reaching for the gate.

"There you are, my young friend," the old man said as he rose from behind an overgrown bush, a pruning tool in his hand. "Here. Hold this ornery branch so I can whack 'er off." He demonstrated by slicing the air with his shears.

Jodi surveyed the yard while she held the limb. The old man had been busy over the past week. Brush had been cleared, bushes had been trimmed, and some pansies were popping up in the flowerbed under the front window.

"Today's chore"—he cut the branch Jodi was holding—"is to till the garden beds." He gestured with his head to the far corner of the small yard. "We're already late getting the seeds planted."

Mr. K rested his shears next to some garden tools. He handed Jodi a shovel and then reached for a hoe. "We need to clear the weeds and break up the dirt clods so that the seeds can germinate and sprout." He swung his hoe into a clump of weeds.

Jodi wedged the shovel into the dirt and turned over a scoop of earth. She used the point of the tool to break up the clods. Soon her arms felt heavy and sweat dripped from her forehead as the searing sun promised another scorching day. The old man's stamina amazed her.

Her parched throat was screaming for a cold beverage when at last he stopped and said, "That's about all these rickety ol' bones can handle for now. Let's take a little break."

He motioned her into house, and she propped herself against an armchair in the living room while he wandered into the kitchen. He returned with two glasses of iced tea.

He handed Jodi a glass. "Now for that violin lesson."

The old man eased into the worn sofa. Jodi removed her violin from the case and started to sit in the matching chair.

"No, no, young friend. You stand. I am old. I can sit. You stand when you practice the violin. Now, let's start with some scales. Start with G major, and then cycle through the circle of fifths."

"Huh?" She knew G major, but what was this circle of fifths?

The old man lumbered up from the couch and adjusted her playing position—her arms, her shoulders, her wrists—as she fumbled through the scale. She felt awkward in this revised stance.

"You must relax," he scolded. "The music can't flow through you if you are tense. Your wrist is rigid. Shake it out and keep that looseness through your bow movement."

Jodi jiggled her wrist and then played the out-of-tune scale.

He returned to his seat. "Now, what is the fifth note of the G major scale?"

Jodi counted on her fingers. "G, A, B, C, D. D is the fifth note."

"So now play a D major scale."

She fumbled through a few more scales, repeating them several times.

"I think that is enough for today. Practice only scales this week. Listen closely for good tone and intonation. Use the full bow. And by all means, relax!"

As Jodi returned the instrument to the case, Mr. K retreated to the kitchen and then reemerged with refills of the tea. Jodi took the glass he handed her.

"You will be a fine violin player," he said. "Consistent practice is the key."

Jodi nodded, skeptical. "I'll never be as good as Kristen, and she'll ridicule me forever about it."

"Whoa, young lady. Music is not about being better than anyone else. It is only about the music. Play only for you."

Jodi now stood by the mantel, entranced by the photo of the old man's wife. "She has the most enchanting eyes I have ever seen," Jodi said, more to herself than to Mr. K. An array of conflicting emotions radiated from the mocha-hued orbs peering from the photo, so real that Jodi felt she was being watched. Happy, yet sad. Joyful and sorrowful. Serious, but playful. "You told me when you first saw your wife, but you didn't say how you met. What was her name?"

Mr. K leaned his head back and after a long pause resumed his story.

CHAPTER 5

The following day my father's chauffer drove Jakub and me across the city to our boarding school. My mother thought it was silly to go to a boarding school in the same metro area where we lived, but my father insisted that this was the only institution that provided the curriculum necessary to meet the demands of senior positions in his business. And his driver had too many other obligations to be shuttling us to and from school every day. Let alone that petrol was a valuable and scarce commodity. I thought he just wanted us away. Although, with most of the schools skuttled by the Nazis, there weren't many, if any, other options.

I couldn't get the girl or the death camps out of my mind. My stomach churned the more I thought about them. After witnessing the Nazis brutal treatment of the Jews at my father's factory, I was beginning to think the rumors were true. I was haunted by recurring visions of those big, sad eyes peering through a wire fence while bodies littered the ground around her. In one scene, a smirking guard pressed a rifle barrel to her ear. I shuddered and squeezed my eyes closed to try to purge the image from my consciousness.

The following Sunday after Mass, I walked to the ghetto to see if I could find her. It was a long walk, and it was late afternoon when I arrived. The ghetto was surrounded by a high wall, the gated entrances patrolled by German guards. I cased the barrier, looking for a peephole while maintaining a safe distance. I kept my gait brisk and shoulders square, trying to act as if I had business on this isolated street. I knew that any appearance of helping a Jew could get one instantly shot, even a fourteen-year-old boy. Crunching footsteps of an approaching patrol spooked me, and I shoved my hands into my pockets and hustled around the corner. Discouraged, I trudged back to my dorm room.

That night, though weary from the long walk, I couldn't sleep. After what seemed like restless hours of staring into the darkness, I bolted upright and blurted, "The work crews!"

Henryk, my roommate, stirred, and I whispered again, "Of course. The work crews."

After classes the next afternoon, I rushed back to the ghetto to wait for my fathers' Jewish workers to be marched back to the slum by the German guards. There were even more soldiers in the street that day, congregating on every corner. I squatted in the entryway of a crumbling building near the ghetto barrier and surveyed the surroundings. Bullet holes speckled the disintegrating structures, and bricks and piles of rubble littered the walk. The charred skeleton of a burned building was a stark reminder of the Luftwaffe air raid on the city four years earlier. Though the day was warm, a chill slithered up my spine.

Daylight was fading when I heard commotion in the distance. Then the figures of the escorted column rounded a corner, growing larger as they neared the checkpoint. I tried to shrink as I crouched against the doorframe and watched the guards poke and cajole the emaciated Jews as they shuffled by. Toward the end of the line, I spied Mr. Bujak holding the hand of the girl. My heart sank as I realized there was no way to approach her. I watched them pass, their worn shoes barely lifting from the disintegrating pavement, as if the street was quicksand trying to suck them under.

One straggler collapsed, and a guard rushed over and struck him in the kidney with the butt of his rifle. "Get up, you filthy Jew, or you'll die here in the street."

Two of the other men in the procession hobbled to the weakened man, hoisted him to his feet, and dragged him back to the scraggly marchers.

I rose from my perch in the doorway and followed the horde, thankful that my dusty clothes helped me blend in. I rubbed some dirt onto my face and cap, hoping my prep-school attire would not draw unwanted attention. I leaned against another building as I watched the last of the Jews funnel through the gate and into the confines of the slum.

Saddened that I couldn't talk to the girl, I trolled the perimeter of the ghetto barrier, fists shoved into my pockets and eyes downcast. I was startled by a rustling behind me. I spun and spied a young boy sliding on his stomach though a hidden gap under the wall. He froze for a moment when he saw me, and then he darted in the opposite direction, as if he expected me to call out to the sentries. I scanned the street to make sure no one was watching and then shimmied through the tight space and into the ghetto.

I emerged from the alley with the secret entrance to the main corridor and stopped cold, stunned. Broken furniture, shattered glass, and other debris littered the street. Deteriorated buildings were bandaged together with scraps of plywood and sheet metal. Frayed curtains fluttered through broken windows. The people milling about were ragged and emaciated, many appeared only steps from death. They cast sunken eyes downward, as if studying the crumbled pavement would keep both the thieves and the police at bay.

Noticing I was within gunshot range of the guarded gate, I trudged deeper into the ghetto. After passing a couple of blocks, I spotted the throng of Jews from my father's factory dispersing into various dilapidated dwellings. Mr. Bujak and the girl, along with a spattering of other stragglers, continued their slog along the street. Mr. Bujak conferred with a group of bearded men as they walked, while the girl trailed behind. I swallowed hard, and my heartbeats hammered in my chest as I gathered the courage to approach her.

As she passed by, I rushed up beside her. Without rehearsing what I might say, I blurted out, "What's your name?"

Startled, she jumped and gasped as she turned to me. Her expression changed when she recognized me. "What are you doing here!"

"I, uh, I just want to know your name?"

She hadn't yet replied when her father turned from his companions and called out, "Karina, come along. We need to stay together."

"Coming. I'm coming," she shouted back.

"So that's your name, Karina?"

"You shouldn't be here. Why are you here?"

"I just wanted to meet you, to know your name."

"Well, you know it now. You better go."

"Come along, Karina. We must hurry home. Who are you talking to?" her father asked as his comrades dispersed.

"There's going to be trouble later," she said in a harried whisper. "You might get hurt. You should leave. You're one of them, and someone might shoot you."

"I'm not one of them."

"I have to go. Bye, uh . . ."

"Michal."

"Bye, Michal." She rotated to follow her father.

"Wait!" I exclaimed.

She paused mid step and whirled.

"I brought something for you." I reached inside my jacket and handed her a brown paper bag that contained some dry biscuits and an apple I pilfered from the dining hall that morning.

Her eyes widened, and she snatched the bag from my hand and ran to her father. I watched her slip the bag under her blouse and reach for her father's hand. She glanced over her shoulder to see me standing in the middle of the filthy street, watching her disappear into one of the crumbling apartments.

She was right. There was trouble. No sooner had father and daughter vanished into the dwelling when shots rang out nearby. Startled, I spun around just in time to see a woman with a pistol in each hand shooting at a guard. The guard cried out, grabbed his leg, and fell to the ground. Another soldier shot the woman, and she slumped to the street, bleeding from the chest.

I ran. Faster than my feet had ever propelled me before. On the next block there was more shooting. Another woman pulled a grenade from under her corset and tossed it at a group of soldiers. She leaped behind a barricade as other nearby sentries sprayed machine-gun fire, splintering her shelter of packing crates. Two men threw rocks and a Molotov cocktail—a homemade grenade—at the shooting soldiers. Blocked by the chaos, I turned and ran the other direction, away from the route to the secret entrance. An explosion blasted ahead of me, and soon black smoke rose from another building. I darted into an alley and hid behind a pile of rubble, trembling. My clammy hands gripped the Saint Christopher's medallion I wore around my neck as I listened to the shots, explosions, and terrifying screams pierce the darkness.

Hours later, the last of the stray gunshots silenced. Then it grew quiet. Eerily quiet. My shallow breaths the only intrusion on the stillness, the lingering odor of smoke and gunpowder hung in the air. A rat scurried from under an overturned trash bin and disappeared into a crevice. The silence frayed my nerves as much as the chaos because I knew I must leave my hiding place.

The breaking dawn burned the eastern sky fiery waves of purple, crimson, and orange as I reached my dormitory, but blackness clouded my soul. I did not know the fate of those chocolate eyes that stole my heart. I wanted to admonish the songbirds as they tuned up for their morning chorus as the heavens were burning. There was no reason to sing anymore. I had been terrified four years earlier when the German Luftwaffe showered their deadly bombs on my city. But back then I had hidden with my family in a dark basement as the outside world crumbled and burned. But nothing had cut so deep into my innocence as the horror I witnessed that night in the Warsaw Jewish ghetto. Little did I know that the horror was just beginning, and my life was about to change forever.

***

"I must have worn myself out," Mr. K said. He stretched out on the sofa and rested his head on a cushion.

Jodi collected the empty glasses and carried them to the kitchen. By the time she returned to the living room, the old man was asleep. She picked up her backpack and opened the front door. She paused and watched the old man, his chest rising and falling to the rhythm of his raspy breathing. She hoped the sweet melody of the Brahms sonata filled his dreams, but she imagined that his sleep instead propelled him to a dark and intimate intersection where angels and demons collide.

Jodi's mind was far away as she walked home. Her heart heavy, almost as if she felt Mr. K's terror as he huddled in that alley on that horrific night. What might have happened had he been discovered? She shuddered.

The path she followed reached the schoolyard, and screeching voices snapped her back to the present. Darn. She had forgotten to take the alternate route home—away from the school. She couldn't believe it. Cheerleading camp was underway, and all the popular girls, Kristen at the center, shouted as they bobbed up and down and shook their blue-and-white pompoms in tandem above their heads. "Rah, rah, Mustangs. Go Mustangs Go!"

Jodi made an abrupt turn. Too late. The taunt immediately started. "Hey, team!" Kristen shouted to the rhythm of her cheer. "It's B-flat Beanstalk. B-flat Beanstalk. Coming out for cheer squad, B-flat Beanstalk?" She stopped bouncing. "Oh, wait. Ugly skyscraper girls can't join cheer squad."

Jodi raced from the hurling barbs. The hollow achiness that had ebbed during her visit with Mr. K erupted as she fled.

"What's the matter, B-flat?" Kristen shouted over the laughter of the other girls. "Where's your school spirit? We have a water girl spot open."

CHAPTER 6

Sunshine and the *hoo-aw* of an annoyed owl weaved their way into Jodi's subconscious the following morning as she dangled in the hazy abyss between sleep and awake. Then a car horn and squealing tires jolted her from her semiconscious state.

The neighbor baby wailed. Jodi lay in bed, aware of every aching muscle in her body. "God, I hurt," she said to the ceiling. She rolled over and moaned as pain exploded in muscles she didn't know she had. Even her toes hurt. She closed her eyes and listened to the stillness of the room, the traffic noise drifting from the street below, the crying baby, the clanging in the kitchen. She had forgotten that this was her mother's day off work. She detected a whiff of bacon wafting through the bedroom door, a foreign aroma in the small apartment.

"Are you going to sleep all day?" her mother called from the kitchen.

"Argh!" Jodi mumbled. "Coming," she shouted back. Her stomach growled as the scent of sizzling bacon filled the room. She wriggled out of bed and hobbled barefoot to the kitchen.

"I get up to make a special breakfast for my favorite daughter, and you sleep right through it," her mother yelled as Jodi came up behind her and reached into the cabinet for a chipped mug.

"Oh, you're finally up. You look like hell. Did you have a fight with the boogeyman?"

Jodi rolled her eyes. Her mother's attempt at humor was sometimes amusing, but seldom funny. "No, Mom. I must have slept crooked." Jodi poured herself a cup of coffee.

"You're too young to drink coffee," her mother scolded. "It'll stunt your growth." But knowing her daughter would indulge anyway, she added, "The milk's in the fridge."

"Too late for that." Jodi smirked as she splashed a generous amount of skim milk into her steaming cup. She added a heaping teaspoon of sugar and carried the creamy beverage to the hideous turquoise Formica kitchen table, a thrift-shop find like the other marred, dated, and mismatched furniture and accessories that filled their snug apartment.

"So, what's the occasion that you're cooking breakfast?"

"Why does there have to be an occasion? Can't I cook a nice breakfast for my daughter?"

Jodi would have to wait to find out what the occasion was. Her mother, Dorothy, spent six days a week on her feet waiting tables at the Sage Grove Café. Jodi couldn't recall a time when she had ever cooked a hot breakfast. Bacon, eggs, and—*sniff*—a whiff of burning toast tickled her nostril hairs. Bribery was definitely on the table, along with the special meal.

"So what are you going to do on your day off?" Jodi asked, assuming the usual chores of grocery shopping and laundry topped the agenda.

"Oh, I don' know." Her mother sighed. "It's still a little up in the air." She carried two chipped plates topped with extra-crispy bacon, rubbery scrambled eggs, and blackened toast to the table.

Jodi nibbled a slice of crumbly bacon while watching her mother position her buttered toast to nudge ketchup-smothered eggs onto her fork.

After a few bites and a sip of coffee, her mother said, "You never asked about my date the other night."

Jodi cringed. She'd hoped the date, like the string of others, had bombed. The grumpiness and aloofness the following few days were far better than the emotional hangover after the breakup, which always happened.

Jodi reluctantly took the bait. "So how was your date the other night?"

"Oh, I'm so glad you asked. It was okay, I guess. He seems nice, but of course it's too early to tell."

"Must have gone well then."

"We're going out again today. He needs to run an errand in Boise and insists that I come with him and spend the day. He says it's a beautiful city and that I must see it."

"Nice." Jodi waited for the bomb to drop. "So how did he react when you told him you had a daughter?"

"Uh, well, the subject really didn't come up, so I haven't had a chance to tell him yet."

"He'll find out soon enough when he comes to pick you up."

Her mother dropped her eyes to her plate. "He's, ah, he's going to pick me up at the café."

"At work? On your day off?"

"It was easier than giving him directions to the apartment."

That wasn't the reason. It wasn't like the apartment was hard to find. The sorry-looking, soot-gray building with the broken railing, peeling paint, and junky cars littering the lot was six blocks the wrong side of Main Street. How hard could that be?

"What's his name? I mean, if he kidnaps you and I have to call the cops, I need to give them a name," Jodi joked.

"His name is Tom."

"Tom what?"

"Just Tom. We got to enjoying the movie and talking, and you know, I just didn't ask his last name. I'll make sure he doesn't kidnap me."

Was her mom crazy, leaving town with a guy she hardly knew? *What if he's a murderer?* She brushed the thought away.

"All right. Tom has a good job and makes decent money," her mother said. "You should see that gorgeous truck he drives! I just don't want to blow it. He may be our ticket out of this dump."

Her mother hoped that every man she met would rocket her to the good life. After years of watching her mom's string of disappointments, Jodi had resolved long ago that she would forever be independent and self-reliant. Who needed a man, or anybody else, to pull her out of anywhere? But her mother came from a different place and time, with a different set of values.

As Jodi helped clear the morning dishes, her mother asked, "Will you go to the store today? I'll leave a list and some money. And could you help with the laundry also? I'm just not sure what time I'll be home, and all my uniforms need washed."

"Sure, Mom," Jodi responded. "Have a good time on your outing. And don't forget to get his last name, license, and social security number."

Her mother grinned and gave Jodi a quick hug and waltzed to her room to get ready for the big day.

Jodi dried the remaining dishes. On the one hand, she was happy for her mother's excitement. On the other, she dreaded the head-on collision with heartbreak that was roaring up the highway. Maybe this time would be different, she thought with a sigh.

Later, after an hour of practicing scales and arpeggios and her fingertips too sore to play anymore, Jodi tucked her violin into the case. She tossed her basketball into the laundry basket on top of the dirty clothes and carried the basket to the first-floor laundry room. She stuffed the clothes in the washer, poured in the appropriate amount of powdered detergent, and inserted six quarters into the slot.

She checked her watch—11:45. "Forty minutes for some hoops." She grabbed the basketball and headed for the lone rim in the parking lot.

As she rounded the corner of the building, she skidded to a stop and leered at the U-Haul trailer hitched behind an old, dented green sedan, clearly parked in front of the NO PARKING sign by the basketball hoop.

"Hey," she shouted to the back of a woman straining from the weight of the box she was carrying. "You can't park here. Can't you read? The sign says 'No Parking.'"

The woman continued toward the building. A boy, who must have been her son, as he shared the same dark hair and silky olive skin, opened the door, and the woman disappeared into the hallway.

The kid sauntered to the U-Haul. "Sorry," he said to Jodi. "My mother doesn't speak much English. We're almost done unloading. Then I'll move out of the way."

Jodi stood with the ball wedged between her forearm and hip, giving the boy her most disgusted look. "How much longer are you going to be? This is a no parking area."

"Sorry," he repeated. "It's taking a long time with just the two of us. There was nowhere else to park. We should be done soon."

Jodi sat on the curb and watched as mother and son removed items from the trailer. The boy, who looked to be about her age but wasn't nearly as tall, moved at the same slug-like pace as his mother. She sat and watched, the ball wedged between her chest and thighs, arms wrapped around her shins, checking her watch every few minutes as mother and son carried—one at a time—a lamp, an old chair, and more small boxes into the building.

Jodi's forty minutes ticked away, and she retreated to the laundry room to transfer the wet clothes from washer to dryer. After inserting more quarters, the dryer started to hum, and Jodi, with basketball tucked under her arm, returned to the parking lot. The U-Haul was gone.

With a sigh of relief, she tossed the ball through the netless rim. "Nothin' but air!" she exclaimed as the ball passed through the hoop without touching the metal ring.

Jodi leapt for a layup as the boy emerged from the hallway with an armload of cardboard and plastic bags destined for the nearby dumpster. After depositing the garbage, he leaned against the overflowing bin.

Jodi was conscious of his eyes on her as she dribbled the ball with a showy bounce between her legs, made a fake on an imaginary opponent, and soared toward the basket. Another two points! The ball bounced off the curb and rolled toward the dumpster.

The kid picked it up and flung it toward Jodi. Although only a few steps away, the ball bounced twice before Jodi scooped it up. "Thanks."

"No prob," he replied.

Jodi started to pivot back toward the hoop, then stopped and eyed the new neighbor.

"Sorry it took us so long unloading," he apologized.

"So, you just moved in?"

"Yeah."

He didn't elaborate, so she asked, "Where'd you move from?"

"Caldwell."

"Oh" was all Jodi could think to respond. She had never been to Caldwell but knew it was another sleepy southern Idaho town somewhere west of Boise.

"I'm Jodi. Thanks for returning the ball."

"Juan," he said.

In addition to not being a basketball player, he was also not a conversationalist.

"Welcome to the Ritz," she said sarcastically. "Maybe I'll see you at the pool later." Of course, there was no pool, or grassy area with a swing set, or picnic tables. The rusty basketball hoop was the only recreational amenity at this run-down complex.

"I better get back in. My mother needs help." He trotted back to the building.

Later that evening, Jodi was lounging on the sofa with a bowl of popcorn and a can of Dr Pepper, watching her Portland Trailblazers in a rare playoff game, when her mother breezed through the door. Swinging her purse and twirling in circles, she made her way to the sagging couch and kissed Jodi on the top of her head.

"Date must have gone well," Jodi remarked.

"Oh yes, I guess so," her mother responded, trying to downplay her giddiness. She dropped her bag on the scuffed coffee table and plopped down on the sofa next to her daughter as Jodi swung her feet out of the way. "Oh, all right, if you must know, it was a marvelous day. We had lunch on the patio of a quaint café by the river. Then we went for a long walk on the Greenbelt River Path. He's just so charming." She reached for a handful of Jodi's popcorn.

"That sounds nice, Mom. So what's his last name, and where does he work?"

"Must you be so inquisitive about such unimportant details?"

"I think they're kind of important."

"All right, all right. His last name is Smith, and he works at Webster's Packing. He's a shift supervisor."

"Smith? His name is Tom Smith?"

"*Smith* happens to be a very common name." Her mother stood and danced the few steps to the kitchen and snatched a Diet Coke from the refrigerator. "He was quite the gentleman. We're going out again next week. And he wants to meet you." She was a bit huffy now.

"Okay. I'm glad you had a nice day, and I look forward to meeting him."

"I've had a long day and have to open tomorrow. I'm going to bed. Don't stay up too late." She picked up her purse and carried the beverage to the bedroom.

"Good night, Mom." Jodi tossed a piece of popcorn into the air and caught it between her teeth. *Hmm. Tom Smith.* Something about the impromptu trip niggled at the edge of her mind.

CHAPTER 7

The next Monday Jodi was kneeling in the dirt pulling weeds from Mr. K's recently planted garden. He had the good sense to use a mini stool to relieve the pressure on his achy knees.

"How did these weeds grow so fast?" Jodi asked. "We just tilled last week."

"Get used to it. Gardens and weeds are like picnics and ants. You can't have the fruits without the pests." He winked at her and then corrected himself. "In this case, you can't have the vegetables."

Jodi's arms glistened with perspiration. Salty sweat stung her eyes, and the bright glare forced her to squint. She'd have to remember a cap and shades next time. Her mind drifted to Mr. K's story of meeting the girl, his future wife, in the Warsaw ghetto.

"Mr. K, I'm curious. What happened next after you met Karina? How did you get together?" Jodi wished she had paid more attention during history class, but she had learned that Jews were rounded up and sent to concentration camps and that anyone caught helping them faced dire consequences.

He paused for a moment, inhaled a deep breath, and resumed his weeding—and his story.

***

The day will be forever etched in my memory. May 16, 1943. I was on my way to the dining hall for the midday meal. A loud group of older boys ahead in the queue couldn't contain their excitement, and my growling stomach was forgotten.

"The whole ghetto is on fire," one boy shouted in rapid-fire gasps. "Flames and smoke everywhere. Explosions! Whole buildings tumbling. Crash!" he added for emphasis while pantomiming with his waving arms.

"Wow!" another boy shrieked, his eyes wide in bewilderment. "Those Jews are done for now!"

I didn't stick around to hear the rest. I raced to my room, grabbed my jacket and cap, and, as an afterthought, a candy bar that my mother had recently sent me. I ran nonstop to the ghetto.

My classmate was right in his description. Buildings were ablaze, broken glass and charred rubble littered the streets, and the thick smoke that hung over the crumbling slum spit smoldering ashes on the weary souls plodding along the filthy sidewalks. Panic set in as I rounded a corner and saw armed soldiers herding Jews down the middle of the street. Frantic, I searched for Karina and her family while still having the sense to keep clear of the soldiers. I skirted to the next block and mirrored the mass of prisoners as they were funneled toward the train station.

When I reached the depot, soldiers were forcing the Jews into boxcars that were fitted with a platform to create an additional level so as not to waste a centimeter of available space. An old man tumbled backward from an overloaded car, and a soldier clobbered him with the butt of his rifle. As he fell to the ground, another soldier kicked him in the ribs. Children were crying. Mothers clutched their fidgeting babies. Even after the rail car was stuffed with distraught Jews, the soldiers crammed more in.

But I could not find Karina. I was torn. Should I stay at the station and wait, or should I backtrack and search for them on the street? Or were they already stuffed like sardines in one of the bulging cars? I decided to wait. I tucked between two posts where I could see most of the Jews as they approached but hidden well enough that I could duck behind a pillar when a guard turned my way.

I don't know how long I waited or what I would do if I spotted her. My heart raced, and my hands were clammy. I had almost lost hope when the listless family crowded through the gate and crept toward the platform, not by freewill but drawn by a cyclone of hatred siphoning them toward a vile underworld. Karina's mother led the family, clasping the hand of a toddler who clutched a tattered stuffed bear that I assumed must be Karina's younger brother. Karina's father held Karina's hand in one hand and a battered suitcase in the other. My panic escalated as the crowd pressed them closer to the overflowing train, the guards keeping a keen watch.

Suddenly someone screamed, and a soldier rushed over and clobbered a man with his rifle. The other guards rushed to assist. This was my chance. Concealed by the confusion, I darted from my hiding place and tugged Karina by the wrist. She resisted, but her father bit his shriveled lip and then whispered to her, "Go with him." He looked at me square in the eyes and pleaded, "Keep her safe."

"I promise." I tugged her away from her family, and we raced from the station. We had just escaped the depot when someone shouted behind us, "Hey! Hey, you kids! Get them!"

I snuck a peek over my shoulder and spied two soldiers chasing after us. I knew we would soon be overtaken.

"This way," Karina shouted as she pivoted and darted into an alley.

I followed her around the corner and panicked when I saw a brick wall that had us trapped.

"Down here," she said as she bent to lift a metal grate from a storm drain.

I helped her wrestle the heavy grille from the sidewalk, and she jumped into the darkness just as the soldiers rounded the corner. I leapt after her as their shots rang out.

"Quick." She ran in the ankle-deep water, and I splashed after her.

BANG! An explosion came from behind us as the hand grenade the soldiers dropped down the storm drain detonated, hurling us facedown into the slimy muck. We scrambled to our feet and, with ears ringing from the deafening blast, sloshed through the tunnel.

The water was soon up to our knees as more feeder lines merged with the main tunnel. The blackness was interrupted by intermittent streams of light as we passed beneath grates on the overhead streets.

"Where does this go?" I gasped as I slogged through the sludge behind her.

"To the river."

We huffed, and our pace slowed to an awkward waddle as we tried to remain upright in the rising water. A spec of light in the distance grew with each labored step, and I prayed it was the discharge to the river. While relieved that the tunnel was coming to an end, I feared what might be waiting for us once we reached the outlet. Whoosh! A torrent of water rammed us from behind and thrust us into the light, where we landed in the Vistula River with a splash.

Fortunately, we were deposited into a shallow cove, and we scrambled to the rocky shore.

"What now?" she asked.

I had no idea, but I tried to appear brave. "My father's factory. It's not too far from here. He will help us."

"You heard what he told my father. He won't help a Jew."

"He might do it for me."

"Might?"

"Do you have a better plan?"

We set off upstream in the direction of the Warsaw Steelworks building, but deep down I knew she was right. My father would not risk his position with the Germans and lose control of his factory, or worse, for a Jewish girl, no matter how much I pleaded.

When we reached the edge of the factory grounds, we clawed up the riverbank toward the soot-stained building. Black smoke billowed from the rooftop smokestacks graying the cool spring air, and Nazi guards patrolled the grounds below.

We lay on or bellies, wet clothes clinging to our shivering frames, and watched the two pacing guards. Their gaits were uneven, their eyes cast downward, as if examining the dust that marred their shiny boots. My father's motorcar was backed into a parking spot near the open gate, his driver not in sight.

Not knowing what else to do, we waited, observing, trembling with cold, teeth chattering. When the paths of the two guards crossed, they stopped and conferred. One pulled a cigarette from his pocket and offered it to the other. Then he retrieved another cigarette and positioned it between his lips, struck his lighter, and offered the light to the second guard. Both faced the opposite direction to protect the flame from the breeze as they lit their smokes.

"Now," I whispered.

We darted to the far side of the car. I peered over the hood. The guards were still enjoying their smoke. I risked another peek through the window, then opened the passenger door and crawled in, Karina at my heels. I skuttled over to the driver's seat and froze as the door hinge creaked when Karina pulled it closed.

I pushed the clutch with my left foot, pumped the choke, and turned the key. "Come on. Come on," I coaxed the groaning Mercedes as the motor struggled to start. Finally, the engine roared, but I was too anxious as I released the clutch and pressed the accelerator. The car lurched forward and stalled.

"Hey!" The two surprised guards rushed toward us, cigarettes dangling from their lips.

Flustered, I cranked the starter again, and this time the car cooperated with my foot maneuvers. With a loud screech, we peeled through the open gate, sideswiping the gatepost as we screamed around the corner and onto the deserted street. I was too absorbed with coordinating my foot on the clutch with shifting gears and steering to peer in the rearview mirror to see the guards raise their rifles.

I jumped in my seat as the first shot shattered the rear window and whizzed past my ear. Karina shrieked as the second bullet pierced a taillight. The tires squealed as I steered around a bend and out of sight of the factory. I slowed the car and tried my best to blend in with the other traffic, which was sparse, as petrol was rationed, and most citizens had to either sell or abandon their automobiles. As a factory president, my father was afforded a generous allotment of the Nazi's fuel.

After another few minutes, Karina raised her head and looked out the windshield. "That was close."

"Keep your head down," I admonished her. "Don't let anyone see you. There's a blanket in the backseat. Use it to cover up in case we get stopped. And take that armband off." I snatched her armband and tossed it out the window.

Karina huddled under the blanket on the floor. "Where are we going?"

I didn't answer. I just knew we had to get out of Warsaw, but as I maneuvered through the dirty streets, I didn't know how.

I followed the traffic signs to the southern suburb of Mokotow and found the main highway that led south. At the town's edge, I slowed to a stop behind the car in front of me. "Oh no!"

"What is it?" she asked.

"A checkpoint."

"We can't get through a checkpoint."

"I know. I know." I panicked, as I watched the guard wave the lead car in the line through the barrier.

As the vehicle in front of me crept forward, I spun into a U-turn and headed back toward the city.

I remembered visiting a farm close by on a school outing years ago. I turned down a side street and, after a few more turns, spied the familiar barn ahead, roof collapsed, door dangling ajar on one hinge, the roaming chickens long gone and the field barren of goats and pigs. I turned down the overgrown drive, crept past the ailing structure, and paused by the fallow field.

"It's going to get rough," I informed Karina while staring through the windshield at the stubbly ground before me.

"Why?"

"We're going to cut through the field." I pressed the accelerator, and the car rocked over dirt clods and clumps of weeds.

"Ouch!" she cried as her head hit the glove box as we drove over a large bump. "Can't you go any smoother?"

"Sorry. My father's going to be steaming mad that I'm getting his car dirty."

"I would think he'd be steaming mad about the back window getting shot out."

"He'll be furious about that too, and I'll be slaving in his factory for the rest of my life as punishment."

After more jarring, we reached a gravel access road. We kicked up a trail of dust as we followed the path until it intersected with the highway. I whistled a sigh of relief when I was sure we were out of sight of the checkpoint, and I eased onto the rutted pavement.

Once rumbling on the main road heading south, I finally said to Karina, "We're going to Venice."

"Venice? That's in Italy."

"I know where it is. I've been there many times."

"Why are we going there?"

"My uncle lives there. He will help us."

"Why would he help us? Why would he be any different than your father?"

"Actually, he's worse. He's powerful, intimidating, and unscrupulous. He's my mother's brother and, in a convoluted way, a business associate of my father. He will help us. I will find a way to convince him."

The kilometers hummed by, my hands wrapped around the steering wheel, eyes focused straight ahead. I wasn't sure where we were. I just knew we needed to go south. The desolate road weaved through naked fields, thick forests, and desecrated villages, where charred chimneys stood as tombstones to the ghostly remains that were once the homes of innocent Polish citizens. I also knew that in German-occupied Poland there were many checkpoints secured by vigilant Nazi soldiers.

It grew dark, and the ruts that the German tanks left in the road rattled us as we rumbled through the dangerous enemy-inhabited countryside.

After a long silence Karina asked, "How did you learn to drive? You're not old enough."

"I used to hang out in the garage and watch my father's driver work on the cars. He sometimes let me help. He taught me to drive. We had a pact never to tell my father. I would have gotten ten lashes, and he would have been fired."

My tattered nerves unraveled with every pothole the tires bounced over, and my heart raced at each oncoming headlight as I anticipated being pulled over for an inspection.

"Take me back," she said, interrupting my focus on the dark road.

"Are you crazy? I can't take you back."

"Take me back. I want to be with my family."

"Karina." I tried to sound grown up. "I can't take you back. Besides, your family isn't there anymore. Those damn Nazis packed them onto that train and took them to a labor camp, probably Treblinka." *Rumored to be the worst of all the camps*, I thought, but did not say it aloud. That was the first time I'd sworn in front of someone other than my school chums.

She started to cry.

"I'm sorry. I really am." I wanted to console her but didn't know how. I'd never been around a crying girl before, only my mother after she and my father quarreled. "I promised your father that I would keep you safe. They will take you to the camp if we go back and probably shoot me for trying to help you."

"That could happen anyway." She sniffled.

She was right.

She remained curled up on the floor, under the blanket, which heaved up and down with each sob. After a while she quieted.

The car sputtered. I looked at the fuel indicator. Empty.

"Great!" I exclaimed.

"What?"

"We're out of petrol." The car lurched.

"Can't we get some more?"

"First, I don't have any zloty. Second, there isn't a petrol station around. And third, even if there was, I don't have a ration card."

The engine backfired, causing us to jump. I steered the motorcar to the side of the narrow road, where it rolled to a stop. The surrounding blackness tightened its grip on us, and I rested my forehead on the steering wheel and stifled the urge to cry. Even though I was scared to my core, I knew that I needed to put on a brave face for Karina's sake.

I inhaled a deep breath, opened the door, and slid out of the car. "Come on. Let's push the car into the ditch, and maybe no one will see it until morning."

I shifted the gear to neutral and pushed from the driver's door while Karina shoved from the rear. The front tire caught the side of the road, and the car drifted into the gully. I cringed at the sound of crushing steel and shattered glass as my father's precious automobile settled to its side.

I looked at Karina as she swung the blanket around her shoulders. "Now we can't go back. My father will kill me."

"What now?"

"I don't know." I started walking along the side of the road, and after a pause, she came up beside me.

The slivered moon, now high in the midnight sky, drifted in and out from behind invisible clouds, as if mocking our misfortune. The night chill seeped through my light jacket. I could sense Karina shivering, and she tightened her grip on the blanket that draped her shoulders.

My legs were heavy, and my feet hurt from my school shoes. And I was tired.

A sound came from the distance. *Hoot. Hoot.* After a few moments it grew louder. *Hoot. Hoot.* The approaching train's headlight flickered as it silhouetted ink-black trees, heading north toward Warsaw.

My heart was heavy as I envisioned cattle cars full of tightly packed Jews on their way to the Treblinka concentration camp. I shivered at the memory of what I had witnessed earlier that day—or was it yesterday? The twelve chimes announcing the new day on the grandfather clock in our foyer must have rung by now. I watched the headlight disappear and realized it was hidden by a southbound train on a side rail waiting for the northbound train to pass.

"Come on," I said and darted toward the waiting train.

As we reached the rear car, a blast from the coal-fired engine thundered at the head of the train, and the car lurched forward. There was nothing to grab hold of, so I ran to the next car, a boxcar like the ones the Nazis used to transport the Jews. The side door was ajar. I could hear the hiss from the powerful engine in the distance as the steam from the burning coal coaxed the giant metal wheels to turn.

"Let me give you a boost." I laced my fingers and bent to give Karina a step, the same way my friends and I hoisted each other up trees or over fences. She inserted her foot, and I heaved her headfirst through the opening of the railcar.

"Eew!" she exclaimed as she wrangled into the car.

I reached for the floorboards and tried to hoist myself up, but I slipped and tumbled to the ground. The train was picking up speed, the metal wheels screeching on the iron rails as the powerful engine tugged the long string of railcars forward. I clambered to my feet and leapt toward

Karina's outstretched hand and grabbed the side of the door. Karina clasped my arm and helped pull me in as I shimmied onto my stomach, my feet flutter-kicking the cold, dark air behind me. My knee hit the deck, and I crawled inside and collapsed, then choked on the horrific stench. We buried our noses and mouths in the crook of our arms, trying not to inhale the putrid odor.

"What's that horrible smell?" she shouted over the racket.

"They must have moved farm animals or something," I yelled back, thankful it was too dark for her to read the expression on my face.

We leaned against the rickety wall of the swaying boxcar and succumbed to sleep as exhaustion overpowered the stench and deafening clatter as the train rambled through the perilous countryside.

CHAPTER 8

The dreaded day arrived. The day Jodi was to meet her mother's new boyfriend, Tom. He was now officially a boyfriend, as the couple had gone on two more dates since the trip to Boise the previous week.

To kill time and to escape her mother's nervous nitpicking, Jodi grabbed her basketball and fled to the back lot to shoot some hoops. "Two. Count 'em," she said out loud as the ball sailed through the rim.

"Nice shot."

Jodi turned as Juan approached. She hadn't seen him since he'd moved in the previous week.

"Thanks," she replied as she trotted after the ball. She picked it up and tossed him a dead-center chest pass.

He blushed as he fumbled the catch and scooped up the wayward ball.

"You play?" Jodi asked, though it was obvious he didn't.

"Nah." He thrust the ball toward the basket, missing by yards.

Jodi retrieved the ball and looped a graceful hook shot. "Don't the kids in Caldwell play basketball?"

"Some of the dudes did, but it's not my thing."

"What is your thing?"

"Uh, nothin', really. Just hangin' out. Sometimes I'd go fishin' with my dad and big brother. Most of the kids play soccer, since that's the big sport in Mexico."

"Soccer's not a big draw here. No good fields, I guess." She took another jump shot. "I didn't think you had a dad. I mean, I didn't see him when you moved in."

"Uh, well, he didn't move with us."

"Did he stay in Caldwell?" Another shot off the backboard and two more points. But who was counting? Juan scooped up the ball.

"No. I'm not sure where he is. He may have gone back to Mexico."

"What about your brother?"

"He may have gone too. I'm not sure." Juan shot another air ball. Jodi chased after it. "Sorry. I didn't mean to pry."

"Was that blond lady I saw you with your mother?" he asked.

"Yeah," Jodi replied.

"Wow! She's really hot."

"What's it too you?" Jodi snipped, wedging the ball against her hip. It hurt when people compare Jodi to her beautiful mother, a frequent occurrence. But each subtle, and in some cases not-so-subtle, remark escalated her self-consciousness of her own plain appearance. "Oh, the two of you are related? I never would have guessed." Or "Really? Mother and daughter? I could see distant cousins perhaps." Or the ultimate zinger, "You must take after your father." She was often embarrassed by her mother's overzealous attempt to flaunt her beauty with her tight skirts, heavy makeup, and bleached hair, not unlike the floozies that caroused the streets and patronized the sleazy bars in downtown Portland, Jodi's former hometown. How could Jodi have turned out so differently?

"Hey, don't take offense. I didn't mean anything by it. It's just that you don't look related."

Wham! Another rung lower on the self-esteem ladder. "Sorry. I guess I'm a little sensitive sometimes." She tossed him the ball.

"What about your father?" He took another awkward shot, and the ball bounced off the rim.

"I don't have one."

"You must have one. It's biologically impossible not to have a father."

"I don't have a father, and I don't want to talk about it, okay?" She sounded just like her mother whenever Jodi asked about her father. No comment. End of discussion. The silence was usually followed by Mom turning her back on her daughter, either by leaving the room, or facing the stove, or searching for something in the refrigerator.

No, Jodi had never learned anything about her father and had come to accept that the topic was an impenetrable steel door that would remain closed and double bolted with no key, through eternity. She'd often fantasized about him when she was younger, imagining him a dashing prince who would swoop in and rescue her from the dingy apartment, buy her the latest toys and stylish clothes, and take her on exotic trips to Hawaii or Disneyland or the ocean, like the family vacations the rich kids took every spring break and summer. Now, being more realistic, she figured that her father must be tall and skinny and not very good looking, as these undesirable traits could not have possibly come from her mother's side.

Juan thrust his hands into his pockets and kicked a pebble. "Maybe you can teach me to play? Some dudes need another player for a game. I told them I was tied up now but could help them out later. There's a little money involved. I'll split the winnings with you."

"So that's your angle. What'll it cost if you lose?"

"I don't know. Maybe a hundred bucks."

"A hundred bucks! You've only lived here a week and you're already getting tied up with a bad crowd? You have that kind of money?"

"Not right now. That's why I need you to teach me—I need the dough." After a pause he added, "And they're not bad dudes. It's just a friendly wager."

"I'm not paying half if you lose."

"You better be a good coach, 'cause I can't lose."

"Well, the first thing you need to learn is to handle the ball. Start by dribbling."

"Dribbling?"

"Bounce the ball." She dribbled as she trotted around in a circle, the ball floating around her back, between her legs, hand to hand. "Do it all the time—while you're walking through town, brushing your teeth, eating breakfast."

"I'll drive my mother crazy."

"Probably."

"Jodi," her mother called from across the parking lot.

"Gotta go." She passed him the ball. "Dribble, dribble, dribble." She trotted toward her mother, gut churning, dreading the upcoming meeting.

"Is that what you're wearing?" Jodi's mother exclaimed as she wedged a picnic basket in the cluttered trunk of the gray Civic.

Jodi looked down at her cutoff shorts, Blazers T-shirt, and sneakers. "I thought we were going on a picnic." She eyed her mother's short skirt, platform sandals, and skimpy halter top.

"Get in the car. We're going to be late."

Jodi and her mother arrived at Riverfront Park at one o'clock sharp. Tom was nowhere to be seen. They carried the basket to a picnic table shaded by a large elm tree and unloaded the contents—a plastic tablecloth, paper plates, napkins, sandwiches, and a bottle of red wine.

"I don't see any Dr Pepper. Does that mean I get wine too?" Jodi smirked, not surprised by the oversight.

"Hello, beautiful," a man's voice called from behind them. He swaggered to the table and placed his hands on Mom's hips, spun her around, and planted a kiss on her lips. "You must be the little lady," he said as he winked at Jodi. "Your beautiful mother has told me so much about you." He grabbed Jodi's wrist and air kissed the back of her hand. "It's nice to meet you, Joanie."

"Jodi," her mother corrected.

"Oh, of course. I apologize, Jodi."

Jodi cringed as her internal jerk alarm dinged. Tom's dark hair curled up around the green John Deere cap he wore tilted low over the mirrored Oakleys that masked his eyes. A thick brown mustache covered his upper lip. A developing beer belly hung over a large silver belt buckle, the kind that cowboys wore, which was obviously needed to hold up his ill-fitting Wranglers. A pair of rattlesnake western boots covered his hooves, and the fringe of a tattoo peeked below the sleeve of his blue golf shirt.

"Pleased to meet you, Mr., uh . . ."

"Tom. Call me Tom. If you call me Mr. Smith, I'll think you're talking to my father." He chuckled.

Jodi grinned. "Nice to meet you, Tom." *Ding ding.*

"Here, Tom." Jodi's mother handed him the bottle of cabernet. "Open this, will you? I'll get the glasses." She fished around in the picnic basket and pulled out two plastic cups.

Tom opened the wine and poured a generous amount into each glass. "Cheers," he said as he handed Mom one of the glasses and clinked his with hers.

"Cheers," Mom repeated while staring at her reflection in his Oakleys. They both took a sip, while Jodi turned away and snatched a sandwich from the basket, jerk alarm rising from a ding to a cymbal crash.

While lunching on ham sandwiches and potato salad, Tom updated Mom on the week's activities at the packing house. Jodi pretended to listen to his complaints of problem workers, an overbearing boss, and a water shortage that was impacting grain prices. Her mother's attention was unwavering, asking an occasional question and overdoing the laughter at the corny anecdotes. Jodi knew her mother wasn't interested in the mechanics of beef production, but she at least pretended to hang on to Tom's every word.

"So how was your week at the café?" he finally asked Mom when he had exhausted his list of problems at the plant.

"Well, it was a very busy week," she began.

"Oh, hey," Tom interrupted. "There's Joe and Tina." He waved to a black convertible passing on the distant street. "Did I tell you about the poker game last Thursday? I creamed his ass. Sorry 'bout the swear word, kiddo." He grinned at Jodi.

Turning back to Mom, obviously not interested in her busy week, he continued his tale on how he pulled one over on poor Joe and raked in the $132 pot. "He's probably eating at McDonald's this week, and I'm gonna take you out for a night on the town."

Tom slipped his cell phone out of his pocket and peered at the time. "I'm so sorry, sweetheart, but I've gotta run. I promised Ed I would stop by and help him move a fridge. I don't know why he picked today to get a new one, but I owe him a favor and need to pay up." He stood and pulled his cap farther down over his shades. "This was nice. And Joanie, it was nice to meet you. You take care of this beautiful doll until I pick her up on Friday." He moved closer to her mother, who was now also standing. "Wear your dancin' shoes. We're going to spend Joe's hard-earned cash on burgers and brews at the Sage Tav."

Jodi looked away as he kissed her mother again. Then he nodded to Jodi. "Little lady, it's been a pleasure."

Jodi and her mother packed up the leftover potato salad, empty wine bottle, and utensils in silence.

"Well, what do you think?" Mom finally asked.

"Well, if you really want to know, I think he's a self-centered, egotistical jerk," she said before she could stop herself.

"Jodi!"

"Well, you asked what I thought."

"At least give him a chance. He was trying to be nice. He just doesn't know how to interact with children."

"First of all, I'm not a child. And he didn't even try to interact with me. He just talked about himself the whole time."

"Well, if he had more time, I'm sure he would've gotten around to it."

Jodi gathered the dirty paper plates and plastic cups and stomped to the nearby garbage can, deposited the rubbish, and gave the lid an extra slam.

When she returned to the table, her mother was stuffing the plastic tablecloth into the picnic basket.

"Who was that boy you were playing ball with?" she asked in a quieter but edgy tone.

"Just some kid who moved in downstairs."

"What's his name?"

"Juan."

"Where is he from?"

"Caldwell. Why?"

"You need to stay away from him."

"Why?"

"You just don't need to hang around with his kind."

CHAPTER 9

Jodi replayed the previous day's discussion with her mother about Juan over and over in her mind as she strung bean vines around a trellis in Mr. K's rapidly growing garden. It didn't make sense to her why her mother was so disapproving of someone she hadn't even met. It wasn't like she and Juan were even friends. They'd only had two conversations. Sure, she had agreed to teach him to play basketball. Did she really agree to that? How did that happen?

"The peas and beans should be producing soon," Mr. K said, bringing Jodi back to her present task. "Look at all those buds."

"Huh?"

"These little flowers. They're all going to transform into peas and beans, kind of like caterpillars turning into butterflies. I can almost taste them now. Have you ever tried fresh-picked peas? There is nothing like it."

"You mean raw?" Jodi didn't really like peas, or beans, or most vegetables, for that matter. She couldn't imagine eating them raw.

"You haven't lived until you've eaten fresh-picked peas."

"Uh-huh." She doubted that.

"What's on your mind, my young friend, that you're so distracted today?"

"Nothing much." She pretended to focus on the vine that she was winding around a string on the trellis. "It's just that my mom and I had another fight yesterday."

"Another fight? You and your mother fight often?"

"Well, maybe not a fight. More like a disagreement. I just don't get it. She doesn't want me to talk with a kid who moved into our building. She hasn't even met him."

"Maybe she thinks you're too young to have a gentleman friend."

"First of all, we're not even friends. And we're certainly not *that* kind of friends. We were just shooting hoops." After a pause, she added, "And she's always pestering me about not having any friends and especially about not having a *special* friend. I guess she had boyfriends long before she was my age."

"Too young, if you ask me."

"I think it might be because he's Mexican. But why would she care about that?"

Mr. K gazed at a quail perched on the rooftop of the house across the street, calling out for its mate. He inhaled a deep breath. "Biases can run very deep and often have no rationale."

Jodi paused from her work and leaned back on her heels and quietly responded, "I guess you do know about that. So what happened after you got on that train?"

***

I wasn't sure what woke us—the cool morning air, the breaking daylight streaming through the open car door, or the changing pitch of the whining rumble as the train slowed.

We both saw it at the same time. She screamed, and I covered her mouth with my hand as we stared, horrified, at the tattered toy bear in the corner, soiled stuffing spilling from a tear that once held a furry limb.

"It's not his. It's not his," I kept repeating. "There's no way it can be his," I said as the memory of Karina's baby brother clutching the stuffed animal flashed in my mind. "That train was going east. There's no way this can be the same train." I removed my hand from her mouth.

She was trying not to sob, but tears streamed down her red cheeks.

The brakes squealed, and the train slowed further, the metal clanking and grinding as cars butted against each other. I poked my head through the open door and peered toward the front of the train. I gasped and drew back. Far ahead was a platform with armed soldiers milling around. I rushed to the other side of the filthy boxcar. I struggled with the latch and slid the door open just enough to squeeze through. I peered out, looking both directions. The tracks were in a clearing, with some woods about a hundred meters away.

"We need to go now. Quick!" I leapt from the train and broke my fall by rolling over my shoulder. I scrambled to my feet and helped her down, and we raced for the woods. I pumped my arms to propel me faster as I stumbled through the rocky field. I could hear Karina heaving at my heels. We reached the trees but didn't stop and didn't look back. The thick brush snagged our clothes and scratched our faces, but still we kept running. The forest opened to a small clearing with a shallow stream. We fell to our bellies, inhaled the icy sweetness of the spring runoff, and spit out the grit and stench of the grungy railcar.

Still on our bellies, we lay there for a few minutes, breathing hard, the hair around our faces wet from the cold water that trickled haphazardly over the smooth pebbles that lined the creek bed. Karina rose to her knees and let out a long breath. "I need a lavatory really bad." She stood, looked around, and paced toward some bushes.

I started to follow her.

"You can't come."

"I, uh, I wasn't. I'm just going to go behind this tree." I wandered over to the tree to take care of my business. Just as I was finishing up, she screamed.

I dashed over and clasped my hand over her mouth to muffle her hysterical cries while she pointed to the bushes.

When her panic eased, I removed my hand. "In there," she whispered, still pointing at the bushes, her voice shaking.

I took a tentative step toward the brush, anticipating a snake or other small animal, and shifted the branches. I jumped back. After taking a deep breath, I returned to the bush and squatted next to a dead soldier's body lying face down in the mud.

"Is he dead?" She peered over my shoulder.

I realized from my night in the ghetto that she had seen a lot more dead bodies than I. "He's dead."

"Is he Polish or German?"

"Definitely German." The torn green-gray uniform and jackboots were a dead giveaway. I rolled the body over, and we both flinched at his maggot-covered face. "Looks like he's been here awhile." I fished through his pockets and scooped all the contents into my arms and moved to a clear area.

"What are you doing?"

"He won't need these anymore." I opened a thin metal cigarette holder. Three smokes left. I snapped the case shut and shoved it into my pocket, along with some matches, a few coins, and chewing gum. I peeked into a crumpled bag. "Damn!" I cried and threw the sack of ant-infested crackers into the bushes. I was hungry, and I was sure Karina was too. I returned to the body and snatched a pistol from his belt. I searched for some bullets but couldn't find any. I put the gun into my pocket with the cigarettes anyway.

Finished pilfering the dead soldier's possessions, we retreated from the stench of the body. I pulled the candy bar out of my other pocket, broke it in two, and handed her the larger piece.

"What now?" she asked after we devoured our treat.

I had no idea, but I wasn't about to tell her that. "Let's follow the stream." Since she didn't offer a better suggestion, we started hiking as the train whistle hooted in the distance.

The trek through the thick forest was difficult. Withered vines attacked our faces and pricked our clothing. We scrambled over felled trees, tripped around rocks, and squished through soppy mud that tried to suck our shoes from our aching feet. I hoped we were going south, but I couldn't be sure.

Late in the day we came upon a narrow dirt road. I motioned Karina to scrunch down, and we crouched in the underbrush and eyed the lane. There were no vehicles. I looked at the sun and tried to determine which way was south. "This way." I nodded my head to the left as I walked to the side of the road.

Karina followed, and we trudged on in silence. I imagined her mind was on the fate of her family and the dismembered toy on the train. She buried her face in her elbow to muffle a sob. I also wondered if my school had notified my parents of my absence. My mother must be worried sick and my father very angry. I winced as I envisioned the lashing that was looming if I were found and sent home.

A faint rumble distracted my thoughts. It took a moment before the sound registered. "Get off the road!" I dragged Karina into the ditch, thankful that the spring rains had provided tall grass and thick brush for cover. We were once again on our bellies, spying through the foliage at a short German convoy traveling in open-air jeeps, a machine gun clutched in each soldier's hands, twitchy fingers poised to fire at the slightest provocation.

After they passed, I released the breath that I had been holding. "That was close," I said more to myself than to Karina.

We rose from the gully and continued down the road, my senses attentive to the slightest noise. I tried not to think about being hungry, but my growling stomach was a constant reminder. The orange ball of sun sank closer to the horizon. My legs ached and my feet hurt. I knew Karina was worse off, but she kept up with me and did not complain.

After rounding a few more curves, we came upon a small farm. A weary cottage stood near the road. Behind it was a dilapidated barn that looked like it might collapse at the slightest breath of wind. The surrounding field was not plowed. We spied a lone tree just beyond the barn. Reckless, we dashed for the tree, which held a promise of ripe cherries. I could almost taste the sweet delicacies. We stood under the branches and searched for red orbs. There were no cherries within reach. Perhaps near the top. I jumped up, trying to grasp a branch, but it was just beyond my reach.

"Let me boost you up." I knelt and looped my fingers in the same manner as I had at the train. She shot me a skeptical gaze, and I understood her hesitation. "I promise I won't look. . ." meaning up her skirt.

She slipped her foot into my clasped hands, and looking down, I boosted her up. She clutched the lowest branch. I willed for her to pull herself up, as she was so thin and weak, but soon she had shimmied up into the heart of the tree. She thoroughly searched every branch but didn't find a single cherry. The birds had left the dangling pits stripped bare.

She wriggled her way down to a lower branch. "How do I get down?"

I looked around for a stool or a ladder, which I knew I would not find. "Hang from the branch, and I'll lower you down."

Just as I wrapped my arms around her dangling legs, the brittle branch of the old, tired tree snapped, and we tumbled to the ground.

"Are you okay?" I scrambled to my feet and brushed the dust from my trousers.

She remained on the ground, clutching her elbow. "My arm. My arm hurts. Argh!" Anguish etched her face.

I stared at the dark house with the drawn curtains, expecting the angry resident to rush out with a shotgun, but everything remained still. I bent and helped her to her feet, wrapped my arm around her, and escorted her to the barn. The door hung ajar from a broken hinge, as if inviting us in for the night. It creaked as I nudged it open farther. A mule in the corner stall watched curiously as we crept in.

I steered Karina to a pile of straw in the far corner and helped her down. The mule snorted. "Quiet there, ol' buddy," I whispered to the mule.

"Let me see your arm."

Karina slid her sleeve up, and even in the dimness I could see it was black and blue and swollen like a balloon. She lowered her sleeve and eased back into the hay, trying to muffle another groan.

"I'm so cold," she said, her voice soft and shaky.

I looked around the barn but couldn't find even a burlap sack. I covered her with straw, the blanket forgotten on the train. Her breath was heavy, and when she closed her eyes, I leaned back on my heels and mumbled a quick prayer. I shuddered as a distant train whistle echoed in the night.

I realized she was asleep, so I crawled in the straw near her, closed my eyes, and buried my face in my arms to smother my sorrow. I had failed in my promise to her father to keep her safe.

CHAPTER 10

The next morning, I woke to the prongs of a pitchfork hovering over my chest. I had no doubt the woman, wisps of graying hair dangling over her angry face, clutching the other end was hell bent to plunge it deep into my heart.

"Who are you and why are you in my barn?" she demanded.

"I ... I ... uh," I tried to slide away from the improvised weapon, but the straw had me trapped. "Michal," I blurted.

"What are you doing in my barn, Michal?"

"I'm sorry. We were cold. Please don't hurt us. We'll leave now. Please let us go."

She looked over at Karina. "What's wrong with her?"

I scooted onto my elbow and looked at Karina. Beads of sweat covered her ashen face, and she was shivering. "Uh, I think she broke her arm."

"She needs a doctor," the woman said. "Is she a Jew?"

"No! No!" My mind was racing now. "She's, uh, she's my sister."

"She doesn't look like your sister."

"She is! She is!" I rambled. "You see, my mother's Italian. She looks more like my mother. I take after my father. She is my sister!" I left out the detail that my mother was only part Italian.

"Let me see your papers." Obviously, the woman wasn't buying my story. I reached into my trouser pocket and slid out my wallet and fumbled for my papers, which designated me as a juvenile citizen of the city of Warsaw of the German-controlled General Government sector of Poland. I held my breath again.

The woman spoke Polish, but with a heavy German accent. I feared that her loyalty could be with the Reich. The one thing that was certain was that we were at the mercy of this woman.

"Says your residence is Warsaw. What are you doing here?"

I didn't want to let the woman know that I had no idea where we were. "We're on our way to Venice. To see my, er, our uncle. We got lost."

She tossed the papers back to me. "Show me her papers."

"Uh, they got lost too."

"They got lost," the woman repeated, furrowing her brow.

We were doomed.

After a brief standoff, she let out a long sigh and lowered her weapon. "Help me get her to the house."

I clambered out of the straw, and the woman and I carried Karina to a small room at the back of the tiny cottage and laid her on one of the two twin beds.

"She needs a doctor," the woman repeated as she left the room.

I knelt next to the bed and watched Karina. She shivered, and perspiration dampened her threadbare clothes. Her breaths were shallow. I touched her forehead with the back of my fingers. It was hot.

The woman returned with a bowl of water and a towel. She dipped the towel in the water and wiped Karina's face. She rewet the towel and placed it on Karina's forehead.

"God help me," the woman sighed. "There is a Jewish doctor in the village, the only doctor in the village who survived the Nazi's purge. Some of the residents have been hiding him. I'll try to find him." She dipped the towel in the water again and replaced it on Karina's forehead. "Try to keep her as cool as you can. The pump is in the kitchen. You can refill the bowl when needed. Come help me hitch the wagon."

My soul burned as Karina's fearful eyes watched me follow the woman from the tiny room.

After we harnessed a wooden farm cart behind the aged draft mule, the woman climbed up and looked down at me. "I should be back by dark. If I'm not, stay inside and don't turn on any lights. If someone comes by, don't make any noise. Don't let anyone see you." She faced forward and picked up the reins.

"Wait!" I shouted. She glared down at me. "What is your name?"

"Maria," she said as she flicked the reins, not offering her surname.

The mule shook its head and snorted. The wagon creaked as the steed jerked it forward.

"Thank you, Mrs. Maria. Pani Maria," I said under my breath as I watched woman and mule disappear around a bend.

I returned to Karina's side and kept the damp cloth on her forehead as instructed. Each time she closed her eyes to sleep, I feared she would not wake up. When she did wake, I wished she would go back to sleep so she wouldn't be in so much pain. She would look at me blankly, as if she didn't know who I was. Once she asked for her mother. In sleep she would often mumble. I could only grasp sporadic words of her muffled cries—"get out," "fire," "help," and "daddy." I'd never felt so helpless, and I feared the woman, Pani Maria, would not return with the doctor.

I must have dozed in the chair by the bed because the squeak of the opening door startled me. I jumped up when Pani Maria entered the room—alone. "Where's the doctor?"

"I don't know," she whispered. "I put the word out to everyone I knew who would be safe to ask. We can only wait and hope that he comes."

I couldn't believe what I was hearing. How could she not bring the doctor?

As if reading my angst, she explained, "It is very dangerous for the doctor and the people who are hiding him. The Nazis will offer food or threaten imprisonment or death to coerce citizens to turn on their friends or neighbors. The doctor's protectors have no reason to trust that my summoning him is not a trap."

She checked Karina's forehead. "Fever is still too high. Did she drink any water?"

"Very little," I responded, shaking my head. "She mostly slept."

"I don't have much to eat, but I'll go make some broth." Pani Maria disappeared into the kitchen, and I heard clanking pans and running water.

She emerged with a tray containing some watery soup and a few bites of bread. "When is the last time you had something to eat?"

"Day before yesterday." I neglected to mention the candy bar from the previous day.

After devouring the meager meal, I decided I had no choice but to trust the woman, so I asked, "Where are we?"

She raised her eyebrow. "Northwest of Krakow, just inside the German territory."

"We're in Germany?" I was terrified now.

"Prior to the war, this province was part of Poland. After the Nazi invasion, the Germans annexed western Poland into Germany. Most of the Polish citizens who lived here were forced to move to the east so that 'racially pure' Germans could be resettled here. That is why you must be careful who you talk to and trust."

I felt a sudden chill. "Are you German? Were you resettled?"

"My heritage is German, but I was not resettled. My husband was Polish, and we raised our two sons as Poles in this house. However, because of my German bloodline, I was allowed to stay."

"Where is your husband?"

She lowered her head. "He is dead." She took a shaky breath. "Soon after the Nazis invaded, he enlisted with the Polish army. He and his comrades raged a brave fight, but the German panzers were too powerful for the underequipped and undertrained Polish fighters, and they were forced to retreat." She studied the backs of her weathered hands resting on her lap. "My husband was shot by a German sympathizer from our very own village during the retreat." She closed her eyes, and her voice was faint. "He never made it home, and I never got to say goodbye."

I tried to digest what she had told me. "Where are your sons?"

"I don't know." Bitterness crept into her shaky tone. "I pray every day that they are safe, but I don't know."

We sat in silence and watched Karina. She seemed more peaceful now. That scared me. The faint light that had twined through the curtain had faded. Night had fallen.

A soft knock sounded on the front door by the kitchen. Pani Maria rose to answer, and I followed her. She motioned for me to stay in the shadows. The knock came again.

"Who is it?" Pani Maria whispered through the door.

"Did someone summon a doctor?" the voice from outside asked.

"Thank goodness," Pani Maria said under her breath as she creaked open the door and peered out. After confirming that it was indeed the doctor, she stepped aside, and a diminutive figure slipped through.

The doctor was a slight, frail man. His dark clothes and shoes were ragged. His sunken eyes were concealed behind broken spectacles and a tattered hat, which he wore low. He was not wearing the armband with the Star of David, which all Jews were required to wear. He gave me a slight nod.

"This way." Pani Maria guided him by the elbow to the back room.

He looked down at Karina. "What happened?"

Pani Maria glanced at me, and I knew she was signaling for me to remain quiet. "She broke her arm," she answered.

The doctor nodded again and turned the bed covers down to Karina's waist. "Bring some scissors or a knife. We need to cut away her blouse."

Pani Maria returned with a pair of sewing shears, and the doctor went to work. "I don't have any plaster to make a proper cast, so we're going to have to improvise. Can you bring some strong sticks or pipe, a clean bed sheet, and some tape or twine?"

Pani Maria scurried away in search of the requested supplies.

"This is going to hurt. I need to set the bone," the doctor said to Karina. He turned to me. "Get on her other side and hold her upper arm as tight as you can. I am going to pull the bone back into alignment." He looked again at Karina. "I don't have any morphine, so you're going to have to be brave." He picked up a towel and rolled it up. "Here. Bite down on this."

Karina squirmed, and her muffled cries cut through me as the doctor forced the bone to its proper alignment. I struggled to keep her elbow steady as he manipulated the limb. Finally, he lowered her arm. "That should do it."

Pani Maria returned with the improvised splint material, and the doctor wound strips of sheet around some kindling and metal kitchen utensils. After securing the last piece of tape around Karina's arm, he leaned back. "Not my best work, but that should hold it in place provided you take care not to upset it. Don't try to use the arm or hand for six weeks. And no hitting anybody," he added as he winked at me.

He reached into his pocket and pulled out a small paper sack, which he handed to Pani Maria. "I could only scrounge up a few antibiotics, not enough to fight the infection, but it might help some. Give her one every twelve hours. I know rations are tight, but she is very malnourished, and her body will not heal without adequate nutrition. Try to get as much food into her as you can, especially protein, but start slow, with only bland foods for the first few days. There is nothing else I can do under the circumstances. You can try a tea with garlic, honey, or oregano oil. It might help with the fever." The doctor stood and reached for his hat.

I knew Pani Maria didn't want me to speak, but I felt compelled to do so, considering the risk he took to come. "Thank you, Doctor." I reached into my pocket and collected the coins that I had taken from the dead soldier. "This is all I have. Please take them."

I held the coins in my open palm, and the doctor studied them for a moment. "You keep the coins and use them for food or medicine for your friend." He put on his hat and shambled to the door. He paused, turned, and said, "Good luck to you, young man." He tipped his hat to Pani Maria and then disappeared into the darkness.

CHAPTER 11

At dawn the next morning, Pani Maria and I hitched the wagon behind the old mule again for a trip to the village. I didn't want to leave Karina alone. She'd had a rough night, weaving in and out of consciousness. She was in a great deal of pain, and her fever still hadn't broken. I was scared for her. I think Pani Maria was scared for her as well, but I wasn't sure. After the doctor left, I had confessed that Karina was not my sister, which she had already presumed. I did not tell her that she was a Jewess. Although she probably determined that as well. It was dangerous to hide a Jew, and I wondered if she secretly wanted Karina to die so she wouldn't have to bear the burden.

The old mule labored, pulling the weight of the cart loaded with me and Pani Maria, so I hopped off and walked next to him, trying to coax him on and to eliminate the boredom.

"What's his name?" I asked.

"Doesn't have one."

"Why not?"

"I don't want to become too attached in case I have to slaughter him come winter. Even as old and gnarly as he is, his meat will be valuable on the black market. If he makes it that long," she added under her breath.

As if protesting his fate, the mule let out a loud snort.

An uneasy chill seeped through the lonely streets as we entered the run-down village. Many of the decrepit buildings were spackled with bullet holes, and heaps of crumbled concrete and debris spilled onto burned-out lots. A few frail souls milled about. Each glanced up to watch us pass but pretended not to see us. No one uttered a greeting.

Upon reaching the market, Pani Maria climbed down from the cart and handed me the reins. "Stay here with the mule. I don't want to leave him alone."

I handed her the coins I had been protecting, and she disappeared into the ramshackle building, its roof sagging, as if weighed down from the worries of the downtrodden villagers, and I hoped it wouldn't collapse while Pani Maria was inside.

After a short time, she emerged carrying a half dozen brown eggs, a small sack of flour, a few potatoes, an onion, some goat's milk, and thankfully, some honey and garlic. "Didn't have any oregano." She stuffed her bounty into a burlap sack, and instead of putting the bag in the back of the cart, she set it on the footbed and tied it to the rail. "Can't be too careful," she said.

She stepped up onto the cart and tried her best to conceal the bag under her tattered skirt.

I handed her the reins and reached for the mule's bridle. "Come on, ol' mule." I gave him a slight tug and maneuvered into a U-turn. I was anxious to get back to Karina.

Two blocks into our return trip, Pani Maria instructed me to turn onto a side street. I led the mule around the corner, and we stopped in front of another droopy dwelling. "I'll be right back. Sit up here while I'm gone." She retrieved another burlap sack from the cart and disappeared into the shop.

I understood I was to guard the rations as well as the mule.

I must have been daydreaming because I didn't see the two boys who approached the wagon.

"Well, well," the taller of the pair said. "Brother, it looks like we found supper." He pulled a knife from his tattered trouser pocket and flicked the blade open.

"I'm so hungry I think I could eat this ol' mule," the smaller boy said.

I tried to swallow the lump that formed in my throat. Although both boys were thin and, like everyone else, wore dirty, ragged clothes, they were both older and bigger than me. I didn't stand a chance.

The older boy took a step onto the cart and reached for the bag.

I whisked the dead soldier's pistol from my pocket and pointed the barrel straight between his steely eyes. He froze. I pulled back the hammer and prayed that he didn't notice my quivering lip or shaking hand as I stared into those eyes, willing myself not to blink.

He swallowed hard and eased to the ground. "I guess I'm not as hungry as I thought." Both boys backed up a few steps and then fled toward the alley.

I lowered the gun and noticed Pani Maria standing in the doorway of the shop, gaping, as if she were about to scream. She composed herself and approached the wagon. I returned the pistol to my pocket, stepped down, and handed her the reins.

As we neared the outskirts of the dreary village, a trio of enemy jeeps crept toward us. Pani Maria motioned for me to move to the side and stop. "Lower your cap and keep your eyes down," she instructed.

I did as she directed, but as the last vehicle passed, I stole a glance to see the doctor being dragged behind it by a rope tightly knotted around his bleeding wrists. My heart ached as I nudged the mule forward. Suddenly a dark shadow swallowed the midday sun, and I looked up to see thick black smoke billowing from the next block. As we passed the flaming dwelling, a slew of bodies, including a tiny one, dangled from a blossoming elm tree, lifelessly swaying in the midday breeze, a chilling warning to other daring villagers tempted to undermine the brutal authority of the ruthless occupiers.

I tried to hide my tears from Pani Maria during the agonizing trek back to her small cottage. She never asked me about the gun, and I never asked her what was in the sack. Neither of us uttered a word to Karina about the doctor.

CHAPTER 12

Pounding on the apartment door interrupted Jodi's morning violin practice. She rushed to the entry and spied Juan through the peephole. She unlocked the deadbolt, removed the chain, and whisked open the door to her fidgeting trainee. She puffed a breath of relief that her mother was at work and wasn't home to create an uncomfortable scene in front of Juan.

"What's so important that you had to try to break the door down? I thought there was an emergency."

"There is an emergency!"

"What is it?"

"The game! It's today!"

"What game?"

"The three-on-three game. The one that you've been coaching me to get ready for."

"The one with a hundred bucks riding on it?"

Juan nodded.

"You're going to play in a three-on-three game today? Against a real team? You're light years away from being ready."

"I know. I know. I didn't think it would be so hard. I figured if you could do it . . ."

Jodi cut him off. "You mean because I'm a girl?"

"No, no. I didn't mean it like that. It's just that you make it look so easy."

Jodi smiled. "Because of my years of dedicated training and superior talent."

"Yeah, yeah. That's what I was trying to say."

"Sounds like you've got a problem. Maybe I'll come just to watch you get clobbered. It would serve you right for getting messed up in such a stupid thing."

Juan gave her his most pathetic look. "Will you help?"

"Will I help what?"

"I could pretend that I sprained my wrist, and you can play for me."

Jodi chuckled. "You want me to play in your place? How long did it take for you to dream up that cockamamie idea?"

"All morning. Just come to the park with me. If nothing else, you can help me figure out how to scrounge up the money."

"You don't even have the money?" Jodi exclaimed in disbelief.

"I wasn't expecting to need it."

"You can't make a bet like that without the means to pay up, especially since your chance of winning is less than zero. Translation: impossible!"

"I know that now."

When they reached the park, Juan led Jodi to a picnic table near the basketball court. Two Mexican kids sat on the table, feet resting on the seat.

"Hola," Juan called out to the pair.

They nodded, and one asked, "Who's the chica?"

Assuming she was just insulted, Jodi placed her hands on her hips, wishing she could think of a comeback.

Juan jumped into his ruse. "Look, guys. I'm really sorry. I hurt my wrist and can't play. Can't even hold the ball in fact." He nodded to the ball Jodi held under her arm.

"Are you kidding me?" one of the boys said as he stood from the table. "Two hundred smackers are riding on this game and you're backing out?"

"You want us to just hand over two Ben Franks?" the other boy chimed in. "Where are we going to get that kind o' dinero?"

Jodi's jaw dropped.

"No, no," Juan said. "This is Jodi. She's going to cover for me. She can kick both your asses."

Jodi shot Juan a piercing gaze, which he pretended not to notice.

The first boy grabbed the ball from Jodi. "You're full of it, Castillo. No chica is going to kick our asses, but we're going to kick yours." He fired the ball back to Jodi, and she expertly caught it, to the surprise of all three boys.

"Look," Jodi said to Juan. "I'm going home. Can't wait to read your obituary in the paper tomorrow."

She started to turn, when three more teens approached. She expected the other team to be Latinx as well, but two were Black, wiry, and identical twins, and the third sported a wavy shock of sandy hair and sparkling blue eyes. They all had a significant height advantage over Juan and his pals. She recognized the twins from school, although they were a grade ahead of her and had not shared any of her classes. They stood out as the only African American kids on campus, among a sea of white faces sprinkled with a dash of Latinos, the second and third generations of the migrant workers who, Jodi knew, labored in the potato, onion, and sugar beet fields that surround the town.

"Well, well, well," the blond player said, grinning. "If it ain't the three banditos just beggin' to get their asses kicked. How about you just pay up now so the nice parks department folk don't have to peel your sorry butts from the pavement?" They laughed and gave each other high fives.

"Ooh, tough guy thinks he can intimidate us. It ain't over till it's over," Juan's teammate said. "Let's get this thing started."

Jodi stared at him as he continued.

"Wimpy Juan over here hurt himself, so Jodi's going to take his place."

Her jaw dropped again, but before she could protest, he kept on talking. "Half court. Play to fifty. Call your own fouls. Opposite team must touch the ball after each point." After a pause he added one more item, "Five-minute warm-up."

"Are you crazy?" Jodi said to the commanding one who filled the role of team leader as they proceeded to the court.

"Probably." He turned his baseball cap backward on his head.

"What's your name anyway?"

"Name's Marco." He nodded to his buddy. "And he's Rodolfo. Goes by RJ."

"How did you get into this mess anyway?"

"You don't wanna know," Marco responded as he took his first warm-up shot—and missed.

Jodi trotted after Marco's wayward ball. She lobbed the retrieved ball to RJ. As she returned to the court, she studied the other team. *We're going to get slaughtered*, she thought as she watched shot after shot swish through the hoop.

After the warm-up, Marco's team won the coin toss, and he assumed the point position and dribbled the ball. He signaled Jodi to make a block. He rushed past her, and Marco's defender ran into her, almost knocking her over. Marco took a jump shot that was batted away by one of the limber twins. The other team recovered the ball and in no time had two points on the scoreboard, which was Juan's job on the sidelines—tallying the points after each basket.

After the other team scored six more points, Jodi's team regained possession of the ball. Jodi maneuvered herself into the open and called out for the pass. Marco ignored her and drove to the basket, only to have the ball stripped from his hand by an opponent.

After three more baskets by the "Sharks," as Jodi had now dubbed the other team, Marco once again had the ball. Again, Jodi yelled that she was open, and since Marco was now double teamed, he had no option but to pass it to her. She caught the bounce pass, drove to the basket, and put in a smooth layup for two points.

Marco, apparently realizing that points on the board trumped machismo, passed the ball to Jodi and set up a block. She took a jump shot over the block for two more points. She, Marco, and RJ high-fived.

The Sharks scored another two baskets, and then Marco once again had the ball. He passed it to Jodi, and she spied RJ open near the basket. She fired him a pass, and he put up the easy shot.

Jodi wiped the sweat from her eyes as Marco took his position at point. She cut across the court, and Marco passed her the ball. She attempted a hook shot over one of the twin's head, when the other twin knocked her arm from behind, an obvious and intentional foul, which sent the ball sailing out of bounds.

"Hey!" Jodi shouted at him.

"What?" He held his arms out in the "what did I do?" gesture. He did not self-call the foul.

The game became a little rougher after that, with more body contact on both sides. Jodi took another shot and an opponent's elbow collided with her eye. She responded with a side bump to a Shark as he blocked for his teammate's jump shot. Her heart pounded, and salty sweat stung her eyes as the fast-paced game continued under the sweltering summer sun. She wanted to call a time-out and quench her dry throat, but she didn't dare.

Juan shouted from the sideline. "Forty-eight to thirty-two."

Marco took a jump shot that bounced off the rim, and a Shark recovered the ball and soon scored the winning basket.

The Sharks fist-bumped and high-fived each other while Jodi and her haggard teammates were stooped over, hands on knees, gasping for air.

The Sharks sauntered over, and the sandy-haired one said, "Awesome playing, Jodi. You're all right. You can play with us anytime." They each gave her a fist-bump.

"You"—he pointed at Marco as he continued—"have until Friday to pay up." And they swaggered off, shoulder bumping and heckling each other as they exited the park.

Juan and his buddies stood in silence as they watched the victors cross the field. Although physically exhausted, Jodi was elated. Sure she wished they had won, but it was the best time she'd had since moving to Sage Grove nearly a year ago. Not only did she get to play the sport she loved, she actually felt accepted, even by the opposing team.

"How are we going to come up with two hundred smackers by Friday? And how come my share is half and not a third?" Juan asked.

"Hey," Jodi responded, "that's your problem. I'm going home."

She picked up her ball and started walking toward the street.

"Hey, Jodi," Marco called after her.

She stopped and turned, and he gave her the thumbs-up gesture.

"Thanks." She pivoted back toward the road, sporting a huge grin.

"Hey, wait up," Juan called.

They had only gone a few steps when a woman's voice shouted from behind them. "Jodi." Jodi spun to see her blond and fit PE teacher jogging toward her.

"Mrs. Wilson," Jodi said with surprise.

"I was watching your game. You're a great player," the teacher replied.

"Well, we lost. But thank you."

"How come you didn't come out for the school team last year? We really could've used you."

"Well, I was, uh, I had some conflicts."

"Can I count on your participation this coming year? You'd be a great asset to the team."

"I'll have to see how things go."

"Well," Mrs. Wilson said, "I'll look forward to seeing you at the first practice. I'll make sure you're informed of the date." Then she added, "You should get some ice on that eye."

Jodi touched her stinging eye.

"Great playing," the teacher added.

"Thank you." Jodi watched Mrs. Wilson return to her young children at the play area.

"Why don't you play on the school team?" Juan asked. "You'd take them to the state championship."

Like a light switch flicking off, the elation Jodi felt moments ago darkened. "My mom doesn't have the money for the activity fee."

"I'm sure if you told the coach, she could get the fee waived."

"I'm not going to ask the coach to waive the fee."

"Well, I bet if your mom would put the money she spends on her hair and nails toward the activity fee instead, you would have enough by the time the season starts."

"That'll never happen. My mom insists that her salon costs are an investment in our future, necessary to attract a man who will rescue us from our poor, miserable life. And it also helps with the tips, or so she claims."

CHAPTER 13

Mr. K was stooped in the garden the next morning, as Jodi often found him when she arrived for her violin lesson and garden chores. As she opened the gate, his eyes brightened, and a smile appeared on his shriveled lips. "Come over here, my friend," he said, waving for her to follow him. "I have a surprise for you. What happened to your eye?" he added.

"It's nothing. Just a minor collision with an elbow during a basketball game. What kind of surprise?"

"Come. Come."

They tiptoed over rows of maturing lettuce and radishes. "They're almost ready to pick."

"Peas?" Jodi said, scrunching her forehead. "That's the surprise?"

Mr. K picked two pods off the vine. "Hold your hand out."

Jodi uncurled her clenched fist. He squeezed the green peas from the pod and dropped them into Jodi's palm, as if they were precious gems. "Go ahead. Try them."

"Raw?"

Mr. K slid some of the delicacies into his own hand, popped them into his mouth, closed his eyes, and tilted his face to the sky.

Jodi followed his lead, but without the drama and with her eyes wide open. What could be so exciting about a silly legume? But he was right. The sweet peas were nothing like the mushy canned vegetable that often appeared on her school lunch tray alongside a glob of pasty mashed potatoes and a chunk of shingle that the cafeteria staff tried to pass off as chicken fried steak. "Sweet," she said.

She picked another pod from the vine and massaged the treasure from its protective shell. "When do we pick them?"

"Maybe as soon as tomorrow, along with the beans, radishes, and lettuce."

"Sweet."

After a morning of tending to the garden followed by a music lesson, Jodi asked Mr. K to pick up his story from where he'd left off the previous week. Her heart was still heavy upon hearing of the fate of the Jewish doctor after the risk he took to treat Karina's broken arm. "Karina obviously got better," she prompted.

***

It took five days for Karina's fever to recede. However, she was still weak and struggled even to rise out of bed. When I wasn't watching over Karina, Pani Maria kept me busy with chores around the farm. Beyond the fallow field was a forest where we scavenged for wild berries and mushrooms. She taught me which were safe to eat and warned me away from the poisonous ones. She had also started a garden, which was hidden in a shallow gully in the field behind the house. When she first took me out there, I asked her why she would keep a garden in such an inconvenient location.

"It used to be over there." She aimed a finger to a level plot of ground near the barn. "But the Nazis looted anything that was edible and destroyed the rest." After a pause, she continued, "So this year I planted the seeds that I was able to salvage in this little hollow, so that it won't be seen from the road."

I took a moment to absorb what she was saying. "Why did the Nazis come here, and why would they destroy your garden?"

"They came looking for Jews. When they found my two sons, they were angry that they hadn't either been resettled in the east with the other Poles or enlisted in the German army."

"How old were your sons?"

"In thirty-nine, when the Germans first invaded, they were fifteen and thirteen. The Nazis let them stay because they were part German and would be groomed to be obedient Nazi soldiers when they were old enough." Her body grew tense, and her voice became flat. "I guess in three years' time they became old enough."

"Where are they now?"

"I don't know."

She worked in silence, concentrating on her weeding and pruning, but I imagined her heart was heavy with worry.

It was late in the day when a rabbit poked its head through some grass at the edge of the garden. Pani Maria and I saw it at the same time. Unflinching, she reached for a nearby hoe without taking her eyes off her prey. I crept in the opposite direction, planning to corner it. The bunny, sensing the danger, darted back into the grass. Pani Maria chased after it with the hoe, took a swing and missed, and tumbled to the ground. Without stopping to help her up, I chased the rabbit into the nearby woods and skidded to a halt when it skirted into the underbrush and dove into a hole.

"What goes down must come up," I said to the hole as I sat nearby and stared into its blackness.

The sun had long set when I returned to the house with a smirk on my face as I presented the dead rabbit, its head dangling awkwardly to one side, to Pani Maria.

"Good boy." She took the rabbit and a sharp carving knife outside.

Later that night, I presented a bowl of rabbit stew to Karina and was pleased that she ate every bite.

After the meal, when Karina was resting, I asked Pani Maria about the rooster I heard crow while I was sitting in the forest waiting for the rabbit.

She told me about the new family who'd moved to the farm on the other side of the woods. "You must not let them know you are staying here. A very nice Polish family lived there before the start of the war. They were our friends, and we helped each other with our crops. Although we had small farms, we shared our harvest with each other and sold or traded the excess in the village. We also made ends meet by working odd jobs in the village, my husband as a roofer and Mr. Lebeski as a blacksmith."

She bit her lip and lowered her eyes. "The Germans took them away. They were given one day's notice to pack what they could carry, and they were moved to the east."

"Were they Jewish?"

"No. They were Catholic, like most Polish people. Their only crime was that the Nazis wanted Germans to live in the land that they had conquered."

"That's why you were allowed to stay," I surmised, "because you are German." *And also why my father is allowed to continue to run his factory.* "Where did they take them?"

"I don't know. Somewhere in the General Government corridor, I imagine, but perhaps even as far as the eastern Russian occupied territory."

I wondered if they were among the people taken to my father's factory after the Nazis started resettling the Jews.

"A short time later a German family moved in."

"Are they good people?"

"Like all Germans, their survival depends on their loyalty to the Nazi Party and war effort." Her stern gaze pierced my eyes as she repeated her warning. "Do not trust anybody, and do not let them see you. And *especially* do not let them see Karina."

My fear returned with a vengeance. Although I was thankful that Karina and I had come upon Pani Maria's barn rather than her new German neighbor's, deep down I wondered if I could trust her. Could she have betrayed the doctor? Would she expose Karina? Another train whistle pierced the silent night, a chilling reminder of Karina's pending fate if she were caught, and mine.

Little by little with each passing day, Karina gained strength, but the pace was like hungrily watching a lone drop of molasses slide from a mason jar tipped over a bowl of steaming porridge, as there was never enough food to provide sufficient nourishment. The rabbit stew was long gone, and I was concerned she wasn't getting enough protein, per the doctor's instruction. I could feel weakness seeping into my bones as well, as simple tasks, such as lifting objects or bending over in the garden, took more effort as the days slipped by. During our daily jaunts to the garden and the forest, I kept a look out for another rabbit. Or a squirrel, or grouse, or pheasant, or anything that moved. But to no avail. Even supplemented with vegetables from the garden and wild treats from the forest, Pani Maria's ration card was not sufficient to feed three hungry mouths.

One night after hearing the rooster again, I had an idea. It was a dangerous idea, especially considering Pani Maria's warning. But I was hungry, and I was worried that Karina would not get strong enough to continue our journey to Venice. I knew it was too dangerous to stay with Pani Maria much longer, not only for us but for her as well.

The next morning Pani Maria's face froze mid-yawn as she entered the small kitchen and discovered three fresh eggs resting in the basin. She stared at them for several moments before reaching for a cast iron skillet. When I called to Karina to come for breakfast, she trundled to the table to discover three plates topped with a hash of scrambled eggs, fried potatoes, and onions. Scrambled eggs never tasted as good as they did that morning in Pani Maria's dim kitchen, perfumed with caramelized onions, dark curtains smothering the morning sunshine.

After we finished our meal, Pani Maria gave me a stern warning. "Don't ever do that again."

I lowered my eyes and nodded, and she proceeded to clean the dishes and grind up the eggshells to eliminate any trace of evidence.

After the egg incident, I limited my thievery to plums and apricots from neighboring orchards.

CHAPTER 14

By midsummer our lives followed a familiar routine, and complacency was fraught with danger in war-ravaged Poland. Once a week I accompanied Pani Maria to the village, where she gathered her weekly food ration and secretly traded her precious garden vegetables for other valuable commodities. My job was to protect the mule. I think Pani Maria had a little more confidence in my ability to carry out this responsibility knowing about the pistol that I carried in my pocket. I never told her that there were no bullets. But maybe she knew. She seemed to have a sense about things.

One warm afternoon Pani Maria and I were tending the garden, when we heard the rumbling of an approaching vehicle. No doubt Germans. There were few civilian motor cars in the village and certainly not on this road.

"Get down," she ordered, and I immediately dropped to my belly. "No matter what happens, don't go near the house, and stay out of sight until I tell you it's okay."

Pani Maria rushed toward the house just as the German soldiers approached the stoop. Ignoring Pani Maria's order, I slithered like a snake through the tall grass and crouched behind the cherry tree so I could see. Karina was inside, and I was so terrified for her that my breath was trapped in my chest, like a fly tangled in a spider web.

"I'm over here. What can I help you with?" Pani Maria called out to the three sentries, trying to draw their attention away from her home.

"Heil Hitler!" the ranking soldier saluted as Pani Maria approached.

"Heil Hitler," she muttered without enthusiasm. "What can I help you with, Sergeant?"

"Just a routine search, ma'am."

"Search for what, Sergeant?"

"There have been reports of Armia Krajowa in the area. Do you live here alone?"

"Yes. My sons are with the führer's army," she lied, as she didn't know the whereabouts of her boys.

"Show me your papers," he demanded.

Pani Maria reached into her apron pocket and pulled out her crumpled documents and handed them to the officer. I was thankful she had her papers on her person, which was the requirement, so the soldiers would not follow her into the house while she retrieved them.

The officer returned the papers, and Pani Maria pocketed them without lowering her eyes.

"Mind if we look around?" the soldier asked. It wasn't a question. Pani Maria had no choice but to acquiesce to the soldier's request.

I prayed that her positive response would convince the soldiers that there was nothing amiss. My prayer, however, was not answered.

Two of the soldiers went to the barn, while the third stayed with Pani Maria. My heart sank, and it took every ounce of restraint I had not to rush out at them when the two soldiers emerged from the barn and approached the cottage. Time seemed to move in slow motion as the sergeant turned the knob and the two uniformed men disappeared into the dwelling. My eyes remained glued to the door, even as I was aware of the third soldier abusing Maria.

Sounds of clanking kitchen utensils and breaking glass indicated that every hidden dust web would be turned upside down and anything of value carried off, including a Jewish girl with a makeshift cast on her broken arm.

Salty tears stung my eyes and streamed down my cheeks when the soldiers finally emerged with their arms loaded with jars of beans and squash that Pani Maria and I had canned the day before and had not yet hidden in the underground cellar. One of them took a bite from an apricot I had stolen just that morning. But no Karina. First I was overjoyed that they had left her, but then terror struck like a poisoned arrow piercing my heart when I realized they must have killed her.

The two soldiers carried their loot to their vehicle and called out to the third, "Come on Hans. We are finished here."

The soldier named Hans was holding Pani Maria tightly from behind, kissing the back of her neck, his hand lost inside her unbuttoned dress while dragging her toward the barn.

"Hans we're leaving. Hurry up."

"Just a minute. I'm not through here yet," Hans shouted back.

The jeep pulled away, and Hans darted after it, leaving Pani Maria in a heap on the ground. I remained still, barely breathing, tears cascading down my cheeks, until the vehicle was out of sight and the rumbling engine faded into the forest. I sprinted from my hiding place. Pani Maria, her dress still unbuttoned, and I reached the open door in unison and darted through the kitchen and short hallway to Karina's room.

It was empty. I looked wide eyed at the neatly made bed, a pair of worn boots upright on the floor under the window and her jacket hanging from a hook. If it weren't for the half-empty glass of water on the nightstand, I would have thought the room hadn't been occupied in some time.

"Karina?" I whispered into the stale, sticky air.

A muffled whimper filtered from the wardrobe closet against the far wall. Pani Maria and I rushed over and jerked open the creaky doors. A heap of old clothes and shoes tumbled onto the floor, and a large stuffed bear twitched. Pani Maria reached in and retrieved the toy animal from the closet, as stuffing spilled from its wounded belly—where it had been stabbed by the soldier's bayonet—revealing Karina curled up in the corner. She had been saved by the toy bear and, as I learned a few moments later, the metal utensil that splinted her broken arm.

CHAPTER 15

Mom was in an unusually good mood when she arrived home from work. Jodi was lounging on the couch browsing through a magazine, the evening news on the TV in the background, when her mother placed her customary evening kiss on the top of her daughter's head.

"Hi, Mom. Busy day today?" The underlying meaning being the level of tip bounty rather than the actual number of customers served.

"Very busy today," Mom responded. "With the holiday weekend starting tomorrow, no one wants to go near a kitchen."

"I'll get dinner started." Jodi swung her feet to the floor.

"No need. We're going to the fair tonight. We'll pick up some greasy, decadent, calorie-infused fair food." She rubbed her hands together in anticipation.

"What fair?"

"The annual Sage Grove Fourth of July town celebration. The fireworks aren't until tomorrow night, but the fair starts today. Half-price ticket day."

"Oh. What am I going to have then?"

"You're coming with us."

"You mean with you and Tom? Do I have to?" Jodi dreaded the thought of another outing with her mother's new boyfriend. She had hoped they'd have broken up by now. She would much rather be dealing with the breakup saga.

"Yes, you have to go. Go change your clothes. And wear something besides one of your ratty T-shirts."

Jodi sauntered to her room and emerged a few minutes later in a new-to-her thrift-shop T-shirt bearing the Nike swish logo, rather than her favorite, comfortable Portland Trailblazer go-to tee. She didn't bother to change her cutoff shorts or frayed Converse kicks.

They met Tom near the ticket booth, and he proudly displayed the three tickets he had just purchased. He kissed Mom on the cheek and then tipped his John Deere cap to Jodi. "Hello again, Joanie."

She forced a smile. "It's nice to see you again, Mr. Smith."

"Tom," he corrected. "Remember, I asked you to call me Tom."

"Oh yeah. Tom." She had not forgotten.

Once inside the gate, Tom took Mom's hand, and Jodi, behind them, wove through the crowd, browsing the attractions. Jodi was soon bored with the silly games and booths stocked with overpriced trinkets. "I'm going to the restroom," she said to her mother and darted off.

After spending longer than necessary washing her hands, she exited the women's room and almost ran into Kristen.

"Omigod!" Kristen cried. "It's Miss B-flat." The pitch of her voice rose on the word *flat*.

As usual, Kristen was surrounded by her entourage of the school's most popular kids, with Julie smugly occupying the premier position on Kristen's right. The other kids chuckled.

"Oh dear," Kristen continued, raising her hand to her cheek in feigned concern. "What happened to your eye? Did you poke it with your bow? Or maybe you hit yourself for being so dreadfully ugly." She shrilled a dainty laugh and turned to her cohorts for affirmation. "Do you guys know why she doesn't have a father?" she asked her friends. "He took one look at her repulsive baby face and was like 'I'm out o' here.'"

The kids roared with laughter.

Jodi spun around to run away and almost plowed into the three approaching Sharks. *Just great!* She expected them to join in Kristen's banter.

"Hey, Jodi," the blue-eyed Shark said. "Problem here?"

"Uh—"

"Are you guys harassing our friend?" the Shark asked while furrowing his brow at Kristen.

"Your friend? Gee, uh, no Matt. We're just hanging out. She just stopped to say hi," Kristen replied, hips swaying and false eyelashes batting at the attractive older classmate.

"Hey, man," one of Kristen's male disciples said to the Shark, "everything's cool. We're just goin' to get somethin' to eat." The group retreated from behind Kristen. Kristen stared at Matt for a few seconds longer and then pranced after her friends.

"Are you okay?" Matt asked.

"Yeah, sure," Jodi responded. "You didn't have to do that."

"Do what? We were just passing by. Great fair, huh?"

"Oh yeah. Great fair."

"See ya around." He gave her a fist-bump, and the other two Sharks copied the gesture. The trio was soon swallowed by the crowd.

When Jodi returned to her mother and Tom, her mother scolded, "What took you so long? We were getting ready to send out an APB."

"Sorry. Ran into some kids from school and stopped to chat."

"Oh, that's nice, honey. I'm glad you're finally making some friends. I just hope it wasn't that dreadful boy from downstairs."

Jodi watched the trampled grass pass beneath her sneakers, wishing she were curled on the sofa, bolted inside to her drab apartment.

"There's the hoops game," Tom said, ignoring the mother-daughter drama. "Let me win my gal a prize." Still clutching Mom's hand, he pivoted to the booth, jerking Mom with him. He handed two dollars to the attendant for three squishy miniature basketballs. After sizing up the basket and mimicking some practice shots, he fired the first shot too hard and it bounced off the backboard. He overcompensated on the second shot, and it air-balled far short of the rim. The third shot hit the rim and bounced away.

"Let me try again. I was just warming up." He coughed up another two dollars. This time he made one of the three baskets, far short of the required trio to win the silly prize.

As they melted back into the crowd, Jodi's mother said, "Jodi likes to play basketball. Maybe she should try."

Tom chuckled. "You see, hon. Those things are tricky. They look easy, but the ball is squishy, and the baskets weave around. They're designed so that you can't win."

Jodi noticed a teenager in the crowd carrying a stuffed lion, like the grand prize at the hoops shoot.

"Now when I used to play football . . ."

Jodi quit listening.

As they passed an olive-green tent, a woman dressed as a gypsy was pacing outside in search of prey. "Fortunes.

Fortunes. Only ten dollars. What's in store for you? Unlock the mystery to your future."

Mom stopped to read the poster pinned to the tent.

"How stupid," Tom said. "She can't read your fortune."

"For you, buddy," the gypsy said to Tom while poking him in the chest with the tip of her long acrylic black fingernail, a string of bracelets jingling on her wrist, "I'll give you a half-price special. Two for the price of one."

Mom looked at Tom. "Don't you think it would be fun?"

Tom reached for his wallet and slid out a ten-dollar bill. "Here. You girls get your fortune read. I'll wait out here."

Mom snatched the bill and handed it to the costumed woman. "He's such a fuddy-duddy. Tell us our fortunes."

Jodi agreed with Tom that it was a waste of money, but she followed her mother through the flap into the dim tent and was assaulted by an overpowering blast of burning incense.

After asking their names, the gypsy had them sit cross-legged on two overstuffed floor pillows as she circled the room, hands in the air, summoning the spirits to grant her plea. She then sat across from them and whisked away a cloth to reveal a crystal ball. She rotated her wrinkled hands in the air above the globe, closed her eyes, and tilted her face to the ceiling. "Sleeping spirits of the ages," she chanted, "wake and reveal your secrets to me. What lies ahead for these two enchanting ladies? Oh spirits, reveal to me Dorothy's future."

The gypsy was quiet for a few moments, eyes closed, face tilted skyward, hovering hands floating around the globe, the footsteps and murmurings of the passing crowd outside filtering through the canvas and thick incense. "I hear something," the gypsy whispered. She inhaled a stream of incensed air. Her hands froze.

"What is it?" Mom asked, wide eyed.

"Shush." The gypsy composed herself and resumed working the orb, although her withered fingers circled slower now. "An accident," she said in a hushed voice. "I see a mangled car and a somber crowd surrounding paramedics hovering over a body on the street. I see feet, one missing a sandal, bright-red paint covering the toenails. Or is it blood? There's a lot of blood. The medics are blocking the face. Speak to me, oh spirits. Who is bleeding in the street? Is it Dorothy?" she pleaded to the ceiling. She waited a moment in silence. Her shriveled hands stilled. "The spirits have no more to say."

The woman resumed working the orb. "Ancient spirits, tell of this young Jodi, her long, fruitful life still ahead of her. Reveal her destiny to me." Hands spinning, eyes closed, head tilted as if the clues to Jodi's future were dangling from the canvas tent top. "I see a gentleman. Tall and handsome, with dark wavy hair and deep-brown eyes. Rich. Very rich. I see a yacht, a Bentley, and a mansion on a hill. Tell me more, oh powerful spirit." She exhaled a deep breath and stilled her hands. The spirits would reveal no more.

Jodi's mother stomped from the tent. Upon spying Tom, she marched up to him. "You were right. A waste of money!"

"Well, what did she say?" Tom asked with a chuckle,

"That I'm going to die in an accident and Jodi is going to marry a tall, handsome, extremely wealthy gentleman."

"First of all," Jodi corrected, "she didn't say that anyone was going to die, and she didn't say that I was going to marry anyone."

"Well, she certainly implied it."

"Well, you're not going to die, and I'm not going to marry anyone, wealthy or not!"

"That's just ridiculous, sweetheart. If some wealthy gentleman enters your future, of course you'll marry him."

"No, that is what *you* want. I'm going to be a doctor and won't need or want any kind of gentleman in my future." Jodi was as shocked as her mother by her abrupt announcement, as the conflict that had been gnawing at her subconscious about the injustice inflicted on Karina's Jewish doctor burst to the surface, crystallizing her life's purpose.

Tom chuckled. "You can't be a doctor."

"Why not?"

"How are you going to be a doctor?" her mother chided. "You know I can't afford to send you to collage."

Jodi crossed her arms in defiance. "I'll figure out a way."

Clearly uninterested, Tom changed the subject. "I'm hungry. The Grove Rib Shack always has the best barbeque beef burgers and corn on the cob. Let's go get some."

The Rib Shack booth also had the longest line. When they reached the counter and without asking, Tom ordered three burgers, three ears of corn, and three lemonades. They each grabbed their flimsy paper plate piled with their meal and found an empty table.

Jodi had just taken her first bite of the messy burger when Juan, Marco, and RJ approached. *Just great.* She pretended not to notice them, hoping they would pass by without stopping, but they didn't take the hint.

"Hey, Jodi," Juan said. "How's the eye?"

"Uh, fine." She tensed at the frown that crossed her mother's face. Jodi hoped they wouldn't rat her out about the black eye. She had told her mother that a wayward ball connected with her eye, but she'd left out a few details, or rather all the details, of the game with the Sharks.

Tom peered over his dripping burger and noticed the bruised eye, "Wow, that's a doozey. You should put a raw steak on it. That'll clear it up in no time. People think it's just an ol' wives' tale, but it really works." He then proceeded to tell Jodi's mother his black-eye story and the healing powers of raw meat.

If Jodi or her mother was fortunate enough to have a steak, it wouldn't be used to cover a swollen eye, but in a frying pan sizzling to a perfect medium rare.

Jodi used the distraction to nudge her friends away. Although just hours away from the payment deadline to the Sharks, she didn't ask them whether they'd scrounged up the money.

CHAPTER 16

Jodi now looked forward to her weekly violin lesson. By midsummer she had memorized her scales and arpeggios, could hear the improvement in her tone and intonation, and had worked through two intermediate violin studies books that Mr. K had lent her. Hand positions and fingerings were becoming second nature. Her shoulders and wrists were still too tense, according to Mr. K, and she still tended to grip the bow too tightly, but overall, her progress was remarkable, at least in her humble opinion.

Two weeks had passed without a run-in with Kristen. She was still trying to teach Juan to play basketball, a hopeless cause, but he still wanted to play with Marco and RJ in a three-on-three tournament later in the summer. Her footsteps marked time with the Brahms sonata as she whistled the familiar melody on her way to Mr. K's house.

"Hey, Mr. K," Jodi shouted as she opened the creaky gate. She didn't know why the peeling paint on the picket fence bothered her so much. Now that the grass behind the perimeter was green and freshly mowed, the flowers under the front window were in full bloom, and the thriving vegetable garden was virtually weed-free, the house and surrounding fence pleaded for a fresh coat of paint.

"Over here," Mr. K called out from the side of the little house. He emerged from the detached garage behind the dwelling, which also begged for sprucing up.

"Will you kindly help me carry these boxes to the car," Mr. K asked.

"What car?"

"My car in the garage," he said, as if it were a silly question.

Jodi had not been in the garage.

"You have a car?" She picked up a box of jarred vegetables off the back stoop and followed Mr. K to the small garage adjacent to the alley. She stepped through the open door and was surprised to see an older-model brown Buick LeSabre sedan. At least it looked brown under the layer of dust.

"Does this thing run?" she asked.

"Of course, it runs. At least, it did last time I drove it."

"When was that?"

"Oh, I don't know. Last year, I think. Might have been the year before."

Jodi put the box in the open trunk alongside several others that Mr. K had already loaded.

"Where are you taking these?"

"To the food pantry. We did such a great job on our garden, and there are far more vegetables than I can use. I have a box set aside for you to take home. We'll pick what is ripe this morning and take those with us as well."

Jodi helped Mr. K harvest some cucumbers and zucchini and pack them into the car. There was a lot of zucchinis. Jodi hoped all the zucchini was destined for the food pantry and not the box for her to take home.

"Who's going to drive you?" Jodi asked as they squeezed the last carton into the backseat.

"What do you mean, who's going to drive? It's my car. I'm going to drive."

"Uh, do you have a license?"

"Of course I have a license." He reached into his hip pocket for a worn wallet and dangled his Idaho State Class D driver's license in front of Jodi's skeptical face.

Jodi took the license and studied it. "This expired six years ago," she informed him as she handed it back.

Mr. K held the license close to his eyes and squinted at the small print to verify the validity.

"When was the last time you had your eyes checked?"

"What, am I on trial?"

"Yes, actually. If you had renewed your license, you would have had to pass the vision test."

Mr. K returned the license and wallet to his hip pocket and extracted a set of keys from another pocket. "We're not going very far. And I can see well enough to get us there."

"Hand me the keys," Jodi demanded, her hand extended.

"You're not old enough to drive."

"Sure I am."

"Let me see your license then." Annoyance seeped into his raspy voice.

"I didn't say I had a license."

"Well, since it's my car and I have the only license, I'm driving. Now get in."

Jodi didn't move. With her hand still extended, she said, "Since I'm the one who can see well enough to pass the vision test, I'll drive." She snatched the keys from Mr. K's hand, walked around the car to the driver's side, and opened the door. "Are you getting in?"

Mr. K shook his head and eased into the passenger seat.

Jodi inserted the key into the ignition and turned it. The engine grunted. She tried it again. The engine grunted again. "Is there any gas in this thing?"

"There's gas," he replied.

"Oil?"

"There's oil." Then he added, "And a few cobwebs."

She turned the key again, and after more groaning, the engine roared to life. Since the car had been backed into the garage, she positioned the shifter to Drive and crept into the alley.

"When did you learn to drive?" Mr. K asked on the short trip to the food pantry, which had required a detour to the service station to add air to the soft tires.

"When we moved here last September. My mom got bored driving through all the dreary sagebrush, so she had me drive so she could read her magazine and do her nails."

"She let you drive even though you don't have a license?"

"I look old enough from a distance. I'm taller than most kids my age."

"Uh-huh." Mr. K focused straight ahead and held a white-knuckle grip on the armrest.

Upon reaching the food pantry, Jodi followed the arrows to the drop-off lane. She and Mr. K slid out of the car as a man with a clipboard approached. "Hello, Mr. Kaszubinski. It's good to see you again. Another donation for us?" He looked over at Jodi as she peered over the roof of the car. "I see you have a helper this year."

"This is Jodi," Mr. K said to the man. "She's been helping me with my garden."

"Nice to meet you, Jodi," replied the man, who donned an ID badge with the name *Bill* boldly printed under an outdated photo of the balding food-pantry manager. "I hope you don't mind helping to unload your donation. One of our volunteers didn't show up today, so we're a little shorthanded." He shook his head and lowered his voice. "I guess you get what you pay for."

By the time the vegetables were unpacked, a long line of foot traffic weaved outside the front door of the metal warehouse. People streamed in to pick up an assortment of staples: bread, canned tuna and soup, boxes of macaroni and cheese—a favorite of the children, according to Bill—as well as some treasures, such as Mr. K's fresh vegetables and excess cheese donated by the local dairy processor.

Soon Jodi and Mr. K found themselves helping Bill pack and distribute the care packages. She was stunned to see such a large and diverse mass of hungry families, far worse off than she and her mother. She pitied the young children who were dirty, wore ill-fitting clothes, and relied on community support because of their parents' choices or situations. After a while Mr. K went to rest in the air-conditioned break room, leaving Jodi to perform double duty.

The row of faces became a blur as she scrambled to fill and pass out the grocery bags to the procession of outstretched hands. Many of the patrons were humble and grateful. Several kept their eyes lowered in humiliation, while others were rude and irritated with having to wait in line for so long.

As the crowd thinned, Jodi paused to take a deep breath and stretch her back. In mid-stretch, she spied Kristen's best friend, Julie, standing in line, fidgeting on her phone. Jodi resumed stuffing and passing out bags and soon she was face to face with her nemesis's sidekick.

"Julie," Jodi said, shocked at seeing Kristen's friend here.

"Please don't tell Kristen," Julie pleaded.

"What?"

"Please don't tell Kristen you saw me here."

Holding the stuffed bag, Jodi stared at Julie's terror-stricken face.

Tears welled in the corners of Julie's eyes. "Please!" she shrieked. "If she finds out I'm poor, she'll shun me, ridicule me, unfriend me."

"She's your best friend, Julie. I don't get it. The violin lessons, cheerleading camp, your smartphone. How could you be poor?"

Julie was crying now. "It's not my fault my dad lost his job. We're losing our home. They just want what's best for me."

Julie snatched the bag from Jodi's hand and dashed for the exit. As she watched Julie disappear through the warehouse door, Jodi became aware of Mr. K's presence beside her.

"It's a tough blow to the ego when your status in life turns upside down," he said quietly.

"I wouldn't know about that," Jodi responded. But she knew Mr. K did.

CHAPTER 17

Jodi and Mr. K stopped for ice cream after their unplanned volunteer shift at the food pantry. It was Mr. K's idea and his treat. "Since the car is out, we might as well get more cobwebs out of her system," he rationalized.

Jodi thought he just wanted to satisfy his sweet tooth, but while standing in line at Carson's Ice Cream Shack, she realized that he yearned to get out and see something beyond the confines of his warped picket fence. Although spry for someone of his advanced years, his only world beyond his house and garden was his weekly two-block trek to the neighborhood market. The loss of Karina's companionship must have left a crater in his soul.

They took their cones—his, plain vanilla, and hers, mint chocolate chip—to Riverside Park across the street and found the nearest table under the shade of a maple tree. Jodi devoured her cone, while Mr. K took his time relishing every lick. In no time the searing summer sun had the sticky treasure dripping down his wrist and onto his neatly buttoned shirt. He wiped his wrist with a handkerchief but didn't seem to notice the white blob staining his shirt.

She waited for him to finish his treat before asking him to resume his story. "So what happened after the soldiers left?"

***

The soldiers who had visited that afternoon were right. Armia Krajowa, the AK, or Home Army, was in the area. It was late that night, well past midnight. I should have been long asleep like Karina, but I was sitting at the kitchen table with Pani Maria as she mended the stuffed toy the soldiers had injured earlier that day. A carving knife rested near her on the table, the same knife she had used to skin the rabbit.

"My mother made this bear for my youngest son when he was a baby," she informed me. She pierced the frayed fabric with the threaded needle. "He named it 'Tiger,' and it was his constant companion, even while he slept, until another kid teased him about it. Then suddenly he was too grown up and it has remained in the closet ever sense." She tightened another stitch around the wound and added, "I'm saving it for his children."

Pani Maria didn't sleep much, and I didn't want to leave her alone, because I could tell she was still shaken from the unannounced visitors that afternoon, hence the knife, and I suspect it was not the first time she had been violated by the barbaric invaders. Or perhaps it was I who didn't want to be alone in the dark with my own demons. Since the incident, Karina had become sullen and melancholy, which I found unnerving. Ghostly shadows bounced off the walls from the single candle that lit the small room, which was concealed from the outside by a blackout curtain that covered the lone window. Another train whistle pierced the stagnant night. I shuddered. The chilling shrieks seemed more frequent with each sleepless night.

We both jumped at a soft knock on the door. Pani Maria motioned for me to be still. She rose and crept to the entryway, the knife gripped in her palm. The knock came again, louder. She stood with her back ramrod straight against the doorframe, the weapon in her trembling hand poised above her head, ready to strike. I slipped my Boy Scout knife from my pocket, flipped open the blade, and positioned myself opposite the door from Pani Maria, my rapid heartbeat thumping in my chest.

A male voice whispered from the outside the door, "Mam. Mam. Are you in there?"

Pani Maria didn't move a muscle.

The voice came again, slightly louder now. "Mam. It's Edward and Piotr. Are you home?"

"Edward?" Pani Maria asked through the door, her voice shaking. "Piotr?"

"It's us, Mam. Please let us in."

Tentative, Pani Maria turned the knob, and two tall figures whisked in. The knife clanked as it hit the floor. The taller one closed and locked the door behind them, and then they were both in Pani Maria's arms. All three were crying.

"Oh my God, oh my God," Pani Maria kept repeating. "It's really you."

Finally, they separated. "I can't believe it's really you," Pani Maria said one last time, tears streaming down her cheeks.

I picked up the forgotten knife and set it on the counter as one of them looked over her shoulder at me.

"Who's the lad?" he asked.

Pani Maria took both their hands and led them to the table.

"Here, sit. Let me take your coats. I can't believe you're both here. And safe. God, I've been so worried about you."

Both sons wrestled out of their tattered jackets and flung them over the back of their creaky wooden chairs.

"Edward, Piotr"—Pani Maria nodded to each son as she said his name—"this is Michal. Michal's been helping me out around the place."

I nodded but didn't say anything. Panic boiled inside me for when they discovered the sleeping Jewish girl in their room.

"You must be hungry," Pani Maria said. "I don't have much but let me fix you something to eat."

"No, no. Not now. Please sit," the older one, Edward, said as he stood and ushered their matka to the remaining seat at the table. "We can't stay long. The Gestapo has learned we are in the area, and it's too dangerous for us to stay here."

"You're with the AK?" Pani Maria asked. "How? The Nazis, they kidnapped you and conscripted you into their army." Her eyes wandered to the door as she added, "And the Gestapo was already here looking for you, so I think you should be safe for the time being."

"After what they did to Tata? There's no way we were going to fight on their side. The first chance we got, Piotr and I escaped from the Nazis and joined the AK. We've been fighting underground with them for the past year."

They looked like they had been fighting and hiding for some time. Tangled brown hair dipped from under their dusty caps, and unkempt beards covered their chins. Edward was missing a front tooth, and Piotr had a gnarly gash across the side of his cheek that was beginning to scar over.

Edward continued with his account. "The Germans had the audacity to turn on their allies and invade Russia. Their army nearly reached Moscow, when the Russians, helped by Mother Nature's brutal winter, forced them back across the border. Now the fighting is back on Polish land. The Russians are pushing from the east, and we're disrupting the Germans' supply chain from behind the enemy line."

"I thought we were at war with Russia after they invaded eastern Poland. Now we're helping their side?" Pani Maria inquired.

"Apparently, it's the lesser of two evils. On the one hand, we don't trust the Russians. On the other, we need their help to drive the Germans from Polish soil," Edward explained.

Edward continued to update Pani Maria on their adventures with the Armia Krajawa, including acts of derailing trains, firing at the retreating Germans, smuggling arms from the Allies to larger AK units across Poland, while complaining about the outdated and inferior weapons and equipment they were forced to rely on.

He suddenly stopped his narrative and looked at me, "Can he be trusted?" he asked his matka.

I remembered Pani Maria's warning not to trust anyone and had the same concern about them.

"God help us if we can't," she said while evading a direct answer.

"You can trust me," I said. "Your matka saved us, and we owe her our lives." I realized my mistake as it was coming out of my mouth.

"Michal and his sister are on their way to Venice," Pani Maria explained. "Somehow they ended up here, and we've been helping each other out while his sister recovers from a fall."

Pani Maria knew that Karina and I were not related, but I was relieved that she played along with my ploy.

"Venice?" Piotr finally said something. "That's a long way off, and you can't really get to Venice from here."

"Besides," Edward added, "the western Allies have invaded Italy. Last I heard, the British and Americans had taken Sicily and are marching up the peninsula. But I think they're still a long way from Venice."

"On the other hand," Piotr added, "we've been smuggling American weapons up from Italy."

"It's a difficult and dangerous trip. Czechoslovakia, Hungary, Slovakia, Austria, they are all German-controlled territory now," Edward pointed out. "Besides, the contraband has been moving from Italy north to Poland."

"Yes, but someone has to rendezvous with the supply chain. And the smugglers have to make the return trip."

"Too dangerous," Pani Maria said.

"We can't stay here," I argued. "We've put you through too much inconvenience." I didn't say *danger*, but she knew what I meant. "And we do need to get to Venice."

The next morning Pani Maria tried to stretch her meager rations allotted to feed one mouth to nourish five, or rather four, as she would not think of not giving her share to her two boys. The love and warmth she shared with her sons was nothing like I experienced with my family. I knew my mother loved me, but her light hugs and pecks on the cheek lacked the genuine affection that this family showered on one another. The physical closeness strengthened after Pani Maria had shooed them out for a bath. I wondered how my mother was coping with my disappearance and if my father has been searching for me. I wondered if my brother, Jakub, and I would have cast aside our petty squabbles and bonded the way Edward and Piotr had, if fate had led us down a similar path. I felt a sudden pang of homesickness, even missing my brother's obnoxious taunts and pranks.

We were at the small table drinking weak tea when I asked Edward, "Will you help us get to your smugglers? I don't have any money to pay them, but my uncle does. When we get to Venice, I can get some money."

Edward and Piotr looked at each other, but before they could respond, Pani Maria restated her apprehension from the previous night. "It's too dangerous, especially for Karina. There has to be a better way."

In unison, the brothers looked over my shoulder as I heard Karina's voice behind me, "What's too dangerous for me?"

I jumped in before Pani Maria could stop me. "These are Pani Maria's sons, Edward and Piotr. They're going to help us get to Italy."

"You didn't say how pretty your sister is," Piotr said, grinning.

"There's no way a pretty girl like her will survive with these types of people," Edward added.

"What do you mean?" My naivety betrayed my attempt to appear older.

"These men have been away from their wives and girlfriends for months, some of them years. They will be climbing all over each other to get their hands on anything that resembles a woman, or especially a young girl."

The image of the soldier abusing Pani Maria the previous day flashed through my mind, and I felt a blast of anger at the thought of anyone treating Karina in that way.

"Unless," Pani Maria said with a mischievous grin, "she was a boy."

"Brilliant!" Edward exclaimed.

"We'll start with the hair." Pani Maria rose from her chair and motioned for Karina to sit.

Karina sat down as Pani Maria retrieved a pair of scissors and a towel from the cupboard. She draped the towel around Karina's slight shoulders while Karina stared wide eyed at the scissors.

"I think you need to do this," I said to Karina. "It's the only way."

Karina closed her eyes so as not to witness the carnage as Pani Maria snipped away at Karina's beautiful wavy dark hair that Pani Maria had painstakingly deloused shortly after our arrival.

After the haircut, Pani Maria led Karina down the hall. A short time later they reemerged. Standing behind Karina with her hands on her shoulders, Pani Maria announced, "Boys, may I present Michal's brother, Karl."

"Wow!" Piotr said. "That's the prettiest boy I've ever seen."

Edward jabbed his brother in the ribs with his elbow. "We can work with this," he said. "I think," he added under his breath.

Piotr was right. Karina did make a pretty boy. She looked like an elf under the baggy shirt that was tucked into trousers held up by suspenders and that were rolled up at the bottom so as not to drag on the ground. Several rags must have been stuffed into a pair of scuffed boots that protruded from under the pants, and an oversized cap shadowed the wary gaze in her eyes.

"Walk over to the door and back," Edward instructed.

Karina awkwardly clomped to the door and stumbled over the clown-like boots as she rotated to return to the table. "You walk like a girl. Michal"—he looked over at me—"you do it."

I traced Karina's steps to the door and back. "See, Karina, you need to imitate the way your brother walks. Do it again."

"Don't call her Karina," Pani Maria said as Karina repeated her trip to the door. "You have to get used to calling her Karl." She gave me a stern look. "You too, Michal. Even when no one is around, you must always refer to her as Karl. Practice."

"Hi, Karl," I said as she returned from another jaunt to the door.

"Hi back, Michal," Karina replied in a bashful whisper.

"No, no, no!" Edward cried. "Maybe you shouldn't talk in front of anybody. But just in case you have to, talk like this," he said as he dropped his voice an octave.

"You mean like this?" Karina growled, sounding like a sick parrot as she tried to imitate Edward's low-pitched example. She and I both giggled.

Pani Maria and her sons glared at us. "This is no joke," she said. "Your survival may depend on you pulling this off, so you need to take this very seriously."

We spent the rest of the day teaching Karina to walk, talk, and act like a boy. We ran around the table, pretended to eat, tossed shoes and pillows at each other, and heckled each other like brothers do. By days end, except for her pretty face and soprano voice, she could almost pass as a young boy.

After a light supper of watery potato and cabbage soup, Edward said, "Let's get some sleep. We leave before dawn."

CHAPTER 18

Jodi dribbled the ball on the jagged sidewalk in front of a neglected brick building on Main Street. She bounce-passed the ball to Juan, who fumbled the catch, and the ball careened into the street. A car screeched to a stop, and Juan trotted in front of it and retrieved the wayward ball.

"You can't ever take your eyes off the ball," Jodi scolded.

"I know, I know. You've been telling me that all morning."

"Then why don't you listen and do what I say? It's like all the practice we did this morning just went down the drain."

"Sorry. Hey, isn't that your friend Kristen over there by the Java Grove?" he asked.

By the time Jodi spied her nemesis and her best friend exiting the coffee shop, each clutching an Iced, King Size Frappuccino with whip—obvious even from across the street—it was too late to turn the other way.

"Hey, look, Julie," Kristen shouted in her most obnoxious voice. "It's Miss B-flat again. Oh, it looks like she's got a new boyfriend. Wait. What am I saying? She can't have a *new* boyfriend if she never had an *old* boyfriend."

Julie stilled, her eyes scanning the surroundings, probably in search of an escape, as Kristen continued the taunt. "What's a matter, B-flat? You can't like find yourself a real man, so you have to like settle for this scrawny wetback instead?"

She looked at Juan. "Didn't I see you working in our yard last week? I'll have to tell my father to upgrade the help."

Before Jodi could process what she'd just heard, Juan's basketball smashed into Kristen's chest, knocking her pricy beverage onto the street.

"Hey, you bastard . . ."

They didn't hang around to hear the rest. Juan scooped up the wayward ball. Jodi sprinted behind him down the street and around the corner before Kristen had finished her rant.

A block later they stopped running, both breathing hard and giggling uncontrollably. "That was the best chest pass you've ever done," Jodi praised between gasps.

"I learned from a pro." But he wasn't laughing anymore.

"Look, I'm sorry she said that. She had no right."

"It's okay, I guess. I'm sort o' used to it. At least she said something. Usually, like when we go to Boise or the mall or something, people just give us condescending looks or pull their young kids in closer to them, like we're going to hurt them or rob them or something. Or turn their noses up when they walk by and act like we're not even there."

"It's still not okay. Besides, it was me she was trying to insult."

"Why does she do that anyway?"

"I don't know. I don't know why she hates me so much."

"Well, I guess she hates both of us now."

They walked slower, eyes downcast, watching the clumps of weeds peeping through the rutted sidewalk pass beneath their feet. Jodi juggled the ball between her hands like a hot potato. Was that why she'd taken so long to warm up to Juan, not even considering that they could become friends, until circumstances had put them together so much that she began to see him as a person rather than the Mexican kid who lived downstairs? Was she just like the racist snobs he'd referred to, or like her mother? Would she have just ignored him if their U-Haul trailer hadn't been blocking the basketball hoop? Was it because they were Mexican that she sat and watched them unload the trailer instead of offering to help? She couldn't answer her own questions.

Juan grabbed her arm, and she froze, thinking Kristen was back to cause more trouble.

"Isn't that your mom's friend over there?" he asked.

Jodi squinted at where he was pointing. She spied Tom sitting with a young blond woman at a cozy sidewalk table in front of the local burger joint. She knew the lunch hour was the busiest time of day at the Sage Grove Café six blocks away, so her mother would not see the lunching duo.

"Maybe it's a coworker and they're having a business lunch." But she could tell it wasn't a business lunch. They were sitting too close, and her skirt was too short for this to be a work meeting.

When they reached the library, Jodi said to Juan, "You go ahead without me. I'm going to do a little research."

"Research? On summer break?"

"Yeah. There are a few things I want to look up. Catch ya later."

"Sure. Adios."

Jodi had wanted to stop at the library for some time to read more on Poland and World War II. She had been fascinated by Mr. K's story and wanted to learn more. But today she went straight to the computer table, pulled up Google, and typed "Tom Smith" and "Sage Grove, Idaho" in the search box. Her eyes widened at each new discovery that she doubted Mr. Thomas M. Smith had shared with her mother—like an ex-wife and two teenaged kids, child support, and alimony payments, a foreclosure action on his house, a repossession notice on his fully loaded Ford F-150 club-cab pickup, nearly thirty thousand dollars of credit card debt, and two DUIs.

She leaned back in the plastic chair and studied the stained ceiling tiles. Clearly not the knight in shining armor who promised to free her mother from their dingy apartment and rescue her from a life sentence of long hours, sore feet, and impatient customers at the local diner. Her mother would be furious if she knew Jodi was checking up on her. How was Jodi going to get her away from this loser without damaging their own relationship?

On her way out of the library, she passed an organized stack of the *Sage Grove Weekly Gazette* on the checkout counter. A front-page headline caught her attention. The chamber of commerce volunteer committee was seeking nominations for candidates for the annual Paint the Town charity event.

The librarian behind the counter finished checking out a book for a gray-haired lady, then asked Jodi, "Can I help you?"

"Uh," Jodi stammered, "I was just reading this article about Paint the Town. How much is the paper?"

"Since the new edition is coming out tomorrow, take this one for free."

"Thanks." Jodi folded the newspaper and slid it under her arm.

"That's a great event," the librarian said as she squinted and nudged her wire-rimmed specs higher up on her narrow nose.

"What?"

"Paint the Town," the librarian clarified. "I'm on the volunteer committee. Each year teams of volunteers paint houses for our elderly residents who can't afford it."

"Where does the paint come from?"

"It's donated by local businesses and other contributors."

"How can you nominate someone?"

"Do you have someone you would like to nominate?"

"Yeah, I think I might."

The librarian helped Jodi fill out the paperwork and said since she was going to a committee meeting that evening, she'd take the application with her.

Jodi grinned as she crossed the foyer to the library exit. She opened the door and stepped into the oppressive summer heat. Now, what to do about Tom?

CHAPTER 19

The next week Jodi was again on her hands and knees pulling weeds from Mr. K's flourishing garden. "I don't get it, Mr. K." she said as she removed her soiled glove and wiped the sweat off her forehead with the back of her hand. "Last week there wasn't a single weed in this garden. How could they have grown so fast?"

"Children grow. Flowers grow. Minds grow. Weeds proliferate," he mused.

"Funny." She slid her hand into the glove and jabbed it into the dirt.

She was dying to tell him that he was going to get his house painted, but she decided to keep it as a surprise. She smiled at the thought of him opening the door to a group of cheerful volunteers wielding paintbrushes. But then the eternal storm cloud that was Kristen ruptured, releasing a torrent that blew away the pleasant thought. She cringed at the memory of their previous encounter. She knew retaliation was imminent and would be far worse than a spilled drink, or a frog in her backpack, or silly string in her hair, or being dragged through the locker room shower fully clothed after gym class and having to endure the humiliation of entering English class late the next period in a clingy wet T-shirt and jeans—just a few of the bully's pranks over the past year. Jodi would never be able to lower her guard. Her stomach churned as the hollow feeling of being the school laughingstock burrowed its way through her being, like the unwanted weeds tarnishing the old man's garden.

Jodi extracted more weeds and hurled them, dirt clods attached, into the compost bin. She'd barely noticed that Mr. K had stopped his weeding to watch her.

"What's on your mind, young lady?"

Jodi fired another clod into the bin and watched it disintegrate as it connected with the hard metal side. She leaned back on her heels and sighed. "I don't get it, Mr. K. I had another run-in with Kristen the other day. Not only did she insult me, but she also insulted my friend Juan. She called him an offensive name."

"So you and Juan are friends now?" He quirked an eyebrow.

"Well, I don't know that we're exactly friends, but we've been hanging out. Shooting hoops, that's all. It's just that she takes every opportunity to make fun of me, or insult me, or degrade me, or . . ."

"Hmmm." Mr. K hummed as he removed his soiled glove and massaged his bony chin with his spindly fingers. "You know, she can say hurtful things, but only you can allow yourself to be hurt by them." He brushed dirt off his trousers. "I think you should feel sorry for her."

"What!" Jodi couldn't believe what she had just heard. "Why should I feel sorry for her? She's the most popular girl in school. Her family is rich. Her jeans cost more than my mother makes in a week! All the boys drool over her." Which Jodi thought was disgusting, but she kept that thought to herself. "And why are you taking her side? You don't even know her."

"I'm not taking anybody's side. But she is obviously hurting."

"Hurting? How could she be hurting? She has everything."

"She may have material things. But emotionally it sounds like she is wounded and is lashing out as a means of getting attention and approval."

"Well, I wish she would get unwounded. And she's certainly getting plenty of attention—at my expense!"

"What would happen if you simply ignored her?" Mr. K asked as he rose from his weeding. He bent over to pick up his mini stool. "Oh dear." He clutched his lower back with his free hand.

Jodi hopped up and took the plastic stool from his hand. "Are you okay, Mr. K?"

"I'll be fine. It's just these old bones protesting again. Although, I think we're done for the day."

Jodi led Mr. K by the elbow to the shaded back porch and helped to ease him into a patio chair.

"Are you sure you're okay? Should I call a doctor or take you to the emergency room?"

"Don't be silly. It's just a side effect of getting old. A nagging pang that rears up every now and then. Nothing to worry about. Why don't you fetch us a cold glass of lemonade? It's in the fridge. I mixed it up this morning."

Jodi soon returned with two glasses of lemonade with extra ice. After a long soothing drink, Jodi prompted Mr. K to resume his story.

***

"We have one more mission to complete before we head to Krakow to meet the shipment," Edward said as we huddled under the tarpaulin in the back of a beat-up army transport vehicle as it trudged over a muddy, rutted back road through the dense forest. There were five other grimy men in the truck, each eyeing us with suspicion.

It was hard to leave Pani Maria's cozy cottage in the middle of the dark night with her two sons. I think I felt worse about leaving her alone than either Edward or Piotr did. She'd given them each a long, hard hug and showered them with kisses.

As Karina and I had followed the brothers out of the cottage into the unknowns, she gave us each a hug as well. Then she'd pressed the three coins I had given her to buy medicine for Karina into the palm of my hand and wrapped my fingers around them. "Be safe," she'd said as she wiped a river of tears from her cheek.

Moisture had filled my eyes, and all I could do was nod as I tried to mask my sadness. I'd slung the frayed knapsack she'd given us, scantly filled with a change of ragged hand-me-down clothes, over my shoulder and followed the brothers into the darkness. A shaving of moonlight and a few stars provided the only illumination as we'd hiked to the outskirts of the village, where we'd rendezvoused with Edward's small gang of resistance fighters.

Pani Maria's warning not to trust anyone hung with me as I watched the five strangers watching us, one of them eyeing Karina as she sat stone stiff, wedged between me and Piotr.

It soon became apparent that Edward was the leader of this rangy band of AK underground fighters.

"What kind of mission?" Piotr asked as the truck hit a bump and we all popped into the air, like slices of burnt toast ejecting from a toaster, and then plopped back onto the hard bench as the driver maneuvered over the rugged path.

"There's a small enemy supply convoy headed for Krakow. Two or three trucks, with a minimal armed escort, transporting food, medicine, weapons. Since we're the only unit in the area, our orders are to prevent them from reaching the city until another squad is available to seize the provisions."

"Sounds easy enough," Piotr said.

It didn't sound easy enough to me. Although excited by the prospect of ambushing the ruthless, murdering enemy, I couldn't fathom how Edward's rangy gang could take on an armed convoy, even a small one.

The truck jolted to a stop, and we all lurched forward. The engine revved, and the rear wheels spun underneath us. We were jostled about as the driver rocked the truck forward and back, gears grinding, tires spinning, then stalling. After two more attempts, the driver poked his head into the covered truck bed and shouted, "Stuck again."

The men mumbled profanities as they hopped from the vehicle. After three heaves, the wheels spun free of the sucking mud and the fighters piled back into the rig, tracking clumps of gooey earth as they scrambled to their seats. The truck crept deeper into the dense forest. Rusted steel and overburdened joints creaked and groaned, as if protesting the strain the driver imposed on the aged transporter.

Sometime later the squealing brakes and the rustling of the other men roused me from a restless slumber. Karina and I followed the others out of the rig. I held out my hand to help her down, but Piotr clasped my arm before anyone else noticed. It took a moment to register that a boy would not offer his kid brother a hand. From then on, I tried to model my behavior toward Karina the way my older brother, Jakub, would have treated me, except maybe not quite as cruel.

We were crouched at the edge of the woods, peering into a large meadow. Near the center of the clearing, a road crossed paths with a river. Too small to be the Vistula, although I knew the mighty river that ran many kilometers north through Warsaw was not far off.

"What do you think? The bridge?" Piotr asked as he and Edward peered through binoculars. The daylight was fading, and the gray mist settling over the grassy field made it difficult to focus.

"The bridge." Edward lowered the field glasses. "Let's get to work."

The men trotted back to the truck and soon reemerged with packs of dynamite, a roll of cable, and an ignition box. Each had a rifle slung over his shoulder.

"Do you know how to whistle?" Edward asked me.

"Of course." I recalled the preferred method my school pals and I used to alert each other of an approaching nun or rector while carrying out mischief.

"Karl," Edward said to Karina, "you go back to the truck with Fredrik, the driver."

He turned to me. "Michal"—he handed me the binoculars—"you stay here and watch for anything that moves. Even though we expect the convoy to approach from the north"—he pointed to the left—"we can't be sure there isn't other enemy presence in the area. So keep watch in both directions. If you see anything, whistle three times. Make sure we acknowledge that we heard it and then get your ass back to the truck."

I nodded, and the men grabbed the equipment and rifles and rushed into the meadow. I took my sentry job seriously. I scanned the field through the binoculars from one end to the other and then back again. Edward's gang soon disappeared into the gully. Occasionally I would see a head bob up, only to disappear again. It seemed like they were taking a long time. My arms tired from holding the glasses to my eyes, but I wasn't about to rest them. I paused my scanning for a moment to watch a doe and two fawns emerge from the woods, but sensing danger, they darted back into the forest canopy.

I heard it first and jerked the binoculars to the north. I spied the faint outline of a vehicle approaching. I dropped the glasses and inserted two fingers between my lips and let out three shrill shrieks. The men were already racing toward me, the last unwinding the roll of cable as they stumbled toward the safety of the trees. Like a flock of wild geese hurtling toward a placid lake, they dove en masse to the ground upon reaching the tree line and scurried into the underbrush.

Edward took my binoculars and watched the column approach. Piotr was now manning the detonator, his index finger hovered over the switch. Edward, still huffing from his hasty sprint, described the scene. "Three supply rigs, two jeeps, one in front, one in the rear, each with two gunners. Hold tight. Hold. Hold."

I held my breath as the convoy crept toward the bridge.

The lead jeep reached the bridge and still Edward held his hand in the air, signaling Piotr to hold. The first supply truck neared the bridge's center, then the second, when Edward dropped his hand and whispered, "Now!"

Piotr flicked the detonator switch, and a moment later a loud explosion sent the jeeps and supply trucks flying into the air in a blast of fire and debris, and the passing convoy disintegrated into a mangled heap of concrete and steel.

"Let's get out of here," Edward yelled, and we all dashed to the truck, which was at the ready with engine running and wheels already rolling as we scrambled inside to make our getaway. The gang whooped and hollered and slapped each other on the back as the truck snaked back into the thick forest.

CHAPTER 20

"Nice shot!" Jodi shouted to Juan as the ball he'd lobbed to the basket teetered on the rim and then fell through the hoop. "Only try to get a little more height and backspin on the ball. That will encourage it to float through the net."

She tossed him the ball, and he took another jump shot from the free throw line. It bounced off the rim. Jodi chased after the wayward ball, thinking that she was glad that they were at the park instead of the parking lot of their apartment complex.

She and Juan preferred the park. Juan because, unlike the rusty hoop at their apartment building, the basket had a net attached, which reduced the need to chase after wayward balls—except when an errant shot bounced off the rim, like now. Jodi because there was less chance her mother would hear from a nosey neighbor that she'd been spending so much time with a boy that her mother has forbidden her to befriend. "You just don't need to associate with those kinds of people," Mom would scold.

But what kind of people? They both lived in the same run-down apartment building on the wrong side of Main

Street, both without fathers. Her mother waited tables at the local café. His was a maid at the local Holiday Inn Express north of town, similar types of physically demanding, meager-paying jobs. Both families had moved to Sage Grove to escape difficulties in their former towns: hers, escalating rent costs and perpetual heartbreak, and his ... well she was still unclear about that. The only conclusion Jodi could draw for Mom's objection was that he was Mexican. But why would she care? There had to be something deeper, but what did that have to do with Juan? This was almost as puzzling as the nonexistent father that her mother was so tight lipped about.

The ball ramming her in the chest jolted Jodi's attention back to the basketball lesson.

"Now look who's daydreaming," Juan said with a grin.

Jodi trotted after the ball. "Sorry," she said upon returning to the court. "Nice pass, by the way. Almost as good as the one you nailed Kristen with last week."

She tossed the ball back to Juan, and he rushed toward the basket for an awkward layup. Juan's buddies Marco and RJ approached the court, and Juan hurled a wimpy pass to Marco. Marco dribbled three times and took a jump shot and missed.

"Hey, guys," Juan said as he returned from retrieving the runaway ball.

RJ passed his ball to Jodi, and she took a similar jump shot that swished through the net. "Looking good," Marco commended. He then turned to Juan and said, "Not looking so good."

Juan frowned and tossed the ball back to Marco.

Marco passed the ball to Jodi. "How about taking Juan's place on our team for the tournament?"

"Huh?" She was stunned that he would ask a girl to play on his team. It was one thing to scrimmage in the park, but she'd learned that this tournament was a big event in town, and Marco seemed to care about his macho image. What would his classmates think? She spied a disappointed frown cross Juan's face.

"We've got a lot riding on this tournament. What would it take? RJ could carry your books for a month after school starts. We could arrange to have your friend Kristen beat up?"

For a moment Jodi was tempted to take him up on that one.

"We could . . ."

A devious smile escaped from Jodi's lips. She tried to hide her excitement from the boys, but she was dancing inside. Her hips might have even started to sway.

"What?" Marco asked as she passed the ball back to him.

"How are you guys with a paintbrush?"

"Huh, you mean like Picasso?" Marco asked.

"No," RJ piped in. "Like Diego Rivera."

"Isn't he an actor?" Marco asked.

"No, idiot. The great Mexican painter."

"No," Jodi clarified, "like Sherwin-Williams."

"The paint store?" the guys said in unison.

"A week from Saturday. You're going to help me paint a house." Then she added, "And a garage and a fence."

"But we don't know how to paint," Marco said.

"I hope you're fast learners." She grabbed the ball from Marco and dribbled to the basket for a layup. "We'll kick butt at the tournament."

After mapping out some plays for the tournament, Marco and RJ left.

Jodi and Juan crossed the lawn on their way home. She sensed the sour mood he had sunk into since getting kicked off the team.

"You know, it takes more than a couple of months to learn to play well. More like years." Jodi tried to cheer him up,

"Then how did you get so good?"

"I used to play at the Y every day after school in Portland before I moved here. They had a great coach, and most of the other kids were older, so I had to work harder to keep up with them."

"I don't even like the game."

"Then don't play it." Jodi knew that he only wanted to play to get tight with Marco and RJ. She tossed the ball in the air. "What do you like to do?"

He fell silent.

Jodi caught the ball and prodded him. "Well?"

"I like to draw." He studied his frayed sneakers.

"No kidding. How come you never told me that?"

"I don't know. It seems kind of dorky."

"What's so dorky about that? You could be the next, ah, who was that guy RJ referred to?"

"Diego Rivera," Juan said.

"Yeah, him."

"Hey, Jodi."

Jodi swung around and saw Matt and the Shark twins jogging toward them, one sporting a cast on his forearm.

"What happened to you?" Jodi asked as they drew near. She was reminded of Mr. K's account of Karina with a broken arm and near death hiding out in German-occupied Poland.

Matt spoke for the wounded Shark. "Jackson here broke his arm. Can you believe it? Right before the tournament."

"Gee, ah, Jackson"—she'd learned the name of one more Shark—"that's really rotten luck. How'd you do that?"

Matt didn't give Jackson a chance to speak. "Stupid accident. Anyway, we're obviously short a player for the tournament. Any chance you could help us out?"

"Help you out how?"

"You know, uh," Matt stammered, "play on our team in his place."

"Ah, well, I just agreed to play on Marco's team. I don't think I can be on two teams for the same tournament."

"Sure you can. We're at different levels and play at different times. Come on—what will it take?"

The devious grin returned to Jodi's lips. "How are the three of you with a paintbrush?"

CHAPTER 21

"Mr. K?" Jodi did a double take as she passed her elderly friend sitting on a bench on the shady side of the street in front of the Sage Grove Pharmacy. One amenity the town provided was a park bench in the middle of every downtown block. The harsh Idaho weather had taken its toll on the aging seat. The slats—splintered and weatherworn—blended right into the grungy buildings so well that Jodi had hardly noticed them. "What brings you downtown on such a hot afternoon?"

"Hello, my young friend. Are you keeping an eye on me?" he teased.

"Of course not. I was just at the library."

"Well, if you aren't in a rush to get somewhere, why don't you sit with me for a few minutes?"

"You look really hot, Mr. K." She noticed the perspiration beading on his flushed face. "Why don't I zip into the pharmacy and get us each a bottle of water?"

"Here, let me give you some money."

"That's okay. This one is on me."

Jodi darted into the building and returned with two bottles of water. She unscrewed the cap off one and handed it to Mr. K.

He took a long swallow.

"Did you walk all the way down here in this heat?" she asked.

"It wasn't so hot when I left home this morning. I went to the nursing home to visit an old friend. She always loved my pickled cucumbers, so I took her a couple jars."

"I'm sorry your friend is in the nursing home. How was your visit?"

"Very unnerving, I hate to say. Her memory is not so good. She recognized me, I think, but she didn't know who I was. It was mostly a one-sided conversation with me doing all the talking, and her nodding, pretending to understand."

"That's too bad."

Mr. K took another swig of water and stared into the distance. "Edna was a piano teacher. She and her husband lived across the street. We spent many hours together playing duets. Karina would join us, toting along a bag full of yarn and her knitting needles." He smiled. "We had so many scarfs. Edna's husband would disappear when we came over. Classical music bored him. He used to say that if you can't dance to it, it's not music. As soon as I put my instrument away, he would appear out of nowhere with a deck of cards and the four of us would play bridge until late in the evening."

He took another sip of water. A trickle escaped from his lip and slithered down his chin. "I told her about you. She smiled when I told her I was teaching you the violin, so I think she remembers the music."

"Her husband must have died?"

"Many years ago. Edna couldn't live alone, so her kids moved her to Sage Grove Living Care. What a dreary place. A collection of old people waiting to die."

"I'm glad you're not a resident of Sage Grove Living Care. Otherwise, we never would have met."

"I am glad too. Enough dreary talk. What would you like to talk about?"

"Actually Mr. K, I would love to hear more of your story."

***

Satisfied and sated best describe my state of being the morning following the attack on the enemy convoy, but the feeling was short lived. Several small tents were sprinkled among the trees at the temporary base camp of the main AK unit. Rocks and tree stumps surrounded a makeshift fire pit filled with smoldering ashes and cigarette butts, the fire extinguished shortly before dawn so as not to reveal our location. Ropes tied between trees served as a temporary corral for a small herd of emaciated horses. Four armed "soldiers" in tattered uniforms and worn boots guarded the perimeter.

Karina and I had slept in the stuffy transport vehicle that carried us from Pani Maria's village in German-conquered Poland across the border to German-occupied Poland, an important distinction with the occupying government but equally dangerous for a renegade Pole and particularly perilous for a runaway Jew.

But what made this morning satisfactory was that it was the first time I'd had enough to eat since deserting the safety of my boarding school, and it was Karina's first complete meal since the Nazi's invasion of Warsaw four years prior. Another branch of Edward's Home Army unit, if you could call this band of renegade fighters an army or a unit, had returned with the spoils of the convoy we had ambushed the previous evening. Although unappetizing, there were enough tin cans of meat, dehydrated potatoes, dried beans, real coffee beans—a prewar luxury—and cigarettes for a hearty, although not tasty, meal.

A brawl erupted over the coffee, and the cigarettes disappeared into the pockets of the weary fighters.

Karina and I kept our distance from the other troops. We sat on the ground near the truck and away from the fire and tents and tried to be inconspicuous as we ate our meal. Occasionally one or more of the filthy men would glance over at us. One, a repulsive-looking renegade with a scarred face, squinty eyes, and a prominent limp held a sinister gaze on Karina.

Piotr stood from the group and approached us, a tin mug of cold coffee cradled in his dirty hands and a cigarette dangling from his lips. Karina smiled as he sat next to her and sucked a long drag from his cigarette. Smoke billowed from his mouth and nose as he exhaled loudly. War had aged him far beyond his seventeen years. The smooth-shaven face that his mother had smothered with kisses was now covered with a layer of dust and dark stubble. The youthful spring was absent from his step, and he held his aching back like an old man as he sank to the ground. I thought of my brother dressed in his Nazi youth garb and how smug and immature Jakub was in comparison. How ironic that I was roughing it in the forest with a gang of underground resistance fighters, while he yearned for the glory of joining the ranks of the barbaric invaders that occupied his country.

After a few more drags on his smoke, Piotr said, "Got our new orders. At dusk we leave for Krakow. Still no word on the smugglers, but we expect 'em within the week. Got another assignment on the river first, so we'll be in the area when they arrive."

"On the river?" I asked.

"Yeah. The smugglers are coming down the river on a fishing trawler."

"Oh," I said after he didn't offer any additional details. "What's the mission?"

"First we distribute some of the bounty the Germans so graciously provided to the underground market so they can get into the hands of the impoverished Polish citizens who desperately need them. The rest is on a need-to-know basis." It was clear that we didn't need to know, since we were already regarded with suspicion. I wondered whether Piotr needed to know.

Piotr sat with us in silence, leaning against a tree, sucking drags on his cigarette and sipping his cold coffee. He had no longer extinguished the smoke by crushing the smoldering end into the dirt when his eyes closed and his mouth dropped open, his heavy breathing indicating a well-deserved sleep.

One challenge that we hadn't considered back in Pani Maria's cottage when plotting our scheme to hide Karina in plain sight was the complexity involved in taking care of one of life's most basic necessities.

"I need to . . . you know," she whispered. Because of a lack of privacy, she couldn't use the crude latrine dug by the soldiers to answer nature's call. She clambered to her feet and disappeared behind the truck and into the woods.

I passed the time by doodling in the dirt with a stick. It seemed like she had been gone a long time, and I worried that she might have gotten lost. I looked at the group sitting by the smoldering ashes and noticed that the scar-faced soldier was no longer among them. Panicked, I leapt from the ground and raced off in the direction that Karina had gone. I scrambled down a path only to find it blocked by a felled tree. I backtracked and fought my way along an overgrown animal trail that led to a stream, but without a place to cross. I reversed course again, and when I returned to where the paths intersected, I stopped to listen. My heart skipped a beat when I heard a gruff voice.

"What's such a pretty lad doin' in such a dangerous place?"

I raced through the brush toward the voice and spotted Karina's terror-stricken face just as the scar-faced soldier clasped her arm. She struggled to break free, but her attacker wrestled her into a bear hug.

Piotr almost knocked me flat as he swooshed past, grabbed the grimy assaulter, spun him around, and punched him square in the jaw. The assailant stumbled backward, and Piotr gave him another blow to the cheek, and the man swirled and fell face down into the thick brush.

Karina tried to muffle her sobs as we walked back to the campsite.

"Next time, take one of us with you," Piotr scolded while shaking his stinging hand. He scanned for any eavesdroppers. "I know it's hard, but you've got to remain tough. Don't let anyone see you till you get yourself composed and your face isn't red anymore."

Karina nodded her understanding.

Piotr kept a watchful gaze on scar face the rest of the day. But I knew he couldn't protect us forever.

CHAPTER 22

An eerie darkness sifted through the moonless night as we lay on our bellies, peering through a wire fence at a wooden dock house nestled on the bank of the Vistula River on the outskirts of Krakow. German sentries patrolling the grounds confirmed Edward's intelligence that this was indeed a temporary arms storage depot stocked with weapons and explosives. Although the enemy chose a poor structure to house such hazardous munitions, they made up for it by reinforcing the perimeter fence and doubling up the patrols.

Edward, Piotr, Karina, and I were on one side, while three other members of Edward's gang were on the other. The truck and driver were staged just beyond a grove of trees, poised to make a swift getaway.

"Even if we could cut through the fence, there's no way to get past the guards," Piotr whispered the obvious.

As the methodical guards protected their precious stash, we watched in silence, our faces coated with gooey black mud to prevent a reflection from a wayward torch beam.

"It would only take one throw if one of us could get close enough," Piotr whispered again, referring to one of the hand grenades Edward carried in a pouch.

"What about the river?" I asked.

"Even if we had a boat, I don't think we could get away fast enough before they saw us and started shooting." Edward gazed toward the black water mere meters behind the shanty building. The gentle whisper of the mighty river lapping against the dock was one of the few sounds other than the crunching of the soldiers' boots that disturbed the silence of the peaceful night.

"Unless someone could swim, toss the grenade, and then duck under the water," Piotr plotted.

Edward glared at him. "You don't know how to swim."

"I know. I was just saying that someone could."

Edward's silence confirmed that he couldn't swim either.

Neither could I.

"I can swim," Karina said in a hushed voice.

"No you can't!" We all whispered in unison.

"Sure I can," she argued. "We had to swim through the sewers all the time to hide from the Nazis, sometimes holding our breath under the gunk for a long time."

It had never occurred to me how Karina had learned to navigate the underground maze during our escape from the train station.

"But you would have to throw the grenade through the window," Piotr said.

"Piece of cake," she replied.

I flashed back to the woman in the ghetto tossing a grenade at a group of soldiers that awful day I'd met Karina. I never imagined that she had taken any part of the aggression against the invaders, but she seemed full of surprises.

She slid off her jumbo boots and set them beside me. "I'll meet you at the truck." Before we could stop her, she grabbed two grenades out of Edward's sack and darted toward the gloomy water.

"Wait" Our hushed protests were ignored as she slipped into the murky river.

All I could see were the two grenades skimming the surface until they too were swallowed by the blackness.

"As soon as you hear the explosion," Edward instructed, "get your ass back to the truck. Piotr and I will pick off as many as we can, as will the others. God, I hope she's a good swimmer," he added under his breath.

I bit my lip until it hurt, waiting for the explosion. I prayed the disruption would be an explosion rather than gunshots into the dark water. Unsettling minutes seemed like hours, when a deafening blast erupted from the dock house and a wave of fire and shattered glass burst through a window.

Within seconds the whole building was engulfed in flames. I wanted to jump and cheer at Karina's success but cowered with my hands clasped over my ears at the thundering blasts from the exploding munitions that the grenade had ignited, along with the bullets spewing from the machine guns that Edward and Piotr blasted into the chaos.

"Run!" Edward shouted, and we headed for the trees.

I stumbled through the dark woods with Karina's boots tucked under my arm when Piotr cried out and fell face down on the ground. Edward and I each grabbed an arm and dragged him with us. *Crack!* A bullet swooshed past my head and pierced a nearby tree. I tripped and dropped one of Karina's boots, but getting Piotr to the truck was critical, so I tightened my grip around his bicep and kept moving. I struggled to keep pace with Edward and felt unworthy for not carrying my share of the weight. I winced at each agonizing cry. My arms grew heavy, and my body ached, feeling like we had traveled many kilometers. We must be close. Please let us be close. I was about to collapse from exhaustion when the faint hum of the idling truck spurred me on. Piotr's cries, however, had ceased.

The other waiting fighters rushed over and scooped Piotr's limp body from us. They eased him into the truck bed and hopped inside.

"Get in!" Edward shouted as I hovered near the idling rig.

"No," I told him. "I'm going to wait."

"Load up! Load up!" the driver yelled. "We need to roll."

"Just a couple more minutes," Edward ordered.

Fighting back tears, I stared into the darkness. Edward circled the truck. Then again. Then a third time a little faster. Finally, he rested his hand on my shoulder and said, "It's time. We need to go."

I shook his hand away. "You go. I can't leave without him."

"You can't wait. They'll be here any moment. You'll be killed too."

I squinted into the darkness, and the shadows moved. Edward and I both ran toward the shivering, dripping-wet girl and carried her to the vehicle.

Unlike the celebratory return trip from the ambush the other night, the ride to our new safe house was somber. Edward sat cross-legged on the truck bed and embraced Pitor's body, which had now become cold and stiff. I felt empty and numb. Karina trembled next to me. I yearned to wrap my arms around her to comfort her but couldn't without tipping off the rest of the gang to her true nature. And I ached for my mother, longed for her to hug me tightly, to feel her warmth, for her to kiss the top of my head and tell me that everything would be all right. But it was not going to be all right. Pani Maria's beloved son would never have the children she dreamed of to lug around a scarred, hand-me-down stuffed toy.

At least our mourning was in darkness so the other filthy fighters with mud-covered faces couldn't see the tears streaking down mine.

CHAPTER 23

Jodi lounged on the sofa, reading a book she had checked out of the library, when her mother pranced through the door.

"Hi, Honey," Mom said as she leaned over the couch and kissed her daughter on the top of the head. "What are you reading?"

"Oh, ah, *The Diary of Anne Frank.*"

"Anne who?"

"Anne Frank. She was a Jewish girl who hid with her family in an attic during World War Two."

"Oh," her mother responded with a frown. "Why read something dreadful like that during summer break?"

"Because I think it's interesting. Think about it. A girl my age had to stay confined for two years just because she's Jewish. She couldn't go outside and sit in the sunshine or hang with her friends. Couldn't make a single sound during the day because someone might hear them and rat them out to the Nazis."

"Uh-huh," her mother grunted as she turned toward her room. Mom's idea of literature was *People* or

Cosmopolitan magazines. She'd frequently peruse the periodicals over the dinner table to pilfer titbits of gossip to share with coworkers and customers at the café.

"Come help me with my dress," her mother shouted over her shoulder, signaling another date night with Tom.

"Where are you going tonight?"

"I'm not sure. He said to dress for a *special* dinner. I think he might take me to Anthony's."

The local steakhouse. "That sounds expensive."

"It probably is." Her mother hugged the dress she had just removed from the closet. "This has some wrinkles in it." She inspected the silky black garment closer. "It's been so long since I've had an occasion to wear it. Can you get the iron out?"

Jodi was setting up the iron when she asked, "What do you really know about this guy?"

"Why? We've been seeing each other for a while now. I think I know him pretty well."

"Have you been to his house, met his family, his friends?" His ex-wife and kids, Jodi wanted to add. "How's his financial situation?"

"His financial situation is just fine," her mother snipped as she snatched the iron from Jodi's hand. "He's taking me to Anthony's, for heaven's sake. He drives a brand-new, insanely expensive truck, and I've been to his house." She slammed the iron down a little harder than necessary, causing the ironing board to wobble. "And why the inquisition? Can't you see that I just want a better life for us? Don't you want me to be happy? He's our best shot at escaping from this dump. And besides, I think he really likes me."

"Sorry. I didn't mean to make you mad. Maybe I just worry a little."

"You don't need to worry. I'm the mother, and I'll do the worrying." She slithered into the skimpy dress and, without Jodi's assistance, yanked up the zipper in the back.

CHAPTER 24

"Mr. K, this is impossible!" Jodi cried as she lowered her violin.

Mr. K emerged from the kitchen clutching a fresh cup of coffee. "What's impossible?"

"This interval. There's no way my third finger will cross over to the C-Sharp and then get back to the G on the E string."

"Try it again."

Jodi clenched her jaw as she raised her instrument and replayed the phase, stopping short of the C-sharp.

"Look at your left thumb."

Jodi cocked her head to see her digit holding up the neck of the violin.

"You need to break the habit of flexing your thumb and using it to support the instrument. That is what your chin is for. The left hand needs to be free to float up and down the neck."

"I'm afraid I will drop it."

"You won't drop it. You're as tense as a rail. No wonder you can't reach the interval. Close your eyes, take a deep breath, and try it again." He held the end of her instrument. "I'll hold the neck up while you play. Don't even touch it with your thumb."

Jodi played the phase again and tried to keep her thumb away from the instrument. It felt weird. She missed the C-sharp. She took an exasperated breath.

"Why are you so tense?" he asked.

Jodi looked down and studied a scratch on an oak floorboard. She hadn't realized that she was on edge, but after taking a deep breath she felt as if she might shatter if pricked by a pin. "You mean because I'm worried about my mom and the jerk that she's been seeing? Or that she's always fretting about how we're going to keep up with the bills every month or whether she is going to lose her job again, which makes me worry? Or the fact that she doesn't like the kids I play ball with? Or that all the kids at school hate me and that I have to constantly be on guard because Kristen is going to hunt me down?"

Mr. K scratched his chin. "Let's analyze these one at a time. I don't know if your mother's friend is a jerk or not, but she needs to live her own life and make her own decisions—even if they are bad ones. You can't do anything about her finances, so they are none of your worry, unless you're starving, and I don't believe you are. You also can't control her bigotry, if that is what it is. And as far as Kristen is concerned, is she in this house or in this room?"

Jodi did a three sixty of the room and shook her head.

"Then she can't possibly cause you any harm right now. So forget about all that and think only of the phase that you are playing. But don't overthink it. Hear the complete phase in your mind, not the individual notes."

Jodi shook out the tension in her arms and tucked the instrument under her chin and played the phrase. She hit the C-sharp. Only the pitch was flat.

"Do it again," he instructed.

She repeated the phase. Better this time, but still out of tune.

"Now do it three more times."

After the third time he said, "Go ahead and put your violin away for today. Each time you practice, after your warm-ups, play the phase five times. Then at the end of your practice, play it five more times."

While she packed up, Mr. K disappeared into the kitchen. As she closed the latch on the case, he returned with a plate of Animal Crackers and set it on the coffee table.

Jodi squinted at the unusual snack.

"These were Karina's favorite. The little creatures amused her from the first time she saw them. We always kept some around and laughed about how frivolous it was to eat a cookie shaped like an animal. Especially considering our memories of scrounging for food."

Jodi picked up an elephant-shaped treat and studied it.

"You're right, Mr. K. It is kind of a silly extravagance." She popped the treat into her mouth. After washing it down with a swig from her water bottle, she said, "Mr. K, can you pick up your story from where you left off?"

He picked up one of the treats, studied it, and set it back on the plate.

***

Edward, Karina, and I waited in the dark on a dock nestled on the Vistula River, outside Krakow, not far from where we blew up the Germans' ammunition shipment and where Piotr whispered his last breaths a week earlier. A sorrow-filled cloud had hung over us during the long days as we struggled with monotonous tasks, waiting for the long overdue trawler that carried additional arms and supplies for the AK fighters as well as the promise of leading Karina and me a step closer to Venice.

I had not yet told Karina that Venice was not our ultimate destination, but rather America. During our time with Edward's unit, news had trickled in that convinced me that Karina would not be safe anywhere in Europe. The resettlement camps—Auschwitz, Treblinka, Chelmno, Belzec, Majdanek—were in fact exterminating Jews as well as "renegade" Poles and other "undesirables." The Germans' intrusion into Russian territory forced the Russians to change sides, and they now repelled the German assault back across the former Poland boundary. Thousands of eastern Polish refuges who had been forced at gunpoint to relocate to labor camps in hideous places in the depths of Russia had either perished or had been exiled to Persia, and the Germans were continuing their mission to rid the country of ethnic Poles with the intent of establishing a racially pure German population in the land that they had conquered. I knew that the only path to safety was to flee the continent entirely. I hoped that Edward's source was correct, and the trawler was only minutes away.

Earlier in the week, Edward had taken us to a small apartment in the center of Krakow to meet an old man who, prior to the German occupation, made his living as an artist. Edward informed us of his circumstances on the way there.

Neighbors had hidden him from the Nazis when the occupiers rounded up local government officials, professors, teachers, doctors, lawyers, and other souls whom they deemed threatening, including artists. Now the old man utilized his talents by creating falsified papers for unfortunate Poles, both Jews and Aryans, who were out of favor with the invaders. His forged documents had saved many lives, as his fortunate clients had avoided resettlement or military conscription by producing civil service work papers to inquiring SS patrol agents. Karina now had official-looking documents that identified her as Karl Techelli, of German/Italian mixed heritage, the son of my uncle Vincent, and a permanent resident of Venice, Italy. Now instead of brothers, Karina and I were cousins. The papers cost me the dead German soldier's three valuable coins.

Before leaving the safe house in a Krakow suburb to meet the trawler that would take us on the next leg of our journey, Edward led me to an adjoining room in the small cottage. "Michal, you have been a great help to both my matka and to us, and I have mixed emotions about what I am going to ask of you."

"You both saved our lives. I'd do anything for you."

"Think very carefully about what I am going to ask before you respond."

"Okay." My curiosity had me bouncing on my toes.

"As you know, Polish government officials evacuated to London after the Nazis invaded. They have been directing our army here in Poland from there. As you can imagine, correspondence is very difficult, since the Germans control all the communication networks, including the telegraph, post, and border crossings. The only way secure messages can be sent and received is by couriers who smuggle documents back and forth through enemy territory."

"I hadn't really thought about that. Why are you telling me this?"

Edward pulled a small brown envelope from his pocket. "There is some very important information in this package that must be relayed to the officials in London."

"What kind of information?"

"I don't even know. It is encrypted and copied onto microfilm so no one can interpret it without knowing the code."

"How did you get it?"

"You ask too many questions. I only know the man who passed it on to me by a name that I know is not his own. That way I cannot identify him if I am caught and tortured."

"Tortured?"

"That is why you must carefully consider what I am going to ask of you. It is very dangerous."

"We are not going to London."

"A contact will meet you in Venice and take the message to London."

"How do I find him?"

"The contact will find you and pretend to be an old friend. This person will call you Jozef and will ask of your brother in Krakow. You will close your left eye and politely tell this person that your name is not Jozef and that you do not have a brother in Krakow. You must remember to close your eye, and it must be the left eye. That is how the contact will know for sure that you are indeed the messenger. The contact will apologize and be on their way. That will be your sign to remove the envelope from its hiding place and have it concealed in your pocket. The contact will accidently bump into you later, and you will discreetly pass the package on. Like this." Edward demonstrated how to hold and transfer the envelope.

I didn't even pause before I held out my hand for the envelope. "After what they did to Warsaw, to Piotr, to Karina's family, I want to help you."

"You're absolutely sure."

"Positive."

"Okay, lift up your shirt. And you cannot tell anyone, not even Karina."

From the dock, I studied the stars in the night sky, searching for clues to the path that might lead us to safety. There must be a message there. I wondered what the stars in the American sky looked like. Karina stared skyward as well, but I imagined she was wondering if her family was also gazing at the same stars. At night she often wept in the darkness, and I knew she missed them terribly. I wondered if they were still alive.

I tried to reassure her that the rumors of the killings in the camps could not be true, that it was inconceivable that a government, even one as brutal as the occupying Germans, would ever do something as barbaric as murder innocent citizens, but in my heart, I didn't believe my own words. I had seen the brutality of the Nazi soldiers and witnessed their cruelty toward the Warsaw Jews, how they beat them in the streets, how they herded them into those filthy boxcars like cattle, stuffed in tightly, like clothes in an overpacked suitcase that had to be sat on in order to close, that I wondered how they could even breathe. I tried to shake the image of the Jewish doctor who'd saved Karina's life being dragged by the German SS like a slaughtered animal. I ached for her and wanted to hold her, comfort her, but I couldn't.

I felt the heavy tape that Edward strapped around my ribs to secure the important message. I wondered what it said. I also wondered how he would get word to the contact in Venice. I felt proud that Edward had the confidence in me to carry out this important mission. I was also proud to serve my homeland. I hoped that my mother would be proud of me as well. I was frightened and afraid of failing them all.

Edward lit a cigarette and inhaled a deep drag, which he expelled slowly.

I let him enjoy another drag and then asked, "Why are you helping us?"

"Huh?"

"You could have left us at your matka's or turned us over to the SS. It is dangerous for you to help us. I was just wondering why you're doing it."

"Everything is dangerous now. Even breathing is dangerous." He took another puff on his smoke. "Because my matka asked me to, and she raised me to always do the right thing."

"Oh."

"You are my brother now, Michal. My matka is a strong woman, but after my tatu's death and Piotr and I were taken away, I wasn't sure how she would survive. I think she needed you as much as you needed her, and I am grateful you were there for her."

"She said she didn't know where you were."

"It was too dangerous to contact her. I couldn't send a post because the Nazis would have intercepted it. It was safer for her to think we were with the German army."

"Does she know about Piotr?"

"No. I must tell her in person. I know she loves us both very much, but Piotr was her favorite son. Growing up, whenever I would get in trouble, I would get the wooden spoon to my hind end. When Piotr got in trouble, he would flash that silly grin of his and charm his way out of the punishment. He had her wrapped around his little finger." He smiled at the memory. "I have to be there for her when she learns he is dead."

I thought of my own mother and realized that I, too, was the favorite of her two sons, although I also knew she loved us both. I remembered how proud she was when she handed me that violin on my birthday only a few months ago, which now seemed like a lifetime and world away. I missed her terribly and yearned to return to my comfortable home, but I had to honor my promise to Karina's father. Although I knew my mother must be devastated by my disappearance, I took comfort that, unlike Pani Maria, my father and brother were there for her.

The puttering engine of the approaching fishing trawler interrupted my thoughts, and a few moments later an outline of the boat emerged from the darkness and crept closer to the dock. The vessel snuggled up to the pier, and a figure on board tossed a rope to Edward, which he wrapped around a pillar.

A grizzled old man with a scruffy beard hobbled over the side of the craft and hopped onto the dock. I could tell by the clanking and scraping of every labored step of his awkward gait that he had a wooden leg. An unlit pipe bobbed between shriveled lips that were nearly hidden beneath the scraggly beard. Tangled gray hair dangled under his captain's hat, which rested askew on his head. It had been a long time since he had bathed.

"How'y, ma'es," he said with a scratchy voice that had been damaged by too many years of unfiltered tobacco. His missing front teeth caused the consonants in his speech to come out muddled.

"Hello, Captain." Edward reached for the burlap sack the captain had lugged from the boat. "Good sailing?"

I sensed that Edward's question had nothing to do with the piloting the vessel but rather to confirm that the contents of the delivery were in order.

"Us good us cou'd be 'spec'ed under da circums'ances," the captain replied.

Edward raised an eyebrow to this comment.

"A crosswin' or lone pirade cou' disrup' any voyage. Ya just hav' da coun' your' blessin's when ya ge' da shore."

Edward shook his head. I suspected this meant that the captain must have traded some of the precious cargo on the black market. Since the contraband supplied by the western Allies was smuggled over several borders to the Polish

AK, Edward was powerless to prevent a little pilfering. Four members of Edward's unit transferred crates from the vessel to a waiting truck while Edward finished the transaction with the captain.

"I've got some return cargo for you," Edward said to the captain.

"Wha' kin' a' cargo?" The captain's voice seemed gruffer now.

"These two boys." Edward nodded toward us. "Michal and Karl will go with you to your next drop point, where you will exchange them for your next shipment."

I hoped the next drop point was outside of Poland, although that would mean German-occupied Slovakia, which was equally dangerous.

"I ain't lookin' af'er a couple a' kids."

"You don't have to look after them. They can even help with your fish, especially Michal. Karl doesn't talk much, so give him some space."

One of Edward's crew members jogged over to us. "Cargo's loaded. We need to get out of here."

"Right behind you," Edward said.

The captain returned to his vessel, and Edward reached into his coat pocket and pulled out something, which remained hidden in his clenched fist. "Here," he whispered as he handed them to me while looking to make sure the captain didn't see.

I held out my hand, into which Edward dropped five bullets. I slipped them into my own pocket. "They might work with that pistol you've been carrying, but I'm not sure." He gave me a quick bear hug and slap on the back, the way a brother hugs another brother who's shipping off to war. "Be safe, my brother." He gave Karina a similar hug but with a much gentler backslap.

"How can we ever thank you for everything you and your matka have done for us? I'll find you after the war's over."

"You do that, my friend. I'll be waiting."

Edward trotted after his comrades. Karina and I climbed aboard the trawler as the impatient captain had the line untied and was at the helm, not interested in welcoming his new passengers.

CHAPTER 25

The night was creepy black. Jodi and Juan sprinted through the thick forest, stumbling over rocks and stumps that erupted underfoot. Sinister trees turned to monsters. Branches morphed into withered fingers that snatched at their clothes as they raced through the menacing woods. Whoever, or whatever, was chasing them was closing in, and each snapped twig broadcast their location. Juan stumbled, and the basketball he was carrying flew from his hands and was swallowed by the dense fog as he tumbled to the ground. Jodi helped him to his feet, and he stood, searching the murky darkness for the wayward ball.

"Leave it. Come on," Jodi shouted at him. She darted off through the blackness, and he followed. She knew from the crescendo of the heavy breathing behind them that they were about to be overtaken. Gunfire thundered in the distance. The breathy presence enveloped them, and the gunfire turned to cannon blasts. The presence was about to pounce, when her eyes popped open and she found herself lying in bed, panting, perspiration beading on her forehead, the unhappy baby wailing through the wall and someone pounding on the apartment door.

She looked at the clock. "Oh crap!" She bolted out of bed and ran to the door in her sleep tee, peered through the peephole to confirm that it was Juan on the other side, and shouted through the door, "I'll meet you downstairs in five." Not waiting for a response, she hurried to the bathroom, splashed cold water on her face, ran a toothbrush through her mouth, squished her ponytail through a hair band, threw on a pair of cutoff shorts, a stained T-shirt and a frayed Portland Trailblazers cap, and was in the parking lot in four and a half minutes.

Upon arriving at Mr. K's house, they were greeted by two adult volunteers who were removing cans of paint and supplies from the bed of a pickup truck. She searched the street for her recruited crew, fearful they wouldn't show.

"You must be Jodi," a man carrying a can of paint said. "I'm John, and this is my wife, Wendy."

"Hi." She shook his hand. "This is Juan."

"Thanks for coming out this morning, Juan." John extended his hand to Juan. "I hope you have some additional volunteers. This will be a long day with just the four of us."

"Me too," Jodi said as she peered past John to the empty street, scanning for her coerced helpers.

"I assume Mr. Kaszubinski is expecting us. Let's let him know that we're here."

"Actually"—Jodi hesitated—"I was hoping to surprise him. So he is not expecting us."

John raised an eyebrow as the front door opened and Mr. K stepped out.

"What's going on here?" Mr. K raised a hand above his eyes to shield the morning sun and squinted at the crowd assembled in his front yard.

"Hi, Mr. K." Jodi skipped up to him. "It's 'Paint the Town,' day and you've been selected to have your house painted."

"Paint the Town?"

"Good morning, Mr. Kaszubinski. My name is John Fairbanks, and this is my wife, Wendy. We're on the town volunteer service committee, and Miss Jodi here nominated you as a 'Paint the Town' candidate this year. You just relax, and we'll have your house freshly painted in no time."

Mr. K shook his head in disbelief. "You mean you're going to paint my house? The whole house? I know it needs to be painted, and I was going to get around to it someday."

"And the fence and the garage," Jodi added with a broad smile.

"I hope white is okay," John said, "because that is what we have. Plus some sky blue for the trim."

By now the other "volunteers" had arrived, and introductions and assignments were made. The last unidentified Shark twin was Jerome, and he flashed a beaming smile. Jodi grabbed a brush and can of paint and headed straight for the picket fence. Marco, wielding a vintage 1980s-era boom box blasting a contemporary fusion of Mexican Mariachi and American hip-hop music, led his team to the garage. Wendy slipped in a pair of earbuds and followed John and the Sharks to the house.

After an hour of painting, Jodi's arm felt like a limp rubber band. It was a tedious process, stroking the brush up and down each rail and then repeating each swipe to fill in the gaps that the thirsty wood had sucked dry. She eyed the fence line and was discouraged that she was only a quarter of the way completed. Marco and RJ had almost half of the garage finished, and the rest of the team fanned around the house were making good progress.

Jackson sauntered over to Marco's radio, and the guitars and trumpets of the mariachi band were replaced by thumping rap music. He looked over at Marco as if to dare him to change it back, and when Marco resumed his painting, Jackson bopped back to the house to the "doo dat" rhythm of a popular rapper, paintbrush and casted arm swinging in time. Mr. K kept the team supplied with cold lemonade and iced tea.

A short time later, Bill from the food pantry appeared with two older teenagers in tow. Paint dripped onto Jodi's shirt as she rose from the sidewalk. She started to admonish herself, but noticed others displayed assorted white splatters on their arms, legs, and clothes. White blobs even highlighted the back of Jackson's tightly clipped 'fro. *How'd he do that?*

"Hi, Jodi," Bill said. "We heard you were painting Mr. Kaszubinski's house and thought you might like some extra hands."

"You'd help us?" She was surprised that he would offer without having been bribed, but she suspected that was not the case for the younger two of the trio.

"After all the help Mr. Kaszubinski has given us over the years, of course we'd like to help." He nodded toward the two youths. "This is Noah and Amber."

"Nice to meet you," Jodi said. "The paint and brushes are over there." She gestured to the jumble of supplies near the porch.

"Grab a brush, kids, and start painting," Bill said.

Heads down, the two youths ambled to the pile of supplies.

"I had a summer job as a painter while in school," Bill said to Jodi. "John and I will tackle the trim, which is the hardest part."

"You know John?"

"Sure. John and I have known each other since high school. We've worked on several projects together over the years. You guys are doing a fantastic job. We should have this wrapped up in no time."

Jodi watched him saunter to the supplies, his hips swaying to the rhythm of Jackson's music. In fact, she noticed that the rest of the crew sported a swagger to some degree, with Matt and the twins performing the smoothest groves. Was that Mr. K dancing up the walk? She smiled and folded back onto the sidewalk and resumed her strokes, head bobbing to the beat.

The team was rinsing the last few paintbrushes with a garden hose, when the librarian appeared, accompanied by a man clutching a camera. "Hello, hello," she hollered as she reached for the gate.

"Don't touch . . ."

"Oh!" the librarian shrieked.

". . . the gate." Jodi grabbed a brush and touched up the smudged paint.

"I guess I should have known there was wet paint. Anyway," the librarian continued, holding her paint-stained hand in the air, "this is Ben Hopkins from the *Gazette*. He's doing an article on the 'Paint the Town' event."

The reporter began snapping pictures with the digital camera.

"Everybody gather around Mr. Kaszubinski." They all followed her instructions. "Everybody smile," she said for the photographer. "Now, one more with just Jodi and the homeowner together."

Jodi wrapped her arm around Mr. K's elbow and stood tall beside him and smiled as the reporter snapped the picture, capturing the sparkling white house trimmed with blue gleaming in the background.

CHAPTER 26

"Look at all that zucchini!" Jodi exclaimed. "How could they grow so big since yesterday?"

"Isn't this wonderful." Mr. K bent over and lifted a giant leaf to reveal a cluster of squash.

"I thought we were through with the zucchini."

"The gift that keeps on giving. Take some home with you. Give some to all your friends."

"Mr. K, I don't even like zucchini."

"How could you not like zucchini?"

"Well, to start with, it's green and it's a vegetable."

"Zucchini is more than just a vegetable. Have you ever had a zucchini muffin? Best thing ever! Karina kept the freezer stocked with shredded zucchini. We would enjoy fresh-baked zucchini muffins all winter long. Mmm-mmm." He rubbed his belly. "I made some this morning. We'll try them out after we get these picked."

Jodi put a handful of squash in a pail and then looked up when she heard voices in the street. *Uh-oh.* She searched the yard for a place to hide. Too late. Three boys she recognized as Kristen's groupies were riding up the middle of the street on bicycles.

"B-flat! B-flat!" they shouted as they sped past. Their laughter hung in the air even after they disappeared around the corner.

"What was that about?" Mr. K asked as he watched the teens pedal around the bend.

Jodi squished her eyes shut and tried not to cry in front of Mr. K.

He watched her as she sank into the dirt and sat cross-legged with her face in her hands. He reached for his mini-stool and eased onto it. He gazed in the distance. Then he removed his soiled gloves and studied the backs of his hands. He leaned forward and rested his elbows on his knees with his chin in the palms of his hands . . . and waited. He didn't say a word.

Finally, Jodi raised her head and gazed at a lone puffy cloud dangling in the blue sky.

She looked down again and stubbed her toe into a pesky weed. "Mr. K," she said, almost in a whisper, "Why am I such a freak?"

He lifted his chin off his hands. "Where did you get a crazy idea like that?"

"All the kids pick on me and call me names and tell me how ugly I am and tease me for being so tall and . . ."

"Stop right there. You mean all the kids pick on you? Even your friend Juan? And the kids at the park that you play basketball with?"

"Well, not them, but all the other kids."

"All those other kids don't know what they're talking about. First of all, you are not ugly."

"How would you know. Your eyesight is bad."

He smiled. "My eyesight is good enough to see that you are an attractive young lady. Besides, ninety-nine-point nine percent of beauty comes from the inside, and I bet you have all your classmates trumped hands down on that point."

"You wouldn't understand, Mr. K. You don't know what it's like to be picked on all the time."

"I choose not to remember what it is like to be picked on all the time. I had an older brother who thought his mission in life was to make mine miserable. And I was one of the smaller kids in my class. I think in today's terms I would have been called a shrimp or a runt. And I played the violin. Not exactly a masculine pursuit, even back then. So I do know what it's like."

Jodi kept her gaze lowered.

"Another thing," he said, "about being tall. I thought that being tall was an advantage for a basketball player." He smiled at her.

She smiled too.

"I watched a women's basketball game on TV not too long ago, and boy were those ladies amazing! I bet each of them was the tallest in their respective classes. I can see it now—Jodi Evans, WNBA star. I wonder how much money those ladies make. I bet it's millions."

She gave him a gentle nudge to the arm.

"All this talk is making me hungry. Let's go try one of those muffins."

Jodi followed him through the screen door into the kitchen and took a seat at the table.

He carried over a tray of muffins. "After you eat one of these, you'll ask me to plant the whole garden in zucchini next year." He scanned the room and then leaned over the table and whispered, "My secret is that I sometimes lace them with chocolate chips."

She smiled and took a nibble. "Wow, Mr. K," she said after she swallowed the bite, "these are really good. Better than chocolate cake."

"I think I've just hooked another addict." He reached for a muffin.

After Jodi finished the treat, she asked, "Mr. K, can you continue with your story? What happened on the boat?"

***

Since the gruff captain didn't offer a tour of the rickety trawler, Karina and I scoured the vessel for a place to rest. It was late, and our weary bodies craved sleep. We felt our way to the lower cabin. The quarters were pitch black, so I climbed the half dozen steps up to the deck and asked the captain for a light.

"No ligh'," he informed me. "Las' thin' we wan' is da draw unwanded eyes. Goo' way a' ge'in' sho'."

"Oh." I tried to shake off a ripple of fear. "Is there someplace we can sleep?"

"Nope." After a pause he grumbled, "You's can sleep anywares on deck, bu' da only cod below is mine so s'ay ou' a' my way." His empty pipe bobbed as he spoke.

I retrieved Karina from the cabin, and we stretched out on the rotting plank deck behind the wheelhouse, hoping that the railings would conceal us from any prying eyes on shore. The creaky rhythm of the swaying vessel lulled me to a deep sleep.

The next thing I knew, dawn was breaking, the engine was quiet, and the wheelhouse was empty. I lay still, gazing at the awakening sky, trying to estimate how far we had traveled. I was startled by what sounded like a snorting dragon, and a vision of a giant mythical beast that I had seen in movies as a young child flashed through my mind. I bolted upright, only to realize that the roar was erupting from the cabin below, and the source was the toothless captain.

Karina slept soundly beside me. I rose and crept down the six wobbly steps to the musty cabin. Streaks of morning sunlight filtered through gaps in the plank flooring above, painting stripes across the prostrate captain stretched out on a cot. Spittle seeped from his gaping mouth onto his scraggly beard, and the tattered captain's hat resting on his stomach, rose and fell to the rhythm of his throaty snoring. I stared, transfixed by the bobbing cap. The intimidating captain looked ridiculous and even vulnerable in this position, and I tried not to snicker at the horrendous sounds expelling from underneath that tangled mass of whiskers that concealed his chin. He mumbled something incomprehensible and shifted his position.

Then his eyes popped open. He blinked a few times and sat upright. "Huh-huh," he mumbled as he leered at me where I sat on the steps.

"Sorry. I didn't mean to wake you."

The captain sat up on the cot and rubbed his hand through his tangled hair. "Uh, no. I w's awake. W's jus' ge'in' up."

The cramped cabin was devoid of any comforts, furnished with the single rumpled cot on which the captain sat. A tin coffeepot, an iron skillet, and a small burner rested on a rotting wooden counter, which was outlined by a ledge to keep the contents from sliding off in rough waters.

"Le' me ge' some coffee an' we's be on our way." He handed me the coffeepot. "Here, make yoursel' useful and fill dis wi' wader."

"Where is the water?" I asked.

He looked at me like I had just dropped from the moon. "We's sittn' on a whole river full a' wader."

I took the pot to the stern and descended the launch ladder and filled it with murky river water. I studied the gnarly skipper as he struck a match and lit the propane burner to heat the tar-looking faux coffee. Since coffee was not included in wartime rations, indulgers had to improvise with seeds, nuts, twigs, or whatever could be ground and boiled. I took a sip when he offered me a cup and spewed it out as the disgusting beverage scalded my tongue. I didn't want to know the ingredients of the captain's brew. Karina snickered behind me.

"Wa'? Ya don' li' my coffee?"

"Uh, sorry. It just wasn't what I was expecting." I took another tiny sip. "Actually, it's quite good," I lied. "I just needed to get used to it."

"Uh-huh." He topped off his dented tin cup and hobbled up the stairs to the aft deck. "You boys pull da anchor whilse I ge' her s'ar'ed. We's go' lo's a wader da cover daday."

Karina and I glanced at each other, and I mustered up the courage to ask, "Ah, where's the anchor?"

"Ain' ya ever been on a boa' before?"

"Uh, no, we haven't"

"O'er dare"—he pointed with his head—"in da bow. Durn da crank da brin' 'er up."

While Karina and I struggled with the rusty crank, the captain worked to start the engine.

After the engine coughed to life, the captain returned to the helm and motioned for us to follow. "Don' suppose ya know how da pilod eider."

"Uh, no." I was beginning to grasp his marbled speech. "But we're fast learners."

"Ya bedder be if ya gonna pull ya weigh' aron' 'ere."

"Yes, sir." I responded. "What's your name anyway? What do we call you?"

"Name's Captain. An' you can call me Captain."

"Yes, sir, Captain." It was amazing that he could say "Captain" with the hard *T*.

He gave us a crash course on how to work the wheel and how to throttle the engine to speed up and slow down. "Keep 'er dea' pan in da middle o' da river. Keep a shar' eye ou' fer logs or obs'icles, an' keep da droddle low so wes don' was'e pedrol."

After the brief piloting lesson, the captain had Karina take the helm and then proceeded to teach me how to fish. I only poked my finger twice before stringing the first slimy worm through the tiny metal hook. We had to use live worms, according to the captain, because the fish were too smart to nip at anything else. The captain monitored the two poles on the starboard side of the boat, and I manned the two on the port side.

Catching my first carp of the day was thrilling, as I had never caught a fish before, but sitting under the sweltering sun waiting for the next bite soon became boring. Each netted fish was strung on a wire and dropped into a tank of river water, where it flapped around for several minutes, attempting to escape before succumbing to its fate as somebody's dinner. I just hoped it would be mine, though I did my best to ignore the pain in my empty stomach.

As tall shadows stretched across the lazy river and the setting sun signaled the pending nightfall, the captain instructed me to reel in my empty lines and took the helm from Karina. We were approaching a small village. The captain steered the vessel to an empty dock, where I helped him tie the rope around a pillar. He then took two carp from the tub and tossed the smallest one to me. The slimy fish slid right through my outstretched hands and landed on the deck with a splat. The captain snarled at me, and I retrieved the fish and blushed as I apologized. He took his fish to the side of the boat, unsheathed the knife that he wore at his waist, and sliced the fish up the middle and spilled its guts over the side. He wiped the knife blade on his tattered pant leg, re-sheathed it, and carried his fish to the cabin. I retrieved my puny-in-comparison Boy Scout knife from my pocket and sliced into our fish.

"Ouch!" I cried as the blade slipped off the gills and into my thumb, crimson drips sliding off the scaly carp.

Karina gasped and raced to our knapsack and returned with a dirty white sock, which she wrapped around my hand.

With Karina close at my heels, we descended the creaky steps into the cabin just as the captain flopped his fried fish from the cast iron skillet onto a tin plate. Without saying a word, he took his meal and sat on his cot and began eating the carp with his filthy fingers. I concealed my injured hand behind my back, and Karina plopped our fish into the same skillet. Minutes later she scraped as much of the charred flesh as she could from the smoking pan onto the only other tin plate, and Karina and I went back onto the deck and shared our meager meal.

As we picked the last morsels off the plate, the captain hobbled up the steps. He scooped the string of fish from the tub and stuffed them into a burlap sack and slung it over his shoulder. "I'd be bes' if ya s'ayed on da boad. Course, if yas go' los' or arresded for bein' ou' pass curfew I wouldn'd ha' da deal wi' ya no more."

"We won't go anywhere." I suspected the captain would prefer we were absent upon his return.

Karina and I sat on the deck, swatting the annoying mosquitoes. Since it was the first time we were alone where she could not be overheard, I began teaching her Italian. The lesson soon faded to a blur as the gentle wake of the mighty river lapping against the side of the trawler lulled us to sleep.

We were jarred awake sometime later by thumping and banging, followed by vulgar language in the captain's gruff voice. I peered over the side of the craft at the captain on his knees in a puddle of vomit, struggling to lift himself up.

It was apparent that he'd fallen while trying to board the vessel. I leapt over the side and helped him to his feet.

"Wha's my ba'. Wha's my ba'," he repeated, his slurred speech as incomprehensible as a baby uttering his first words. He swayed, and I righted him and coerced and shoved him over the side, where he landed with a thud in a heap on the deck. "Wha's my ba'."

I looked around and retrieved the burlap sack he'd used earlier to carry the day's catch to the village.

"Here's your bag." I leapt back into the boat and dropped the sack next to him. "Let's get you to bed." Karina and I wrestled him to his feet and dragged his weighty bulk to the top of the stairs, where he tumbled headfirst into the cabin. We gazed at each other, as if to ask the other whether we should leave him there, but in a gesture of resignation, I scrambled down the steps into the darkness and hoisted him onto his cot. When I returned to the deck, Karina handed me his captain's hat and I scuttled back to the reeking cabin and rested the cap on his chest.

Back on deck, Karina was untying the string on the burlap sack.

"You can't do that!" I exclaimed.

"Why not?"

"Because it's not yours."

"Didn't you catch half the fish, and didn't I pilot the boat all day?"

"Yes, but . . ."

She spilled the contents onto the deck. I looked toward the cabin, but the thunderous snorts confirmed the captain had passed out. We took inventory of the bounty: a half-empty bottle of vodka, a pouch of tobacco, two small loaves of bread, and some dried meat. Whatever else the fish bought on the black market had already been consumed by the captain, including the vodka. Karina set a loaf of bread aside and returned everything else to the sack.

"Here." I reached for the bag. "Let me tie it up. It needs to look like it hasn't been touched."

She eyed my bandaged hand and proceeded to retie the sack.

We shared the stale bread as we listened to the roaring-dragon snorts stream up from the cabin.

The next morning, long after the rising sun had melted the meandering fog from the lazy river, the captain woke to me handing him a cup of lukewarm coffee. The beverage had been steaming hot when I'd choked down my first cup hours earlier as I'd sat on the deck, watching the hungry fish jump in the placid water and disappear beneath a wake of evaporating rings.

"Who's dere?" the captain stammered as he rubbed his eyes and let out a belch as he sat upright. "Oh, i's jus you." He tried to shake the drunken remnants from between his saucer-shaped ears as he moaned and held his head in his hands. The cup the captain took from me shook in his fist, spilling some of the black sludge on his lap as he brought it to his lips.

I hoped he would offer some breakfast from his bounty in the burlap sack, but he slurped the faux stimulant, tossed the empty cup to the counter, and grunted something incomprehensible as he hobbled up the steps.

I untied the line, and the engine started with a sputter. We repeated the previous day's routine as we trolled up the river. Only, the fish weren't as hungry, and the catch was meager compared to the previous day. I gaped in awe at one point as we drifted by a magnificent castle towering from a nearby hill, and then shuddered at the thought of the Germans using it as a lookout for approaching enemy threats, like the medieval rulers who built the mighty stronghold centuries earlier. Later, I lowered my head in sorrow as we puttered past the charred carcasses of a recently burned village. The putrid stench of smoldering ashes and sizzled flesh hung heavy in the air, the wrath of vengeful Germans as punishment for Polish citizens hiding Jews or retaliation for an AK ambush. I felt sickened that the carnage could have been revenge for the attack on the supply convoy or the arms storage depot by Edward's underground resistance unit.

Like the previous evening, after setting the anchor at dusk, the captain fried himself the largest fish from the day's catch, and Karina and I shared the runt.

The plate was picked clean and the fine bones tossed overboard when the captain stormed up the stairs, red faced, shouting, "How dare you!"

I had hoped that he was too inebriated the previous night to remember what was left in the sack. "How dare you," he repeated as he towered over us. "How dare you," he belted out again as he slapped me across the side of the face.

"What's the matter, Captain?" I felt my stinging cheek start to redden.

"You liddle dief," he shouted as he swung at me again. Like a Ninja, I swerved out of his reach. The force of his swing knocked him off balance, and he tumbled onto the deck.

"Did you steal from the captain, Karl?" I asked Karina with a hint of sarcasm.

She shook her head.

As the captain struggled to his feet, I asked in all seriousness, "What are you accusing us of stealing, Captain?"

"You smar' ass. You s'ole my bread."

"You have bread?"

"You mus'a daken i' while I was sleepin'."

"Maybe you ate it before you went to bed or while you were out." I could see the confusion on his contorted face as he tried to remember the events of the previous night.

His impaired memory saved us from being thrown overboard.

CHAPTER 27

"So how did you meet the old geezer?" Juan asked as he and Jodi strolled through town after a sweltering morning basketball practice.

She wiped the sweat off her forehead with the back of her hand and then tried to spin her basketball on her fingertip. The ball teetered off her digit, and she caught it before it hit the ground. "He's not a geezer. He's an interesting man with an incredible past and is an amazing violin player."

"Violin?"

"He's teaching me how to play the violin."

"And I thought drawing was dorky."

"It's not dorky. It's actually quite beautiful when played well. If only people would take the time to really listen."

Juan rolled his eyes. "Whatever."

Jodi spun the ball on her finger again. It wobbled, and Juan snatched it away. "What do you think the about *The Banditos*?" he asked.

"What?"

"The team. What do you think about *The Banditos* as the name for our team?"

"Fine. I guess Marco will have to agree."

"He'll be okay with it. He said he really doesn't care as long as we have a name to sign up with."

Juan stopped and peered into the storefront of Hank's Tackle and Supply Store. "Cool," he said as he admired the assortment of fishing rods and reels displayed in the window.

"What?" Jodi asked. "It's just fishin' stuff."

"What a rad rod. A hundred bucks!" He exclaimed after he cocked his head and read the price tag. "How can a simple fishing pole cost a hundred bucks?"

"It's probably not just a simple fishing pole," Jodi responded. "It's probably a magic rod constructed of carbon or titanium or some other precious metal and covered with golden flakes. It's probably so high tech that it can cast and reel in a fish all on its own."

"That's stupid."

"What do I know about fishing poles? I don't even like fish, and I can't imagine why anyone would want to catch one of the slimy things."

"Some of us take pride in being able to catch and cook our own meals." In a more somber tone he added, "And it beats going hungry."

"I guess you have a point," Jodi replied as she recalled Mr. K's story of his escape on the fishing trawler with the seedy captain and the single carp the fleeing duo shared as their only meal of the day.

"I miss fishing with my dad and brother."

"What happened to them anyway?"

"I don' know. They were at work when ICE raided the plant. They're probably in Mexico now, but they'll be back." He bounced the ball and spun on his heel to resume the journey and stumbled over a crack in the sidewalk.

Jodi snatched the ball before it could roll away and started to dribble as they resumed their walk home. "Is that why you and your mother moved here?"

Juan didn't answer.

"Sorry. None of my business."

Jodi halted as she saw Tom Smith approach the driver's side of a red Mustang convertible that had just zipped into the parking lot across the street. Tom opened the car door, and the same woman who Jodi had seen him with at their previous clandestine sidewalk lunch date emerged from behind the wheel. Tom gave the woman a quick kiss on the cheek, the same way she had seen him greet her mother. Her appearance mirrored a younger version of Jodi's mother: bottle-assisted blond, overapplied makeup, colorful salon-crafted nails, a tight skirt that accentuated her curvy hips, a snug knit top that revealed ample cleavage. She watched them enter the Burger Hut.

"Do you want something to drink?" She darted across the street toward the restaurant. Juan trotted after her.

At the entrance, Jodi handed Juan a ten-dollar bill and said, "Get two Cokes and an order of fries. I'll find a table." This was not how she had planned on spending her allowance.

Juan flashed a devious grin and filed in line behind Tom while Jodi proceeded to an empty table near Blondie.

Jodi watched Tom as he carried his tray topped with two giant burgers, a heap of greasy fries, and two large drinks. She snickered as the overloaded tray he tried to balance with one hand teetered while he fumbled for straws and napkins from the counter by the soda machine. The broad grin under his bushy mustache soured, and he almost spilled his meal onto an innocent patron when he spotted Jodi sitting alone at the table adjacent to his date.

"Tom!" Jodi exclaimed. "What a surprise to see you here."

"Hello, kiddo," Tom replied, eyes wide as he righted the tipping food carrier. "What are you doing here?"

"Just stopped in for a cold drink and a snack. What about you?" She wasn't going to let him off easy.

"I, um," he stammered. "I'm having lunch with my sister."

"Oh, my mother never mentioned that you had a sister. I'll have to meet her." Jodi leapt to her feet. Juan approached with their drinks.

"Uh, maybe another time, kiddo. We have a lot of catching up to do. Uh, family stuff, you know."

"Oh sure." Jodi returned to her seat. "Another time."

Juan sat down and slid one of the drinks across the table to Jodi. "You have a malicious streak in you." He grinned.

Jodi removed the wrapper from her straw and took a sip of the icy beverage.

Juan leaned over the table and whispered, "You know, it was kind of weird."

"What was weird?" Jodi asked, still gazing over Juan's shoulder at the nervous couple.

"It took him three times to pay for his order. The first two credit cards he tried to use wouldn't go through. He kept making some lame excuse about his wife always canceling cards without letting him know."

"He doesn't have a wife."

"So he says, but do you really know that?"

"I checked him out. He's a conniving dirtbag but definitely does not have a wife, at least not right now."

Tom glanced over at Jodi, and she smiled and waved at him.

CHAPTER 28

"Mr. K, are you here?" Jodi shouted as she rounded the corner of the house and peered in the garden. Waist-high corn stalks crackled in the breeze. Loaded beanstalks tugged at leaning trellises. The zucchini plants must have grown another foot in the past two days. But notably absent was Mr. K. He was always stooped over a row of vegetables in the morning when Jodi arrived. The southern Idaho afternoons were much too hot for any strenuous outdoor activity, especially for an elderly gentleman like Mr. K.

After searching the yard, she climbed the back step and peered through the screen door. "Mr. K!" she screamed and bolted into the kitchen. She knelt next to the old man, who was on his hands and knees near the table.

"What? Don't scare me like that," he said.

"Are you all right?"

"Of course I'm all right. It's just some spilled milk. Can you hand me that towel by the stove? I seem to have made quite a mess."

Jodi picked up the empty milk carton off the floor and set it in the sink. Then she grabbed the towel and helped Mr. K clean up the mess.

"What happened?" she asked.

"Just a silly accident. I was setting the milk on the table, and then suddenly it was on the floor."

"Just don't scare me like that again. Maybe you should make an appointment with the eye doctor."

"My vision is fine enough, thank you." He grasped the edge of the table and pulled himself onto his feet. "But now I am out of milk," he said as he carried the soiled towel to the sink. "I was going to make a raspberry custard this evening to take to Edna tomorrow for her birthday."

Jodi handed him her rag.

He rinsed and rung the water out of the towels and hung them over the edge of the sink to dry. "Instead of pulling weeds today, why don't we walk to the store."

"That works for me." Although Jodi enjoyed helping Mr. K in his garden, she could do without pulling weeds—again.

"Let me just grab my wallet and we'll be off."

"Will you continue with your story? How did you get away from that awful captain?" she asked as they strolled through the glossy white gate.

***

The next evening, we reeled in our lines as the trawler puttered toward another village. I was plotting my own escape into the parish in search of food while the captain did his carousing, when he shouted, "Ge' down!"

Karina and I plopped onto our bellies.

The captain hobbled over to the fish tank. "Help me move dis."

I scuttled over and helped him slide the heavy tank about a half meter to one side, revealing a hidden compartment. "Quick, ge' down dar' and don' make a soun'."

Karina and I squeezed into the dank compartment, and with me assisting from below, the captain scooted the tank back in place, leaving our hiding place in blinding darkness. The secret enclosure reeked of rotting fish, mildew, and gunpowder, the hiding place for the smuggled contraband supplied to Edward's unit revealed. The space was too small to stand, so I scooted next to Karina, and we sat shoulder to shoulder listening to the sputtering engine as the boat crept toward the enemy-patrolled dock. I removed the dead German's pistol loaded with Edward's bullets from my pocket and clutched it in my clammy hands.

"Permission da dock?" I heard the captain say in broken German. I didn't hear a reply, and then the vessel clunked against the pier. "Could ya gimme a han' wi' da line?" After more silence the captain mumbled, "Ne'r min'. I'll ge' 'er myself." I listened to the captain's peg leg drag on the deck as he wrestled with the rope.

"Papers," a deep voice demanded from the dock in German.

"Uh, ya. Here."

The boat rocked, and heavy footsteps thundered above as the sentry boarded the vessel.

"Hey. Wha' ya doin'?"

"What's your business here?"

"Jus' redurnin' from fishin'. Caugh' a couple ex'ra for ya."

I sucked in a terrifying breath as the captain raised the tank lid and pulled out the string of fish. Karina grabbed my arm. The clomping footsteps then descended the steps to the cabin and after a few minutes reascended. "Looks like we got something here," the German voice shouted. "Tobacco. Vodka. These are banned substances. Where'd you get these?"

"Dey's yours," the captain said, voice shaking. "Dake 'em."

"I plan to. What else do you have for us?"

"No'hin' else 'sep' these fish." The squeaky cover opened again.

Karina tightened her grip on my arm.

The German spit. "I wouldn't eat that crappy carp. Would you eat that slimy stuff, Eckert?"

"No, sir. I wouldn't eat that garbage," replied a voice from the dock. "I wouldn't even let my dog eat that crap."

I heard a splash, which must have been our day's catch being tossed overboard.

"Hey, wha' ya doin'? I didn' do no'in da deserve dis." The fear resonated in the captain's quavering drawl. "You wouln' shoo' an unarmed cripple."

"No good godforsaken Pole." The explosion of the gunshot rang in my ears. Karina gasped as the thud of the captain's body hit the deck. I prayed the German didn't hear.

"Stupid cripple." The thundering jackboots pounded on the deck, and the boat rocked again as the guard hopped over the side and clanked on the dock.

The stillness was deafening. I didn't move a muscle, and I was hyper-alert to the sounds around me—the gentle wake whispering against the side of the trawler, a crow cawing a warning to a passerby, Karina's fearful breathing in the darkness.

Karina's grip on my arm tightened each time the pounding steps of the patrolling guards passed by. I knew it was only a matter of time before we were discovered or perished from starvation, dehydration, or suffocation in the stifling compartment. My trembling hand hurt from clutching the metal gun, and I willed myself not to cry.

Minutes and hours and panic swirled like debris trapped in a funnel cloud, churning in my brain as I tried to devise an escape plan. The tank was too heavy to move, the empty compartment void of tools. Even if my measly Boy Scout knife could slice through the wooden slats, we were below the water line and would drown long before a hole could be cut large enough to slide through. I didn't know how many endless hours we sat trapped and terrified in the reeking blackness, when the boat shifted as someone boarded. I held my breath as the muted footsteps creaked the aged planks. "Help me move this," a voice whispered in Polish.

I gripped the gun in both hands, aimed at the widening gap above, and gritted my teeth. Karina squeezed my trembling arm tighter.

"This sucker is heavy," a hushed voice replied as the tank above us shifted. Then I was blinded by a bright light.

"Don't shoot!" one of the intruders whisper-shouted.

I couldn't see the trespasser through the blinding torchlight, but the fact that he knew to look under the tank and that he spoke Polish led me to believe, or was it hope, that he was part of the smuggling network. I lowered the gun, relieved that my trembling finger hadn't squeezed the trigger, and the strangers helped us from our hiding place.

The quarter moon splayed its golden glow over the captain's body sprawled across the deck. Dried blood coagulated around the bullet hole in the center of his forehead. I wanted to feel sorry for him but couldn't pity the crotchety ol' soul. I crossed myself as we hustled to the dock.

"Hurry," the stranger said in a hushed voice as he coaxed us over the side of the vessel. Two bodies were heaped next to a dock house, which must have been the

German guards whose pacing I had been monitoring the last several hours. I didn't cross myself for them, as their souls could rot in hell as far as I was concerned.

We hid in the shadows and evaded patrolling guards as we weaved our way to the outskirts of the small village. "Who are you?" I asked as our rescuers led us into a small rustic shack nestled in a grove of trees.

"The captain was to bring you to us," the stranger said. "Looks like our network may have been cracked, as the SS was waiting for him."

I was relieved that this was indeed the contact and that we were safe, at least for the moment. "What happens now?"

"We stay here for a while until we find the source of the leak. The chain may need to be scrapped for the time being."

"Was the captain supposed to take another shipment to Krakow?" I asked.

"It would be best if you don't know what the captain's mission was. If fact, don't even tell us your names or where you are going. My job is to get you to the next drop point safe and sound."

I noticed some crates in the far corner of the dark shed. *And collect another load of contraband to smuggle downriver*, I thought but knew better than to say out loud. My heart skipped a beat at a crackling sound in the other dark corner, where a radio transmitter was set up. I shuddered, as I knew the Germans had special teams that prowled for illicit communication posts. Now I knew how Edward messaged the smugglers to expect us.

"Make yourself at home," he said. "Smokey and I will take turns at guard. Might as well get some sleep." The rescuer settled onto the dusty floor near the door and nudged his tattered cap down over his eyes.

In unison, Karina and I shrugged our shoulders and did

the same. How I longed for a soft bed with fresh sheets and a feather pillow. I closed my eyes and imagined my mother tucking me in and giving me a soft kiss on my forehead, like she did when I was a small boy. The pleasant memory was eclipsed by a vision of the bloody bullet hole in the captain's forehead.

CHAPTER 29

"Do you have to make that racket so early in the morning?" Jodi's mother yelled from the hallway through Jodi's bedroom door.

Startled, Jodi jumped and then lowered her violin. She had been struggling with the opening runs on the Brahms sonata. All those crazy accidentals! She had printed a copy at the library from one of those free sheet music sites for pieces with expired copyrights. She hadn't yet told Mr. K that she was trying to learn the sonata.

She looked at the clock on her dresser—8:43—and opened the door to see her mother, still in her skimpy nighty, uncombed hair, and no makeup. "I thought you were at work."

"Charlotte and I switched shifts today. She has to take her son to the doctor tomorrow."

"Oh. Sorry. I didn't mean to wake you."

"That's okay. I probably forgot to tell you."

A few minutes later, Jodi sat with her mother in the kitchen, eating Cheerios and drinking coffee.

"So how was your date last night?" Jodi asked.

Her mother dropped her spoon into her bowl, splattering the little Os and skim milk on the tabletop. "It was one of the most humiliating nights I've ever had!"

"Why? What happened?" Jodi's heart rate quickened as she anticipated the breakup announcement.

"We were having such a good time. Dancing, laughing. We were getting ready to leave when the bartender reminded us that we hadn't paid our bill. Tom apologized and said that he probably had one too many beers and that he was having so much fun it had simply slipped his mind. The bartender agreed that it was an honest mistake. Tom gave him a credit card, and the bartender brought it back and said it had been denied. Then he handed him another one, and that one was rejected also. He said he didn't have any cash and asked if I would pay the bill. It was forty-five dollars! Do you know how much I bust my butt to earn forty-five dollars? At least I had my debit card with me."

"Gee, uh, I'm sorry, Mom. I'm sure he'll pay you back." Though Jodi was pretty sure he wouldn't. There went her allowance for the foreseeable future. She didn't dare tell her mother about the incident at the burger joint.

"He'd better." After a few more bites of cereal, Mom changed the subject. "So yesterday Charlotte showed me the front page of the local paper. Do you know who was in the picture?"

"Who?"

"You! There was a picture of you standing next to an old man, surrounded by the United Nations of Sage Grove!"

"I told you I was going to help paint someone's house last week. Remember all the paint splatters I had on my clothes when I got home?"

"You said you were going to help a friend. According to the article, you organized the thing."

"I didn't organize it. It's an annual charity event. I just recruited some kids to help."

"And who were all those kids? Black, Mexican. We moved here to get away from the gangs and trouble those filthy people bring."

"I thought we moved here because you lost your job when the restaurant where you worked closed, and they raised the rent on our apartment. Your friend Charlotte moved here and got you this job."

"There are a lot of decent white kids in this town. I see them every day. I serve breakfast to their parents."

That's part of the problem. Her mother served breakfast to their parents, and therefore Jodi was unworthy to associate with them. The Mexican kids didn't care what her mother did for a living or the fact that she didn't have a father with a good job.

Jodi took her empty bowl to the sink. "Gotta go. I'm meeting some kids to play ball."

"Black kids or Mexican kids?" her mother asked sarcastically.

"Both," she replied as she dashed out of the room before her mother could protest.

CHAPTER 30

"Nice shot, Jodi!" RJ shouted as her jump shot swished through the net.

RJ scooped up the ball and passed it to Marco. Marco dribbled the ball, executed a fake against Juan, and drove to the basket for a layup.

"Awe!" he clutched his hands against the sides of his head as the ball spun around the rim and dropped to the outside of the basket.

Jodi nabbed the rebound and put up the easy shot.

"That's it for today." Marco wiped the sweat off his forehead with the sleeve of his T-shirt. He removed his backward baseball cap, rubbed his hand through his wavy dark hair, and replaced the cap with the brim shading his eyes. "Next practice is Thursday, same time. RJ and I are going to get a Coke if you guys want to come."

"You bet," Juan said. "I could use an ice-cold drink right now."

Jodi looked over at the picnic table near the basketball court where she left her pack. The midday sun forced her to squint. *Is that Mr. K?*

"Jodi, are you coming?" Juan asked.

"Ah, you go without me. I'll see you on Thursday,"

She paced to the table. "Mr. K, I didn't expect to see you here." Upon noticing the distant look on his face, she eased into the bench across the table from him. "Are you okay?"

"Oh yes. I'm fine." He lowered his head. "I went to see Edna again this morning."

"Did you walk all the way to the nursing home again?"

"No. Bill came by to pick up some vegetables this morning. For the food pantry. When I told him that I was going to drive to the nursing home, he insisted on taking me."

"Good. I'm glad you didn't walk. And I'm really glad you didn't try to drive."

"I guess it is time to give up the car. Anyway, when I got there, they told me she had taken a turn for the worse and that she was in the hospital."

"What happened? Is she going to be okay?"

"I don't know. Since I'm not family, the hospital won't tell me anything."

"Gosh, Mr. K. I'm sorry. I know she is a good friend."

"Thank you. I just wish I knew how she is."

"The nursing home is a few blocks away. How did you get here?"

"She hasn't been in good health for some time, and I shouldn't have been surprised, but it took me aback. After a staff member told me the news, I just started walking. When I realized I was near the park, I came over just to sit and think. I don't know how long I was here before I realized that you were one of those kids playing basketball."

Jodi reached into her backpack for her water bottle. She was thirsty. She twisted the lid open and handed the bottle to Mr. K. She'd quench her thirst from the park drinking fountain later.

He took a drink of the water and set the bottle on the table. "You really gave those boys a run for their money."

"I'm just happy that they let me play."

"You really get into a flow when you play. Your concentration is intense, and yet you're relaxed."

"I never really thought about it."

"That's the point. Now we just need to get you in that same state with the violin."

Jodi put her elbows on the table and rested her chin in her hands. "Hmm."

"I'm glad I found you here. I needed something to take my mind off Edna."

"Well, when you're ready, can you tell me more of your story. Did the smugglers get you to Venice?"

**

Demons haunted the sleepless nights in the dilapidated shack, spinning my sanity into a mangled web of terror. Piotr's ghostly image weaved through the walls, his gentle nature, his toothy grin, his blue eyes pleading, accusing, amplifying my guilt for failing to carry him to safety. The captain's angry face burned into my eyelids, fire and blood spewing from the bullet hole centered in his forehead, flaming eyes hunting for vengeance. Crimson blood dripped from his scraggly beard and splattered my dusty boots. The haunting train shrieks followed us up the Vistula and smashed right through the flimsy shed, scooped us up, and packed us into a reeking, bulging cattle car.

The days were monotonous. When both smugglers were away, Karina and I would resume our language lessons. Because of my parents' heritage, I had learned both German and Italian in conjunction with my native Polish. I was surprised and frustrated by the difficulty Karina had reciting even simple Italian phases.

By the fifth day my feet were sweltering in the heavy, ill-fitting boots, hand-me-downs that Pani Maria's sons were not around to grow out of, so I tugged them off to give my toes some freedom. The dirt that spilled onto the dusty floor and the gunk that clung to my soles reminded me that it had been some time since I had bathed. No sooner had I wiggled my filthy toes when the smuggler called Smokey barreled in and shouted, "SS on the way. Get out now!"

I grabbed my knapsack and boots, and Karina and I chased after the smugglers into the woods. *Of all the time to give my toes some air.* I cursed as jagged rocks and prickly brambles cut my naked feet. Smokey and his partner darted into some dense brush, and Karina and I dove after them. I pulled on my boots and vowed not to remove them again until my feet touched the free soil of America.

A loud explosion blasted from where we had just come, and we dropped to the ground. Black smoke drifted upward from what I surmised was our hiding place, when Smokey said, "Boy, that was close."

"I'll say," replied his companion. "How in the hell did they find it, and who snitched us out?"

"I don't know." Smokey shook his head. "But we need a plan B."

We rose from the underbrush and took only a few steps when Smokey whispered, "Get down!"

We dropped to the ground again. I heard the approaching voices of the German SS searching for us. Karina and I slinked on our bellies deeper into the thick brush. I couldn't see the other two smugglers, but I knew they were hiding close by. Karina gasped, and I spun my head and froze when I saw a coiled viper, its forked tongue flicking, its marble eyes centimeters from Karina's nose.

The guard's footsteps grew nearer, and I could hear them rustling through the brush as I held my breath, immobile like a stone statue, eyeing the poisonous reptile, knowing that the slightest twitch would provoke the snake and reveal our presence. The thrashing grew louder, and the branches overhead shimmied. My heart thundered as my eyes followed the tip of a machine-gun barrel as it poked through the brush and slid the brim of my cap sideways. An oversized black boot crunched the snake's tail, and like a bolt of lightning, the serpent whipped around, shot up, and struck the soldier in the thigh. He screamed, and the other soldier rushed over to help. Two gunshots rang out, and both soldiers dropped to the ground.

"Let's go," Smokey shouted, and we scampered up and chased after the smugglers.

Once we determined enough distance had passed, we stopped. Wheezing, the lead smuggler said, "Well, now I guess it's time for plan B. I just don't know how we're going to get the next shipment to Krakow now that the Nazis have destroyed the network."

"What's plan B?" Smokey asked.

I was anxious to know the backup plan since our escape route to Venice had been thwarted.

"Let's go," the lead smuggler said. "We've got a lot of walking to do. I'll fill you in on the way."

He was right. We did have a lot of walking to do. We walked the rest of the day and through most of the night. My injured feet swelled from the cuts and bruises from my barefoot dash from the shack. By evening I was hobbling like an old man and struggling to keep up. At dusk we stopped for a rest by a stream. I was tempted to soak my aching feet in the cool water, but then I cringed at the agonizing memory of my barefoot escape earlier in the day and wisely kept my inflamed hooves safely shoed. Smokey cut a branch off a tree and crafted a walking stick that helped me a little. I was reminded of my grandmother, hunched over her cane as she shuffled about in her small apartment in Warsaw.

Upon reaching our destination, my pain was forgotten. In a clearing illuminated by a full moon and a sky full of stars, about two dozen peasants, men and women wielding shovels and hoes, were clearing a strip of land down to the dirt.

"What are they doing?" I asked.

"Making a temporary runway," the smuggler answered.

"Wow! You mean an airplane is going to land here?"

"Many of the supplies we receive are air dropped by the Allies," the smuggler explained. "As soon as they hit the ground, we hide them before the Germans can get to them, and we smuggle them to the home army, the AK. Generally, landing is too dangerous since enemy scouts are always on the lookout. However, there is something on this shipment that can't be dropped, so the pilot is going to land, offload, and take off again. Our job is to get the supplies removed and hidden before the Germans track us down."

I watched the harried workers as the smuggler talked. "What can't be dropped?"

"I don't know. And one more thing," the smuggler added. "You're the return cargo."

"Wow!" I said again. "You mean we get to ride on a fighter plane?"

Karina glared at me as if I had purple horns sprouting from my ears.

"It's not a fighter plane. It's a cargo plane for transporting troops and supplies. And yes, you get to ride in it, assuming it arrives safely."

"Wow!" I exclaimed again.

"Keep in mind," he continued, "it could be dangerous. If the Germans see or hear it taking off, they will try to shoot it down."

I nodded my understanding.

"Now, let's get to work and help clear the ground so it can land."

I heard it long before I saw it. Dawn was moments from breaking as the thunderous engines drowned out the clanking tools. My heart thumped like a base drum, a combination of excitement and fear. As the plane drew nearer and the roar grew louder, my fear intensified. Everyone in Poland and beyond must have heard the Allies' plane as it approached the secret landing strip.

The workers scattered as the plane screamed nearer and flicked on its landing lights. I watched the wings wobble as the pilot steadied the aircraft as it crept toward the runway. I held my breath as it hit the ground with a thud and bounced and shuddered over the lumpy runway. Its breaks squealed, and its hull creaked and moaned. I was sure it would run right past the end of the makeshift strip and crash into the trees.

To my surprise, the craft screeched to a stop only centimeters from the end of the runway, made a 180-degree turn, and rested, with propellers humming. The rear cargo door opened, and the workers rushed to the plane and, in assembly-line fashion, unloaded crates into waiting trucks. A tank sporting an antiaircraft gun rolled off the ramp and followed the train of loaded trucks as they disappeared into the awakening forest.

"Quick." The smuggler rushed us to the ramp. "Good luck, boys," he said as a soldier on board hustled us into the dark bowels of the aircraft, with no time for handshakes or goodbyes.

CHAPTER 31

Jodi popped into the library after her morning practice session with the Banditos. She had a couple of hours to burn before her next practice session with the Sharks. She enjoyed the library. It was air conditioned, didn't cost anything, and as a bonus, had an unlimited supply of books. She had returned *The Diary of Anne Frank* on her way in and then browsed the aisles for her next read. She headed for the History section and selected two books on World War II. Her next stop was the Health and Medicine aisle, where she selected a book on basic anatomy and another on alternative healing.

Mr. K's account of Karina's broken arm and illness and the fate of the last village doctor who'd sacrificed his life to help her touched Jodi deeply. It was as if his story swirled the dust off a crusty trap door to a dark, musty dungeon cluttered with a tangled mass of sticky cobwebs and rotting bones, buried deep within her soul, and streamed in a ray of light to illuminate the heart of her very existence. Helping just one Karina in the world would bring meaning and purpose to Jodi's being, as if to make amends for the unfortunate souls the doomed Jewish doctor was unable to treat. She hoped she would be worthy of the responsibility.

She carried the four books to an empty table to read the jackets and decide which one to put back, as she could only check out three at a time. Scattered on the table was the latest edition of the *Sage Grove Gazette*. She skimmed the front page, and a headline caught her attention: "Stolen Credit Card Ring Hits Town." The article reported that there had been numerous credit card thefts in the area and that the stolen cards had been used at local stores, gas stations, and restaurants. Some were used in other southern Idaho towns, including Boise, Pocatello, and Twin Falls as well as for internet purchases. It warned regional citizens to be aware of their surroundings, not to leave purses or wallets unattended or in unlocked vehicles, and to report any suspicious activity to police. A number was listed.

Jodi stared at the ceiling and thought of Tom and his problem with credit cards. Her research on him didn't reveal any criminal activity, just irresponsibility and problems managing money. But then, if someone had financial troubles, stealing credit cards would be tempting. Was the blond lunch date, obviously not his sister, in on it as well? Should she call the number? What would she tell them? She hadn't witnessed anything herself. She'd only heard of his cards being rejected from Juan and her mother, but she didn't have any evidence that they weren't his cards.

She glanced at the clock on the wall, jumped from her seat, replaced the alternative medicine book, and headed for the checkout counter.

CHAPTER 32

"Something's just not right, Mr. K," Jodi said as she and the old man picked green beans and tossed them into a plastic washtub. The peas had been long harvested, the treasures de-podded and frozen. The rows that had been crowded with radishes and lettuce were now bare. It had been a fruitful year, according to Mr. K, as Jodi had no frame of reference.

"What's not right?" he asked.

"With my mom and Tom. My mom wants so badly to find the right guy that I think she is blind to his faults. She would sacrifice just about anything to improve her economic and social status. I really think he is the credit card thief that I read about in the paper the other day. Only I don't have any way to prove it. And even if I did, to be honest, I don't think she would believe me. She would go on deceiving herself so that she could marry the guy, just for money."

"That seems shallow to me."

"Me too. Only, if I try to interfere, she will think I'm trying to drive a wedge between them. That I only care about what I want and not what she wants."

"Do you? Care more about what you want?"

Jodi sat back on her heels. "In this case I think it's both. On the one hand, I don't like Tom. On the other, I do want my mom to be happy. I can't imagine living in the same house with that guy though. That would be horrible. I really don't think he's the right guy for her—crook or not."

"So the key is to get some proof."

"How do I do that?"

"Besides catching him in the act, I don't have any good ideas. I'll tell you though, evidence of wrongdoing can come in handy in the right situation."

"Mr. K, now I'm curious. Someone in your story? Will you continue where you left off? You just got on the plane."

***

The soldier who'd hustled us into the belly of the plane, who I soon learned to be the navigator, said in a harried tone, "No time to get you strapped in before takeoff. Grab a handle and hold on tightly with both hands till we level off. I'll let you know when it's safe to let go."

The pilot working the controls was silhouetted by the glow of the cockpit instruments. The navigator slid into the empty seat in the cockpit, buckled himself in, and slipped a helmet over his thinning hair as the pitch of the engine intensified and the plane lurched forward. The light was dim, but I could see the terror in Karina's eyes.

I was excited and afraid. Prior to the air raids on Warsaw four years earlier, I had never seen an airplane. I was so fascinated that I would sometimes sneak out of the shelter of our basement to watch the planes fly low over the horizon to drop their terrifying bombs on the city. Upon noticing my absence, my mother would come after me, grab me by the collar, and scold me as she hustled me back to the dark cellar. After seeing the devastation that the Luftwaffe bombs inflicted on my city and learning of the death of many of my classmates, fear had drowned out any fascination.

The engine's crescendo intensified as the pilot thrust the throttle forward and the wheels bounced over the rugged surface of the peasant's improvised airstrip. My body shook like popcorn in a frying pan full of hot oil as the aircraft accelerated. For once I was glad for my empty stomach because the twisting summersaults kicking around down there would have caused an embarrassing mess. Maybe it was the glow from the cockpit instruments, but Karina looked green.

The plane teetered as the wheels lifted from the ground. At one point I thought it would tip over, but the pilot compensated. The metal fuselage creaked and popped as the craft bobbled in the turbulent morning air, and I was sure it was going to break apart and crash. My sweaty hands hurt from gripping the cold metal handle.

"You boys okay back there?" the navigator yelled over the roar of the engines.

Afraid to talk, I nodded my head, then realized that, of course, he couldn't see me. I let out the breath I had been holding and shouted back, "We're doing okay." I didn't know if that was the truth or not.

"Just a few more minutes and we'll be at cruising altitude. Then you can sit back, relax, and enjoy the flight," he shouted.

Karina gave me a look that said, *He must be out of his mind.*

Minutes later the pitch of the engine changed, the plane leveled off, and the thinner high-altitude air became smoother. The navigator unstrapped his harness and crawled back to join us. "Sorry," he shouted over the roaring engine. "That was a little rough. Landing on a real tarmac will now seem as graceful as a hawk gliding over a cornfield crawling with mice."

Not knowing what to say, I nodded. He opened the lid to a metal container and asked, "Are you boys hungry?"

We hadn't eaten anything since the previous morning, but the thought of food sickened my queasy stomach even more. Both Karina and I shook our heads.

"Well, when you're able to eat something, help yourself. I remember my first time up. You get over it pretty quickly."

He snatched a candy bar and jerky from the compartment and tossed them to his seat in the cockpit. "Let's get you strapped in. The skies aren't always so friendly." He showed us how to buckle into the harness attached to the hard metal benches that lined the shell of the plane. I imagined a nervous battalion of fidgeting paratroopers being transported to the front, anticipating their leap into a raging battle.

"Name's Mac, by the way," he introduced himself.

"I'm Michal," I shouted over the thundering, "and this is my cousin, Karl." It was still hard for me to call Karina Karl, but I could now say it without flinching.

Karina kept her eyes lowered as Mac shook both our hands.

"Are you taking us to Venice?" I asked.

"Well, not quite. But we'll get you close."

"How long till we get there?"

"You got a hot date or something?"

I glared at him.

"Lighten up. I was just kidding. Three, maybe four hours, depending on the wind speed and assuming we don't fly into any unforeseen circumstances. Flying over enemy territory during the daylight sometimes requires a deviation from our flight plan."

"Oh." I didn't want to know what kind of unforeseen circumstances might be lurking on the horizon.

"Better get back to work. Do get something to eat when your stomach is up to it, even if it's only a few bites. You both look famished." He crawled back into his copilot chair. The morning sunlight flickered through the pilot's side window, and I felt a little comfort knowing that we were headed south and would soon be out of Poland, if we weren't already. I wasn't sure where we were. Depending on where we took off, our path would fly over German-occupied Slovakia, Hungary, or maybe Austria—all equally dangerous—to reach Italy.

From my perch on the hard bench, I watched the pilot massage the controls of the American made Douglas C-47 Dakota transport plane (according to the placard bolted to the bulkhead). Lights flashed and dials spun, and I wished I knew what they meant. I could only see a sliver of blue sky through the cloudy cockpit window. Crackling and static filtered through the radio, sometimes accompanied by a voice that spoke in a language I didn't understand. I assumed it was English, as I knew that many Polish pilots flew with England's Royal Air Force. I had a hundred questions: How high were we flying, how fast were we going, where were we, and most important, were we out of range of the German antiaircraft guns? The deafening engine noise made conversation impossible, so I leaned my head against the vibrating hull and plotted our upcoming encounter with my uncle. I hoped I would find the nerve to stand up to him.

Hours later the changing engine pitch jerked me awake. I watched Karina sleeping across from me. How I wish we could abandon our ruse and she could be a girl again. She looked silly in her baggy boy's clothes, scuffed boots, and short hair. I had a sudden urge to jump out of my seat and kiss her swollen lips, which were still blistered from her long days in the sun piloting the dead captain's boat. I thought of Edward and hoped he was safe. I said a quick prayer for Piotr and felt a twinge of jealousy, knowing that Karina had had a soft spot for him. And I thought of Pani Maria and how devastated she must be with the death of her beloved son.

The plane dipped slightly, and Mac yelled back at us, "We're starting our descent, so make sure you're strapped in tightly."

Karina's eyes popped open as the maneuver jarred her awake.

"Gunners two o'clock!" the navigator shouted, and the pilot banked the plane in the opposite direction to avoid the threat.

The engines screamed in protest as the pilot thrust the throttle forward. "Come on, baby. . . come on, baby," he cried as he coaxed more speed from the overburdened engines. Rapid gunfire thundered from below, and bullets pinged the metal hull. Glass shattered, and a gust of air swooshed through the damaged windshield in front of the pilot. Blood streaked down the side of his neck, but he held a tight grip on the throttle with one hand and the yoke with the other.

A thunderous boom exploded. All my breath whooshed from my body, as if a heavyweight boxer thrust a powerful punch into my gut. The navigator yelled, "Left engine out! Left engine out!" A hissing sound came from the left wing, and the pilot wrestled with the controls to steady the craft. Finally, the firing from below ceased and the navigator said, "I think we're out of range."

"We're losing too much fuel," the pilot shouted. He tapped on one of the gauges. "Hydraulic pressure is low."

He tapped another gauge. "Losing oil. Landing gear is damaged. We're going to have to crash land!"

The plane groaned as it streaked toward the green canopy of trees below. "Everybody hold on!" the pilot shouted.

I closed my eyes and prayed with all my might as the plane sheared through the tops of the trees and then convulsed over the rough ground. It stopped with a thud, and I was thrust forward. Lying on the floor still strapped into the harness, feeling a painful lump developing on my forehead, I opened my eyes. Except for a hissing noise, everything was quiet. Too quiet. I looked over at Karina still buckled into her seat. Her eyes were closed, but her chest heaved up and down, and I thanked God she was still alive. I unhooked my harness and crawled into the cockpit. The pilot's face was covered in blood, and he didn't move.

The navigator groaned, and I skuttled over to him and shook his arm. He groaned again and turned his head and squinted at me. In a forced whisper he asked, "Are you okay?"

"I think so."

He lifted his arm and groaned again. He rotated his head toward the pilot and crossed himself with his other arm. I did the same. "We need to get out of here," he said. "They're going to come looking for us."

I unbuckled his harness, and he moaned as he reached for a pack near his feet. I glanced through a gaping hole that until moments ago held the tail section of the plane, and gasped in bewilderment at the trail of debris littered across the serene meadow the pilot had miraculously landed in. I helped Karina out of her harness, scooped up my knapsack, and stuffed it with rations from the bin. I grabbed a canteen of water and with Karina at my heels, hopped to the ground.

The navigator followed, clutching his elbow and

limping as we darted into the forest.

CHAPTER 33

I was gasping for air as we raced through the woods when I heard a *cur-plunk* behind me. I spun and dashed to the navigator, who lay face down in the dirt. His broken arm dangled uselessly at his side as Karina and I helped him rise. He clutched his ribs with the other hand and coughed uncontrollably. When his hacking subsided, I handed him the canteen. Water dribbled down his chin as he sucked in the hydrating fluid.

"Thanks, pal." He hacked some more. Sweat dripped from his face, and perspiration stained his torn British RAF shirt.

"Are you all right?" I asked. "You don't look so good."

"I think I have some broken ribs. Probably bleeding inside. And the arm's no good."

I stared at the purple hand dangling beneath his shirt sleeve. There was a lot of blood.

"Need to get the bleeding stopped. In my pocket"—he nodded to his left side—"is my knife. Get it out and cut off the sleeve."

He slithered back to the ground.

"I have a knife." I fished my Boy Scout knife from my pocket, knelt beside him, and cut and ripped the sleeve away from his battered arm. Karina cringed and turned her head away. I was tempted to do the same, but I tried to put on a brave face, knowing we would never find our way to Venice without him.

He looked at Karina and instructed, "See those branches over there?"

She nodded.

"Find a strong one that is about a half a meter long. Quick."

Karina soon returned with the perfect-sized stick and handed it to me.

The navigator continued with his instructions. "I need you to make a tourniquet. Tie the sleeve around my arm just above the elbow."

I followed his instruction, remembering that I'd learned this technique at a Boy Scout outing years ago. I wish I had paid more attention to the Scoutmaster's instructions. "Now," the navigator continued as I tied the knot. "Slip the stick through the center of the knot and turn."

We both cringed as I tightened the tourniquet a quarter turn.

"Keep going," he said through gritted teeth, "till it stops bleeding."

I prayed for the bleeding to cease, and I feared that he would pass out from the intense pain.

"Think that oughta do it," he concluded through his clenched teeth.

"There's a compass in my pack. Fetch it out, and let's see where we need to go."

I wasn't sure he would be going anywhere, but I fished the compass from his pack and held it in front of him. We both watched the dial spin. He squinted at the sky to pinpoint the sun's direction, then looked at the compass again.

"That way." He nodded.

"Where are we?" I asked. "Are we in Italy?"

"Not sure. We could still be in Austria. We were approaching the border when the pilot changed directions."

I slung his pack over my shoulder, Karina took my knapsack, and we helped him to his feet. Progress was slow as we descended the gravelly limestone and steep slopes of the Southern Alps, oblivious to the spectacular scenery and breathtaking vistas as we assisted the struggling navigator. I hoped we had made it across the Italian border, and I could almost taste the sweet Mediterranean warmth and feel the misty spray of the salty sea. But alas, the navigator's assessment made me realize that it was only my imagination.

We stopped frequently for the navigator to catch his breath. He coughed up blood and became delirious. By late afternoon he was hallucinating, calling for us to duck and take arms against each grove of trees on the horizon. At dusk we stopped by a stream for the night. Karina and I shared two-thirds of the rations, saving the remainder for Mac, for when he would be well enough to eat again. I doubted he would make it through the night. Karina thought otherwise and told me to have faith. If I prayed to my Catholic God and she prayed to her Jewish Yahweh, then one of them might listen and heal the navigator by morning. She reminded me of her recovery from her broken arm and infection back at Pani Maria's cottage and argued that the navigator was much stronger and healthier, so he would obviously pull through.

I didn't mention that she wasn't coughing up blood and that she'd had the help of an underground doctor—who she still didn't know had been captured and killed—black market antibiotics, home remedies, and rest in a clean bed.

We made him as comfortable as we could, used my spare shirt to wipe his forehead with the cool stream water, and hoped for the best.

I was greeted the next morning by the warm sun kissing my cheeks, the sweet serenade of the waking songbirds, and the gurgling stream meandering down the mountainside. The cool morning mist seeped to my bones as I lay still, gazing at the lanky pine trees stretching for the hazy blue sky and the glittering leaves of the creek-side birch trees dancing in the morning breeze.

I could hear Karina's soft breathing nearby. I couldn't hear the navigator's breaths, and I was afraid to turn my head and look.

Karina stirred and, almost as if questioning the hushed breeze, she asked, "Is he…?" She couldn't bring herself to finish the question.

"I don't know," I whispered as I watched the playful leaves frolic above me.

Anticipating the worst, I took a few deep breaths, then sat up and gazed at the navigator. He was stone still. Was he dead? I squinted at his hardened face. No movement. Then an eyelid flickered. Or maybe it was the breeze, or a gnat, or my eyes playing tricks on me. I slid over to his side and placed my hand on his chest. I thought it may have moved. I felt for a pulse on his neck. I cringed when I didn't feel one, but just as I was about to remove my fingers, I detected a blip. I pressed a little harder and was relieved when I felt a faint pulse.

"He's alive, I think," I said to Karina.

"What do we do?"

"I don't know. But we need to get him to a hospital."

She surveyed the surrounding forest. "Do you see anything that resembles a hospital? Besides, we can't carry him."

I thought back to my Boy Scout training. I wish now that I had been a better Scout. My brother was the good Scout. He loved the outings and the adventure. I only went because my father insisted it was vital to my becoming a real man, whatever that meant. I would have rather been home with my books and my violin. I was glad my father let me drop out when the Nazis banned the Polish Scouts, although my troop continued in a new capacity underground as the eyes and ears of the Home Army.

"We make a stretcher."

"Out of what?"

"Sticks, branches, and vine."

It took an hour to scrounge up the materials and the rest of the morning to fashion two large logs as a frame, several smaller, sturdy ones as cross supports, which we then lined with leaves and brush. We used a rope from the navigator's pack and vines to tie them together. The navigator mumbled some incoherent gibberish as we struggled to slide his heavy body onto the makeshift stretcher. With the difficult task accomplished, Karina and I each took one of the protruding poles and heaved forward. The sled didn't move. We counted to three and heaved again, and the stretcher lurched with us—and the navigator slid right off the end. Dejected, we sat, head in hands, on the ground.

Then Karina's eyes lit up. "I have an idea?"

"What?"

"Hand me the pack."

I watched her work. Soon I understood what she was doing and used my knapsack on the other side. Now with the navigator secured to the stretcher with the straps from the two bags and the sleeves of our jackets, we were off.

CHAPTER 34

Progress was slower than a slug scaling a gnarly tree. Every few meters we stopped and cleared the way ahead of fallen logs, thick brush, and rocks. Then we dragged the navigator over our makeshift path and repeated the process. I made frequent checks with the compass to make sure we were still headed south as best as the terrain would allow.

We passed the time by teaching each other songs we had learned as children. Even though I didn't understand the words, I decided her Hebrew songs were far more colorful and uplifting than my Catholic hymns or Boy Scout tunes. I also taught her to hum the violin part of the Brahms sonata. She didn't like it much since it didn't have any words, so she made some up to fit with the melody.

By midafternoon my body felt like one of the aging pines that towered around us, my wilting arms dangling like weary limbs being sucked from the gnarled trunk by a howling wind. We both collapsed to the ground from exhaustion. I thought of Pani Maria's unnamed mule and wished he were here to help, but at the same time felt a twinge of guilt for the burdens he was forced to haul. No wonder he was going lame.

"I can't do this anymore." Karina moaned.

"I can't do this anymore either. But what do we do now? We can't leave him."

"Maybe one of us can stay here with him while the other goes for help."

"I'm not leaving you alone," I argued. "And besides, even if I found help, how do we know it's not the enemy? And how do I find my way back? We'd both be lost then!"

"I know. You're right. We're just not strong enough to pull him much farther. I wish we had wheels for this thing."

"Wouldn't that be great," I agreed. "We should have taken them from the plane."

She gave me that "you're really stupid" look. "I have another idea."

We found a strong, sturdy branch and used our extra shirts to tie the branch to the extended poles to make a harness. Now we had the extra leverage of our bodies to help haul the heavy load.

"Let's get moving," I sighed, feeling foolish since I was the one studying engineering. We lugged the stretcher like mules towing a cart.

We struggled around fallen trees, cut through thick brush, slid over loose scree, and were scratched by brittle branches. Sweat dripped off my chin, and my perspiration-soaked shirt clung to my aching back. Late in the day we came to a narrow dirt road. We stopped to rest and decide our next move. Dragging the stretcher would be a lot easier on the road. On the other hand, we would be more exposed if someone passed by.

Our debate was interrupted by the sound of clanking hooves. Realizing it was too late to dart back into the woods, we turned and faced the approaching horse-drawn wagon that appeared from around the bend.

My heart thundered as the old man at the helm pulled back on the reins to stop the lumbering steed. We must have looked like a sorry bunch, two ragged boys hovering over what must have appeared to be a dead soldier. I cursed myself for leaving the pistol in my knapsack that tied the navigator to the stretcher.

"What 'r' you boys doin' here?" the old man barked in Italian in a dialect that was difficult to understand.

"At least we're in Italy."

I hadn't realized I had vocalized my comment until he muttered, "Only by a horse's hair."

He looked down at the navigator lying on the ground.

Karina knelt beside him. "He needs a doctor," I informed the man.

"Looks like he needs a morgue." He climbed from the wagon, hobbled over, knelt next to the motionless navigator, and pressed his ear to his chest. "Can't tell if 'e's alive or not. He Italian or German? Or one of them English chaps?"

"Ur, ah. I don't really know. Not German." I wasn't about to tell him that he was Polish. "Can you take him to a doctor? Please?"

I studied the old man as he pondered my request. His soiled clothes, leathery skin, stained teeth, shaky hands. I went to the stretcher and rummaged through the knapsack. My knuckle brushed against the hard metal of the pistol, but I nudged it aside and instead pulled out the tin cigarette holder that I had taken from the dead German soldier. "Here." I opened the tin and offered it to the old man, who greedily eyed the contents. "Please take them and get our friend some help."

The old man grabbed the tin, cursed, and put one of the smokes between his shriveled lips. "Don't suppose you got a light?" The crumpled cigarette bobbed as he spoke.

"Sorry." I shrugged. I was certain the navigator had one in his pack, but I wasn't about to take the time to search for it.

"Let's get 'im in the wagon." He shuffled some of the crates of produce to make space, and the three of us hoisted the stretcher into the back of the creaky farm cart.

"Where are you headed?" I asked as we struggled with the heavy load.

"Paularo."

"Paularo?"

"Udine Province. On the border with Austria. How is it that you don't know where you are? Did you just drop out of the sky or something?"

I flinched. I hoped he didn't notice. "We just got a little disoriented. We're on our way to Venice."

"Venice? Or Vienna?"

"Venice." I remembered the train trips my mother, brother, and I took to visit my uncle. I recalled that we spent a lot of time winding through canyons and climbing and descending mountain passes. As I watched the scenery pass by, I never knew whether we were in northern Italy or Austria until the last trip when my mother said, "Welcome to Italy, boys." I was tired of the train by then. After the border crossing, we had spent a long time descending the mountains before we reached the lush checkerboards of farms and orchards. I frowned as the old man's comments indicated that we had a lot more rugged terrain to struggle through.

The old man noticed us eyeing his cargo as we talked. "You can have one potato each," he said with a warning. "Me and the misses picked 'em all by han', and I know exactly how many are there. I need to have an accurate counting when I get back from the market. Or I'll need to find another place to sleep," he added under his breath.

"Yes, sir." I grabbed two of the largest spuds and handed one to Karina.

"How long till we get there?"

"Couple hours," he replied. "Longer if we don't get movin'."

Karina and I sat in the bed of the wagon with the navigator, our feet dangling out the back, while the old man flicked the reins and coaxed the draft horse into a gentle stroll. I devoured the potato without even tasting it.

An eerie stillness hung over the dark village as we clomped along the deserted cobblestone street, past quiet cottages and vacant shops. The old man maneuvered the steed around some turns and came to a stop and slunk down from his perch.

Karina and I hopped to the ground.

"See that house over there with the front light on?" He pointed to a dilapidated structure not much larger than a small cottage. "The doctor lives in the back. We'll take your friend to the front door and set him down. Then after I get the wagon out of sight, you"—he aimed his finger at me—"bang on the door and then hightail it out of there."

"You mean leave him?" I asked.

"As a doctor, he's bound by his code to help your friend if he's still alive. Can't say the same for you, dependin' on which side he supports."

I nodded. We slid the stretcher from the wagon and dragged it to the doctor's cottage—which had a faded Red Cross symbol painted on the door—and rested it on the stoop. I watched Karina and the old man walk back to the wagon and listened to the familiar clip-clopping fade into the darkness. Then I pounded on the door and darted for some nearby bushes.

The door creaked open. A face poked out and looked left, then right, and then down. The doctor yelled in Italian when he saw the navigator lying at his feet, "Camellia,

Camellia, we have a patient. Come help me get him inside."

With the navigator's fate now in the doctor's care, I waited until the door closed, whispered a quick prayer, and sprinted to the wagon.

CHAPTER 35

Saturday morning Jodi and Juan rode bicycles to basketball practice. The bikes belonged to Juan and his older brother. They had seen better days. Chipped paint, dings, and spots of rust spackled the frames, yellowed foam spilled from the split saddles, and some of the spokes were bent. But after the chains were lubed and the soft tires filled with air, they still served their purpose, even with the wobbly front wheel on Jodi's ride.

The parched desert air was stifling hot, and after the last basket, Jodi wiped the sweat from her forehead and guzzled water from the park drinking fountain. She plunked down on the brittle grass under the shade of a nearby maple tree, next to Juan and their rides.

"Tell me again why we need the bikes?" Juan asked.

"We need to find Tom and tail him. I need to know if he's the credit card thief."

"Why don't you just tell your mother your suspicions?"

"She'll just think I'm trying to break them up."

"Actually, you kind of are. You could just go to the police."

"Not without some proof. All we know is that his cards keep getting rejected. We don't know if they're stolen cards."

"I still don't know how we're going to catch him."

"We'll figure something out. First we have to find him. Let's go."

It took two hours of pedaling up and down the grid of Sage Grove's potholed streets before they spotted Tom's truck parked askew over two spaces in the lot of the Sage Grove public golf course. At least there was no chance of an encounter with Kristen and her groupies here, as her family were members of the elite Sage Grove Private Country Club on the rich side of town, a fact that she bragged about to anyone who would dare question her privileged status.

"I didn't know your mother's boyfriend plays golf."

"Neither did I."

"Is your mother with him?"

"She's working today. That's why I wanted to watch him today."

"Oh. How are we going to find him? We can't just walk on to the fairway and look for him."

"That would be a surefire way to get a golf ball plastered into your skull," Jodi said. "The bike path partially circles the golf course, so let's just ride around and see if we can spot him."

"What if he sees us first?"

"We're just out for a bike ride. It's a small town. Just a coincidence. There is no reason for him to suspect we're looking for him."

Jodi was discouraged when their lap around the course was nearing full circle. Then she spotted Tom getting ready to tee off. His back was to the chain-link fence and the bike path, so they stopped and watched as he balanced the little white ball on the peg and stepped back and took several practice swings before stepping up to the tee. He took his time, repeatedly bringing the driver back a few inches and softly swinging until almost touching the ball with the club's wooden head to dial in his swing. The others in his group looked annoyed, and the waiting foursome next up were unable to mask their impatience. Finally, Tom took a swing, and the ball sailed to the right of the fairway.

"Wow, buddy," one of the other golfers said, "at least you're consistent. That's six in a row!"

"Not exactly," a second player corrected. "Three sliced in the other direction."

They all chuckled, and Tom shook his head and swung his club in the air like an out-of-control batter swinging at a wild pitch.

Jodi and Juan watched the foursome play the rest of that hole and then the next.

"This is really boring," Juan said, faking a yawn. "Remind me never to take up golf."

"Someone should have reminded Tom not to take up golf," Jodi responded. "It looks like they only have one more hole left."

"The way he's playing, it may take the rest of the day to get through the last hole." Grinning he added, "Is it dark yet? I think I feel winter coming on."

"Cute."

It did take a long time to complete the last hole, as Tom's ball got stuck in a sand trap. He glanced toward his peers, who were conversing among themselves, then slipped a new ball onto the grass and managed to get the next shot close to the green. Three putts later he joined the rest of his party at the cart, which they rode to the parking lot.

Tom lowered the tailgate on his accessory-loaded, jet-black F-150 pickup and heaved his clubs into the bed. "Here," he said to one of the other golfers, "I'll get yours also." He took a second set of clubs from the cart and slung those into the back of his truck as well. "Let's go get a beer. I'm so thirsty, I feel like a parched camel in the middle of the Sahara."

"My wallet is in my bag," the second golfer said, making a motion toward the truck.

"It's on me, fellas. Go ahead and find a table, I just need to fetch a stick of gum, and I'll catch up."

Jodi and Juan crouched behind a parked car as Tom glanced in both directions. They peered over the hood and watched Tom reach into the side pocket of his golf partner's bag, pull out a folded wallet, remove some cash and plastic, and shove the loot into his pocket. He returned the lightened wallet, slammed the tailgate shut, and sauntered toward the clubhouse to his unsuspecting friends.

"How is it that we are the only two teenagers on the planet without a cell phone with a camera?" Jodi said.

"I can't believe he was so obvious. In plain daylight. What are you going to do now?"

"I don't know."

CHAPTER 36

"By Jove, I think you've got it!" Mr. K praised as Jodi completed the introductory phase of the Brahms sonata.

Jodi tried to maintain a neutral expression, but she couldn't control the wide grin that exploded across her face.

"Play it again."

Jodi repeated the passage.

"Good. Now a little bit more crescendo through the run and then taper the end of the phase."

Jodi played the passage again.

"Not quite so much crescendo. Just enough to add some tension."

After repeating the phrase several more times Mr. K said, "You are making remarkable progress. I think you will be ready to play this for your chair audition."

"I don't know, Mr. K. I still don't sound the way you do when you play it. Or the way Isaac Stern sounds on the recording you play for me."

"Don't be so hard on yourself. You've only been playing the instrument for a short time. Isaac Stern probably started when he was four years old. And you know that I've been playing for nearly a century." He rubbed his chin. "Gosh, that's an awful long time. Anyway, I don't know of anyone who's advanced as much so quickly. Remember at your first lesson when I said you would be a fine violin player?"

Jodi cringed at the memory of her awful playing that day. She nodded.

"Well, I was right. You have the talent and the tenacity to take your music wherever it leads you."

"You know, Mr. K, I never thought I would like playing the violin. Now it's almost like this instrument, crappy as it is, is my best friend. Besides my basketball, of course," she added.

"That is a trait of a true musician. In my life, I've had two best friends and great loves, Karina, and my violin. Even during those trying times when my instrument and I were separated, it was still intertwined with my soul."

"Speaking of, how did you finally get to Venice?"

***

At dawn the next morning, we helped the old man set up his booth at the open-air market. The commune was small, not much different than Pani Maria's village prior to the invasion, sans the charred bones and mangled skeletons of grenade-ravaged dwellings. For our help, the old man gave us each an additional potato.

"How do we get to Venice from here?" I asked the old man as I hoisted my pack over my shoulder.

"I've never been to Venice, so I'm not exactly sure."

I frowned.

"I imagine if you keep south, follow the streams downhill, you'll eventually get to the sea. You should be able to find a traffic sign by then."

Not very helpful. I could have figured that out on my own.

On our way out of the market, I stole some eggs, carrots, and apples from distracted vendors.

Then we walked. And walked and walked and walked. Following the streams down the rugged slopes of the Italian Alps was arduous—as much slipping, clambering, and stumbling as walking. The trek became less strenuous when we reached the foothills. We followed a road but decided we were too exposed. We hopscotched through a fallow field and trailed a railroad line. We dashed into nearby bushes for cover at each passing train. There were a lot of trains. We ate wild berries when we could find them and pilfered fresh fruit from the patchwork of orchards and vineyards that checkered the hillsides, although most fields lay barren, the farmers away fighting with Mussolini's army. Once we passed an untended barn and I was able to steal more eggs. I was tempted to snatch a chicken, but remembering Pani Maria's stern warning, decided against it.

We rummaged for scraps when we traveled through the many small villages along the way. At stream crossings we filled the navigator's canteen with fresh water. At night we slept under the stars, using my knapsack and rolled-up shirts as pillows. We suffered through blistered feet, painful sunburns, snagged clothing, scratched faces, a twisted ankle, and drenching downpours. It took twenty punishing days of coaxing and cajoling our weary bodies, and each other, to reach the outskirts of Venice.

"Wow!" Karina exclaimed at her first glimpse of the Adriatic Sea.

Even though I had seen the vastness of the sparkling blue waters many times as a small boy, I was overcome with emotion at the sight of the sun's rays skipping over the silvery, dancing ripples. "For you, my dear, I present the Adriatic Sea and our gateway to America."

"America!"

"America." I let out a sigh. This was not how I'd planned to tell her about our ultimate destination.

"I thought we were going to your uncle's."

"We are, temporarily. He's going to get us to America."

"Michal, I can't go to America." She furrowed her brow and thrust her hands to her hips. "After the war is over, I have to go home to my family."

I sank to the ground. "Karina"—I motioned for her to sit—"the war is never going to be over. You don't have a home anymore. The Germans destroyed it. You may or may not have a family. I don't know. But it's not safe for you anywhere in Europe. You heard me promise your father that I'd keep you safe, and I intend to do that—or die trying."

"You'd do that for me? Die, I mean. Why?"

"Yeah, I guess so." I looked at the ground and mumbled, "Because I kinda like you."

"Oh." After an uncomfortable silence, she added, "I guess I kinda like you too."

"Really?" I glanced up and smiled.

"Yeah, really. Kinda."

"I really wasn't sure, because I know you kinda liked Piotr."

"Yeah, I did kinda like him too. But he was too old. And with that smile, I bet he already had a girlfriend somewhere."

"Yeah, probably." I tried to hide my relief.

"And besides, it looks like we're stuck with each other, so I guess it's a good thing we like each other."

"Yeah." I grinned. "Definitely a good thing."

"Look, Karina, after we get to America, we'll do everything we can to find your family. When we do, we'll bring them to America too."

She stared off into the vast sea, and if she had any tears left in her, they would have been streaming down her dirty, sunburned cheeks.

"We better get moving." I rose to my feet.

The countryside melted into a labyrinth of urban chaos as we neared the sea and hiked along the shore. I felt the disgusted eyes of weary citizens on us as we passed by. I would have rather traveled at night. But not knowing if there was a curfew, we crawled under bushes to hide from any passing sentries while we slept.

The sun touched the horizon when we reached the shore of Laguna Venetia, the obstacle that stood between us and my uncle and our ticket out of Europe.

"So where is this Venice? All I see is water," she asked.

"It's out there. It's in the middle of this giant lagoon. Quite amazing. A city built on pylons over a giant swamp, with canals for streets."

"Where?" She squinted, trying to locate the island city.

"Let's keep walking. Mussolini built a bridge to it. We can't miss it."

The night was deep by the time we reached the long bridge, built right over the lagoon to the island swamp city. I was already on edge for being on the streets after dark. Then terror struck when we spied a German checkpoint blocking the passage ramp. We concealed ourselves behind a dumpster and watched the diligent soldiers search the vehicles lined up behind the lowered crossing arm.

"We can't go across there," she whispered. "What do we do now?"

"I'm thinking ... I'm thinking." The answer was obvious. "We have to go by boat."

"We don't have a boat."

"We'll have to find one. We passed a marina earlier. Let's check it out."

A quarter moon shed just enough light to prowl along the marina docks and inventory the available craft. My ill-conceived plan was to convince a fisherman to take us across at first light, but the presence of the Germans caused me to scrap the idea. I knew that the Italians under Mussolini were aligned with the Axis powers, and the information that had filtered its way to Edward's AK unit confirmed that the Allies were invading southern Italy, but I never expected to see German troops near Venice.

After lurking around the dock, we spotted a small motorboat. I motioned for Karina to hop in, and I untied the line. I pushed the dingy from the dock, picked up an oar, and started paddling. I nodded my head to the other oar, and Karina picked it up.

"Why don't you just start the engine?" she whispered.

"Not until we get farther away." I wanted to make sure we were out of gunshot range should the owner happen to hear the engine fire up and come out shooting.

In my weakened state, my arms felt like rubber when I determined we were far enough from shore to start the motor, so I put down the oar and pulled the engine crank. It coughed a puff of smoke and died. How stupid of me not to check for fuel. I pulled again, and after a sputter, the motor roared to life. Karina clapped her hands. With one hand gripped on the rudder, I guided the dinghy through the murky lagoon parallel, although not too close, to Mussolini's German-occupied bridge toward the pylon city.

I killed the engine as we neared the pier, and Karina and I paddled the boat to the towering dock. I tied the dinghy to the iron ladder, slung my pack over my shoulder, and climbed the dozen rungs to the landing of Techelli pier.

"My uncle owns this pier," I informed her as we climbed.

I poked my head over the landing and ducked back down as I caught the sight of two uniformed guards patrolling the dock. Wide belts snuggled around their buttoned jackets, and trousers puffed from knee-high jackboots. Not guards on my uncle's payroll. "Germans," I muttered.

By now I considered myself skilled at avoiding German sentries, but Edward had taught me well that each encounter posed significant risk. Not the time to get cocky. I studied the lay of the wharf and observed their patterns. Twenty-two paces in each direction. When they stopped to light a cigarette, I jumped to the dock and signaled for Karina to follow, and we darted behind a shed that served as the customs/receiving office. My ears focused on the pacing footsteps. I counted the twenty-two steps, and when they paused to change directions, we dashed behind a row of crates waiting to be loaded on the next vessel.

By the time a streak of pink in the east announced the pending daybreak, we arrived at the landing of my uncle's mansion. Viewed from any casual passerby on the Grand Canal, the building mimicked the other colorful dwelling stacked side by side, towering over the marshy lagoon. The distinguishing factor, however, was that rather than rows of apartments above the galleries and shops that lined the canal, the whole structure was my uncle's mansion, an expansive dwelling with a wing for the family, quarters for the household staff, and a suite of guest rooms.

I waited until the morning sun cast its long shadows over the city before I reached for the brass knocker and tapped it three times against the solid mahogany door. It was some time before the door opened a slit, just enough to see a dark eye squint down at us. "Get out of here, you mangy kids," my uncle's butler barked as he slammed the door closed.

I turned to Karina and shrugged. "He probably didn't recognize me. I haven't been here since before the war started."

I clanked the knocker, louder this time. The door did not open. I tried again.

"I told you filthy beggars to scram," the butler shouted through the door. "There are no handouts here."

"I guess I didn't tell you that my uncle is not exactly a nice guy," I said to Karina.

"Great," she replied. "You said he would help us."

"He'll help us. He just won't like it." I shouted through the door, "Please open the door, Anthony. It's Michal Kaszubinski. I need to speak with my uncle Vincent and aunt Sophia. Please let us in."

The door cracked open, and the towering butler glared down at us.

My aunt shuffled to the door behind him. "Michal?" she asked, wide eyed as she tried to verify my identity.

"Hi, Aunt Sophie. It's me, Michal."

"What are you doing here?" She nudged the butler aside. "Come in, come in." She hustled us inside, and the butler whisked the door closed and eyed us with disgust.

"Oh my God!" my aunt cried. "You look dreadful. Your clothes, they're so . . ." She couldn't find the right word. "My how you've grown! You're so skinny. How did you get here? Oh my! You're so filthy and skinny, and your hair . . ." She raised her hand to her cheek in shock. "And you smell bad too. Come in and get cleaned up, then you can tell us what this is about. I'll ring the doctor." Noticing Karina, her jaw dropped, "Who's your friend?"

Karina gave me a startled look. "Karl," I said for Karina. "This is Karl. He traveled with me from Warsaw. He doesn't like to talk much." Then I added, "No doctor."

"Mommy, mommy." A young girl around three ran into the room, bare feet pattering on the exotic tile floor. "Anton be mean."

"Anton don't be mean to your sister," my aunt shouted over her shoulder.

The toddler slid to a halt and pointed. "Who dat, Mommy? Pee-ewe, dinky." She pinched her nose closed with her miniature thumb and forefinger.

Squatting next to the youngster, my aunt made the introductions. "This is your cousin Michal. From Warsaw." Looking at Karina she said, "And this is . . . I'm sorry. I didn't catch your name."

"Karl," I answered again for Karina.

"This is your cousin Marissa. Marissa was born after your last visit," she informed me, as if I hadn't figured that out. Turning to Marissa she said, "Michal and Karl are going to have a bath and some breakfast. Then they are going to tell us why they came to visit."

I hoped for some breakfast first, but I knew that we would not be allowed at the table in our unpresentable state.

"What's going on down there?" my uncle growled from the balcony above the grand staircase.

"Hello, Uncle Vincent."

"Michal?" He squinted at us, as if trying to make out a fuzzy object on the horizon. "What are you doing here, and why do you look like a starving street urchin?"

"Michal and his friend are going upstairs to get cleaned up," my aunt interjected as she directed us through the elegant foyer to the staircase. "Please have Anthony fetch the doctor," she instructed her husband.

"No doctor," I repeated.

My aunt hustled us into the elaborate lavatory and turned the brass faucet in the fancy copper claw tub to draw the bath. She left some plush towels and two oversized luxurious robes. "Put your filthy clothes in the hamper, and I'll have Anthony burn them. While you're bathing, I'll have him pick up some fresh clothes for you."

After my aunt left us alone, Karina glared at me. "I'm not taking a bath with you."

"I, uh, no, of course not. She has to think you're a boy, or my uncle will rat you out." I turned and faced the opposite wall from the tub. "You go first. I promise I won't look."

"Promise?"

"Promise."

"Here." She handed me one of the fluffy towels. "Sit on the floor and face the wall and wrap this around your head so you won't be tempted to peek."

"I won't peek. I promise."

She put her dirty hands on her bony hips and stared at the towel. I faced the wall and sat cross-legged on the floor and swirled the towel around my head.

When it was my turn, I scrubbed the layers of dirt and sweat from my skinny body, taking special care not to further damage the fraying tape that still secured the secret message to my ribs. I had lost so much weight that I was afraid that the message, along with its fastener, would slip right off. I dried off, used my fingers to comb the tangles from my wet hair, and Karina and I, wrapped in the oversized robes, plodded barefoot downstairs to the kitchen.

My aunt was sitting at the table, her hands wrapped around a cup of steaming coffee, waiting for us.

I inhaled the aroma. Real coffee.

"That's a little better. We'll have to see if we can get you to the barber this afternoon. The doctor is not able to come until later, but he said to only give you small amounts of bland food at a time." As if on cue, the cook appeared with two small plates of scrambled eggs and buttered toast, set them down, and scurried away.

Like Oliver Twist and his orphaned tablemates, we devoured the small meal, and when our plates were empty, a maid whisked the dirty dishes away.

My aunt continued with the doctor's instructions. "He said that if you can tolerate food, to give you a little every few hours for several days until you regain some strength. Also, rest. So upstairs with you both, and when your uncle returns, you can tell us why you're here." As she led us to our rooms, she asked, "Does your mother know you're here? I'll cable her and let her know you're safe."

"No. Please don't tell her yet."

"All right, I'll wait until I hear your tale first. She must be worried sick."

Aunt Sophie was right. My mother must be distressed by my disappearance. And I so much wanted to tell her myself that I was fine. At least I thought I was fine. But after observing my skeletal limbs in the bath earlier, I wasn't so sure.

The maid scurried from the guest wing as Aunt Sophie stopped at the door of the first room and waved us in. She had us to sit on the bed as she closed the door. She pulled up a chair. "Karl, you can sleep here. And Michal can take the room across the hall." Looking at Karina she said, "It is obvious to me that your name is not Karl. I can't imagine what kind of trouble you are in. I'll keep your secret for the time being, but you're obviously not a boy, but a beautiful young lady. Men can be easily fooled, and you had me for a while. I just hope you're not a Jewess, because the Germans stormed in last week and are taking them away. Even threatening to arrest anyone trying to help them."

Karina flinched. I hoped my aunt didn't notice.

I sat on my hands, took a deep breath, and closed my eyes for a moment. I exhaled another deep breath and gazed at the plush rug. "I thought the Germans and the Italians were on the same side."

"Well, apparently Germany's Hitler got tired of rescuing Mussolini's incompetent army, first in North Africa and then in Greece. So his soldiers just marched right in and took over. Mussolini didn't even try to stop them."

"Did the Germans invade all of Italy?"

"Not yet. The Allies still control the south, but the Germans are fighting hard, and if you believe the propaganda in the news reports, they're gaining the upper hand."

"Aunt Sophie, you wouldn't believe how the Nazis devastated Poland. They've relocated all the Jews to concentration camps, where they're being forced to do hard labor or are killed. The Poles they haven't killed or sent away are starving because the Germans hoard all the food for themselves. Warsaw was nearly destroyed. Villages we've passed through have been burned to the ground. They shoot people for no reason." The captain's body lying on the deck of his trawler with the bullet hole in his head flashed through my mind. "No one is safe there."

She appeared disturbed, though I didn't know how much she believed. I had trouble believing some of it even though I witnessed it myself.

"You look exhausted. Get some sleep, and we'll talk later." She showed me to my room.

It was clear she didn't want to discuss or acknowledge what I had just told her.

As fatigued as I was, I lay in the comfortable bed for some time before drifting off. After all those nights longing for a soft bed and a feather pillow, I felt an unease I couldn't explain. It was odd trying to sleep without Karina near, even though I knew she was just across the hall. I missed her soft breathing and didn't want her to be alone when she cried. I hoped she slept peacefully.

It was dark when I woke. I remained still for some time staring into the blackness, trying to determine what time it might be. Giving up, I reached for the bedside lamp and flicked it on. Someone, Anthony I presume, had put fresh clothes on a nearby chair. It disturbed me that someone could enter the room without my being aware.

I slipped into the crisp garments and tightened the belt to the last notch to keep the trousers from slipping off. I figured I'd grow into them once I regained some of the weight I had lost. I poked my head into the hallway. Karina's door was closed, but there was light streaming up from downstairs. I descended to the main floor and found my uncle and aunt lounging in a pair of matching chairs by the fireplace in the library, enjoying a nightcap.

"Well, well," my uncle said. "I thought you boys were going to sleep forever."

"What time is it?" I didn't know why the time mattered, as I didn't even know what day of the week it was and wasn't exactly sure of the month, although I was pretty sure it had slipped into September. I felt a pang of guilt as I realized I must have missed the start of the new school year.

I noticed the considerable girth that had expanded my uncle's midsection when he slipped a gold pocket watch from his vest pocket and glanced at it. "It's about twenty-two hundred hours."

"Thank you," I replied, as if that was an important piece of information.

"Tomorrow is Sunday," my aunt said. "We'll leave for Mass at eight. I assume your friend will want to join us."

"Uh, yeah. I'll be sure to let him know."

"I'll leave the two of you to talk then," my aunt said as she stood to leave the room. "Be ready by seven so that

Anthony can cut your hair before we leave. He was unable to find the barber."

After Aunt Sophie left me alone with my uncle behind the closed door, he rose and moved behind his desk. He rested his palms on the shiny ebony surface and leaned into them. His expression became stern. "What in God's name are you doing here, showing up unannounced looking like a homeless street beggar? I ought to string you by the collar and flog you before shipping you home."

I stood opposite the desk from him and laced my fingers behind my back through the verbal lashing. When he ran out of insults, he finally asked, "What have you got to say for yourself?"

He eased into his crinkly leather chair.

I remained standing. I swallowed hard, took a deep breath, and began to recite the narrative I had been crafting over the last few weeks. "Uncle Vincent, I am very sorry. I really don't have a choice. It is a matter of life and death for both me and my friend."

"Life and death? That's a bit over melodramatic. What is it that you want?"

"Actually, Uncle Vincent, it's the truth, but I'll spare you the details for now. I need your help to get us to America."

"America! Are you insane?"

"Not insane, just desperate. We really need to get to America."

"Why? And why do you think I would help you? Even if I could. You're just a child."

"I'm not a child. You can't have seen the things that we've seen and remain a child. And you can help us. I know you control all the shipping that goes through the Laguna Venetia. Not just in Venice, but the port of Marghera as well. Get us on one of your ships to America."

"Why would I do that? Besides, these are merchant ships, not fancy passenger liners with luxury cabins and endless buffets. Those damn German U-boats are blowing up merchant ships like duck hunters blasting at a flock of fowl. Even vessels with armed escorts. Why would you even consider crossing the Atlantic on a ship? Your mother would march down here and wring my neck if she knew I helped you in such a ridiculous scheme. Why would I do that?" he demanded again.

"First of all, we don't have to tell my mother. She'll never know. And second, I'm sure you don't want me to tell my father about all the substandard materials you've supplied to him over the years. And third, I don't think you want your government or your customers to know about the kickbacks you take to get your ships unloaded by the dockworkers you control or the undeclared merchandise you smuggle in and out of the country. Do you want me to go on?"

"You have a pretty active imagination, and those are some pretty bold accusations."

"My imagination is not that good. Even though I don't really like the engineering studies my father is forcing me to take and all the weekends and summers I've spent working in his factory, I did learn a few things. I did confirm that some of the parts you delivered to him didn't match the manifests, and I did learn to recognize materials that aren't structurally sound. And by the way"—my eyes drifted to the ceiling—"the ventilation system from this library where you make some of your shady business deals filters right up to the guest room where I stayed the last summer my mother and I visited. I know exactly what I am talking about."

"Are you threatening me?"

"A filthy street urchin like me, threaten a well-respected businessman like you? Let's just call it a business arrangement. Kind of like the ones you make, only without the secret under-the-table cash transactions that aren't recorded in the ledger." I balled my hands into fists to keep them from shaking and hoped he attributed the crack in my voice to normal teenage growth quirks. "Good night, Uncle Vincent." I gazed into his black eyes for a moment and then pivoted toward the door. I could hear my father's voice in my head—*stand tall, shoulders back*—as I crossed the hand-woven Persian rug and closed the solid door behind me.

CHAPTER 37

Rap. Rap. Rap. The pounding on the apartment door caused Jodi to jump as she spread peanut butter on a slice of bread in the kitchen.

Rap, Rap, Rap. "Come on, Jodi. We're going to be late," Juan shouted through the door.

Jodi trotted to the entrance and swung the door open. "Why are you here so early? We weren't going to leave for another half hour."

"I know, I know. I thought you'd be ready by now." His hands were shoved deep into his pockets, and he was bouncing on his toes. "This tournament is such a big deal that I hardly slept at all last night."

"Let me just grab my breakfast and I'll eat it on the way." Jodi went to the kitchen and put the lid on her sandwich, leaving the unpeeled banana on the counter.

"Why are you so nervous?" she asked him as they rounded the corner onto Main Street. Volunteers hustled about setting up portable hoops, chalking boundaries, and stocking check-in stations. On the next block, street vendors and food trucks displayed their wares and fired up their grills.

"I don' know. We've been practicing all summer for this. I just want to win this thing."

"You're not even playing. And the prize is a just a silly ribbon and bragging rights."

"You mean you're not even a little nervous?"

"Why should I be nervous? It's just a game." But that was a lie. She was nervous. She wanted to win. She had checked the rosters for the other teams. Many included the jocks who blindly followed Kristen around like little puppies, obeying her every command and partaking in the pranks and insults that she inflicted on her unfortunate victims, Jodi being the prime target. She wanted to upstage them all and embarrass the queen tormentor in the process.

Jodi poked her head in the front door of the Sage Grove Café and waved to her mother, who was busy with a customer. Mom pocketed her order tablet, hustled to the front, and gave her daughter a quick hug. "Good luck, honey. I'll come watch you on my lunch break."

"Thanks, Mom."

"See ya, Ms. Evans," Juan added as he pivoted toward the street.

Jodi caught the sour look her mother gave him before she headed to the counter to clip the customer's order to the cook's queue. Fortunately, Juan didn't notice the slight.

Jodi sucked in a deep breath. She was tired. Only minutes remained in the third and championship game of the Junior division. She stood at the free throw line. Her opponent had batted her arm as she whizzed past him on a drive for a layup. An egregious foul, one that the otherwise liberal referee couldn't ignore. The dislodged ball had sailed out of bounds. The Banditos had easily won the first two games of the tournament. But the wins, and the rising temperature, sapped her energy. It must be at least ninety degrees by now. She wiped the sweat off her forehead with the back of her hand. She was also nervous. *We're only up by two. Don't blow it.* She bounced the ball three times to calm her nerves. It didn't help. She fired the shot—and missed. The ref tossed her the ball for the second shot. She dribbled the ball twice, took a deep breath, and shot. The ball swished through the net.

An opposing team member whisked the ball away before it hit the ground. He stepped out of bounds and tossed it to the team's point guard, Jodi's opponent for the one-on-one defense. The guard called out a play and dribbled the ball. He drove toward the basket. Anticipating the move, Jodi side-stepped ahead of him. She backed into his blocker and stumbled. Marco rushed over to try to block the jump shot, but his reach was fell short. The other team scored.

Marco was now at point with the ball. He nodded to RJ, who rushed up to block as Marco rolled off him and drove for the basket. Instantly, RJ's defender jumped in front of Marco's path to the hoop. He was trapped. Jodi rolled off her defender and cut through the key. Marco put a fake on his blocker and bounce-passed the ball to Jodi. Still in motion, she scooped up the ball and made the layup at the buzzer.

Cheers erupted from the crowd, which had swelled along the sidewalk, the Banditos victorious by a slim three points. Jodi high-fived her teammates and shook hands with the defeated opponents. The player she had outwitted sneered at her and refused her outstretched hand.

In his excitement, Juan rushed onto the court and gave each team member, including Jodi, a bear hug. He whooped and hollered as if he had slammed-dunked the winning bucket. From the other end of the court came a string of boos and hisses. Jodi turned to see Kristen and her gang shaking their fists and cursing the victors.

"Ignore them," Juan said.

Kristen stuck her tongue out at Jodi.

Juan shook his head. "How childish."

"Yeah, childish," Jodi repeated under her breath, head down, studying her sneakers.

"She must be flaming mad that you beat her snobby friends," Juan surmised. "I think I see smoke billowing from her ears."

The euphoria Jodi felt just moments ago was sucked from her bones as if a cannonball rammed into her gut. Maybe beating Kristen's friends wasn't such a good idea after all. Sure, it felt awesome to win, but would this cause Kristen's harassment to elevate to a higher level? She followed her teammates through the crowd, oblivious to the accolades and congratulatory pats on the back the fans showered upon her.

Her mother and—*Oh crap*—Tom stood waiting on the sidelines, Tom leaning against a street sign that read LOADING ZONE ONLY.

Jodi's mother gave her a giant hug. "Congratulations, honey. You didn't tell me you were playing with all those boys! At first I was appalled, but as your fans cheered louder, I shouted to everyone around: 'That's my girl!'"

Tom, however, ignored them, his eyes scanning the crowd behind his mirrored Oakleys, as if searching for a lost puppy.

"Thanks, Mom. I'm glad you could come."

"Nice playing, Jodi." Jodi turned to see Matt and the Shark twins snaking through the crowd toward her. "I just hope you have more of those great moves for us this afternoon."

"You're playing again?" Jodi's mother asked in surprise.

"Uh, yeah. Jackson here broke his arm." She tipped her head toward the injured Shark as he waved his plastered arm in the air. "So I agreed to sub for him."

"I'm going to get something to drink," Tom interrupted. He asked Mom, "Do you want some lemonade?" Without waiting for a response, he strolled off toward the food trucks.

Jodi noticed Juan suck in a tense breath and fade into the crowd as a police officer approached.

Matt's eyes brightened. "Dad, I didn't think you'd be here."

"I hope I didn't miss anything," the police officer said.

"No. We haven't started yet." Turning to the twins, Matt said to his father, "You know Jackson and Jerome. "

"Nice to see you again, fellas." Noticing Jackson's injured arm, he asked, "How are you going to shoot with that cast on your arm?"

"This is Jodi," Matt said. "She's going to sub for Jackson."

"It's nice to meet you, Jodi. It looks like you've already played."

"She did," Matt said for her. "She's doing double duty today."

"I didn't know this was a co-ed competition," Matt's father commented.

"It's not. But girls can play on the guy's team. Just not the other way around."

"Makes sense, I guess," the police officer reasoned. "I'm on my lunch break. Can I buy you boys, and young lady, a burger before your game starts?"

"You bet. I'm starving," Matt said with a broad smile while rubbing his lean belly.

The twins fist bumped.

"Come on—let's hurry before the line gets too long."
The three older boys followed Matt's father toward the row
of food vendors.

Jodi hesitated, and Matt turned and called out, "Come
on, Jodi."

"Go on," Juan said. "I'm going to hang with Marco and
RJ. We'll get some authentic Mexican street tacos later."

Jodi turned to her mother, who coaxed her on as well.
"I'll eat at the café. Don't want to waste my free meal. Go
and get a burger with your friends."

Jodi smiled and pranced after the group. Her *friends*,
her mother called them. Jodi hadn't considered the Sharks,
or even the other Banditos for that matter, her friends, just
some kids she played ball with, like the kids at the Y back
in Portland. But maybe they were friends. They were the
only people she'd known since she moved here, besides
Mr. K, who accepted her as she was. She didn't have to
keep her guard up around these guys or try to act like
someone she wasn't to gain their approval. They didn't
belittle her, call her names, or play silly pranks. She even
liked hanging out with them, even if it was just to play ball.

Jodi joined her teammates in line at the Grove Rib-
shack barbeque truck, directly behind Tom. He seemed
impatient, tapping his foot, arms folded around his chest,
while the woman ahead of him at the counter placed her
order. When she was finished, Tom approached the
cashier. "Burger with the works, large fry, and two
lemonades." He slid his leather wallet from the hip pocket
of his Wranglers. As he lifted out some bills, a basketball
smashed into his hand, and the wallet and its contents went
flying.

Juan dashed through the line of hungry patrons. "Oh,
I'm so sorry, Mr. Smith." Before Tom grasped what had
happened, Juan had scooped the wayward wallet from the

ground and "accidently" spilled its contents on the pavement. "Let me clean this up for you."

"No, I'll get it," Tom barked.

Before Tom could react, Marco and RJ blocked his path to the wallet and its littered contents as they feigned helping to pick up the mess. "Wow, Mr. Smith," Juan exclaimed, his voice projecting, as if reciting a Shakespeare soliloquy in a crowded theater, "you sure have a lot of credit cards." He read the names as he picked up each card. "Elizabeth Bishop, Warren Jones, Patrick S. McCormick. Who are all these people?"

Matt's father tuned in to the commotion.

Tom shoved through the boys and shouted, "Leave it alone, you stupid brats, and get your asses out of here."

The police officer inserted himself between Juan and his buddies and Tom. "Everybody calm down." He looked at Tom. "Is this your wallet, sir?"

"Yes, officer," Tom replied. "And these filthy gangbangers were trying to steal it." Tom bent to pick up the mess.

"Leave it there please."

"What?" Tom looked up and furrowed his bushy eyebrows.

"You heard me. Leave it on the ground." Looking around, the police officer said to the gathered crowd, "Please back away." He instructed his son and his friends to surround the "crime scene" while he made a call on his cell phone, keeping an eye on Tom as he talked.

Jodi's mother weaved her way through the crowd and stood next to her daughter, watching in horror.

In less than ten minutes, what must have been the whole Sage Grove Police Department was on the scene, and soon after, Tom was led away in handcuffs.

The Sharks remained hungry when the referee's whistle signaled the start of the next round of games.

CHAPTER 38

"You must learn to concentrate," Mr. K scolded for the third time.

Even with the reprimand, Jodi couldn't focus on her violin lesson the next Monday morning. She would play a few measures and then make a mindless mistake. The Saturday afternoon drama clogged her mind like plugged up storm drain.

"Life will always have its little bumps. Music gives you the opportunity to escape from them for a while. Close your eyes and visualize all your problems funneling into a little box."

"I don't think Kristen, or my mom or Tom will fit in a little box, let alone all three of them," she interrupted. "Even a giant crate won't be big enough."

"They will all fit in the box. Keep your eyes closed and visualize everything funneling into the box one by one. Now close the lid and tie a string around it and set it aside."

Jodi tried to visualize Kristen stuffed into a shoebox, but all she could see was Kristen's face, tongue sticking out, bursting through the lid that would not close. She imagined wrapping the string around her neck and tying a knot and yanking it tight. She stifled a chuckle as in her mind's eye, Kristen's eyeballs bulged from their sockets and her face turned blue.

Her mind couldn't squeeze her mother into the imaginary box. Tom, on the other hand. . .

"Now, slowly open your eyes," Mr. K instructed. "Let's start again at the second phase."

The box trick helped, a little. After the lesson, as Jodi packed her violin, she updated Mr. K on the events after Tom's exit from the scene in the back of the police cruiser.

"Matt was disappointed that his father couldn't watch him play. We eked out wins the first two games, but we had to work hard for them. Every time Matt scored, Kristen would cheer from the sidelines. One time she even rushed onto the court and kissed him. Unbelievable! I don't think he even likes her. Then every time I would score, she would boo or shout some insult. I don't get it. I mean, I know she doesn't like me, but if she wants Matt's team to win, why would she hiss when I score points for his team?"

"Because," he rationalized, "you are a threat to her."

"How could I be a threat?"

"Because she likes your friend Matt, and he's your friend, not hers."

"But she's cute, popular, and rich, and I'm not."

"And you're right up close to him playing on his team, and she's not. What about the last game?"

"We lost the last game. In fact, we got slaughtered. I think it was because we didn't get any lunch and were running out of energy."

"And you had already been playing all day."

"Yeah, that too. And boy, Kristen blamed me for that also. It was all *my* fault that we lost. Forget that the other team was older and played on the high school JV squad last year."

"But you had fun."

"Yeah." Jodi smiled. "I guess I did have fun. I really had fun watching Tom get arrested. That made my day more than winning the Junior I championship."

"How's your mother dealing with her gentleman friend's situation?"

"She's in denial. She's convinced that he's innocent. And because I'm certain that he's guilty, she isn't speaking to me."

"I imagine she'll get over him soon."

"The thing is, Mr. K, she really thought he was the one."

"Well, if they truly love each other, they may be able to work through this."

"Don't even say that! I know she doesn't love him, and I'm pretty sure he doesn't love her." She didn't mention Blondie. "I think they were just using each other."

"That's not a basis for a good relationship."

"Tell me about it. My mom is the queen of bad relationships and dramatic breakups. I know this will pass, but then the next guy will come along."

"I think it's time for some tea." Mr. K waddled to the kitchen.

It might have been Jodi's imagination, but it seemed as if his hobbling pace had slowed, and his shoulders were a little more stooped from when she had first met him that stormy afternoon only a few months ago. She followed him to the kitchen and retrieved two glasses from the cabinet while he fetched the pitcher of tea from the refrigerator. As he poured them each a glass, Jodi said, "Mr. K, I've been waiting all week to find out how your uncle got you to America."

***

The next morning Karina and I were dressed in our crisp new clothes, ready at seven to go to Mass. I had spent the previous fifteen minutes before we went downstairs giving her instructions—when to kneel, when to stand, how to take Communion.

"Just follow my lead. During the prayers, just move your lips."

"Michal, I don't want to pray to your God or your Jesus or your Virgin Mary."

"Just pretend. Pray to your God instead. If we're going to get through this, everyone has to think you're Catholic. You heard that the Germans are looking for Jews here too. We must be very careful. When we get to America, you can be Jewish again, and a girl."

She frowned and followed me into the hallway.

My aunt was waiting when we reached the landing. "Turns out the barber's Jewish. Who knew?" she said, raising her shoulders. "Anthony is waiting in the kitchen to cut your hair. You can't go to Mass looking like that!"

Karina and I looked at each other and marched off to the kitchen, where a scowling Anthony stood wielding a towel and a pair of barber shears.

While other worshipers exited the ferry from the Grand Canal at the Basilica Plaza, we disembarked from my uncle's boat at his private slip adjacent to St. Michaels Cathedral. I didn't think anything of traveling the water streets through the rows of towering pastel-colored buildings, but I sensed Karina's unease. As we weaved our way through the pigeons and crowds of the Cathedral Piazza, her eyes were wide with awe at the giant arches, towering gables, intricate statues, and golden mosaics of the opulent house of worship.

Karina and I dawdled behind my uncle and his family when a woman, in a stylish pink dress with matching hat and pumps, bumped into me. "Oh, I'm so sorry," she said.

"Jozef, is that you? What a surprise. What's of your brother in Krakow?"

A lump formed in my throat, and I feared my voice would fail. I swallowed hard and spit out the code that I had rehearsed each day since Edward entrusted me with the secret message. "My name is not Jozef, and I do not have a brother in Krakow." I almost forgot to close my left eye.

"Oh, I am so sorry," the woman said. "I thought you were someone else."

My aunt turned around. "What was that about?"

"I don't know," I lied. "I guess she mistook me for someone else." I turned to look for the woman, but she had evaporated into the crowd.

I hoped we would sit near the back of the grand sanctuary for the service, but we followed my uncle to a reserved pew near the pulpit. After we were seated, I fidgeted, a hurricane raging in by brain. When the clouds started to clear, I whispered to my aunt, "I'll be right back. I need to find the washroom."

I locked myself in a private stall and wrestled the important package from the frayed tape around my ribs, grimacing when the adhesive tore at my sensitive skin. Latecomers filtered into the few empty pews when I slid onto my seat between my aunt and Karina. I was restless through the whole service. I remembered to kneel and pray at the proper times. I was afraid I would drop the message when I approached the alter for Communion.

After the lengthy service, during the passage back across the Grand Piazza, the woman, dressed in a conservative blue suit brushed passed me, and when she was gone, I no longer carried the important document. I slowly exhaled a deep breath. I felt proud to have provided this one small service for my country, which I was fleeing, and relieved not to have to worry any longer about the dangerous burden I was carrying.

***

The tedious days were almost unbearable. Karina and I spent over a month cooped up with nothing to do. Each morning I watched from my upstairs window the boats arrive from the mainland and transfer their cargo of fresh meat and produce to waiting gondolas for transport up the Grand Canal for distribution to the street vendors, who provided the only source of fresh food to the island residents. The German guards patrolling the docks pilfered the premium goods as they inspected the incoming cargo. At least at Pani Maria's I'd been busy helping with the garden and other chores around the farm. My uncle employed a household staff to do the chores, and a garden would have been beneath his dignity. The older two of my cousins were off at school during the day, and I felt both guilt and envy. I wondered how long before the Germans closed the Italian schools like they had in Poland.

Following my morning baths, I examined my bony frame in the mirror of the elaborate lavatory and squeezed the droopy skin that hung from my ribs, willing for an outline of a six-pack to develop underneath. I would make a fist and curl my arm like a victorious boxer, probing for a budding bicep muscle.

My daily push-up regime increased from one to twelve. If nothing else, we were getting three nourishing meals each day, and even though I didn't see much development in my own frame, Karina's gaunt appearance gained more color and fullness.

Aunt Sophie's salient requirement was that we attend Mass each Sunday morning. Even though Karina wasn't comfortable with the pageantry, she was now able to follow the protocol. I no longer had to nudge her when to kneel, stand, or sit. She even used the occasion as an opportunity to pick up on some additional Italian, although sometimes the Latin interjections confused her.

I had let my guard down, bantering with my cousins, that fourth Sunday morning as we crossed the Grand Piazza after the morning service, when we were approached by two German guards, their rifles slung over their shoulders, pistols and knives visibly fastened to their thick belts.

"Papers please," one said in heavily accented Italian.

"What?" my uncle asked, as if he didn't understand the request.

"Papers," the guard demanded. His hand slid toward his pistol.

"Do you have any idea who you're talking to?" my indignant uncle inquired.

"Some nerve," my aunt chimed in.

I tapped my aunt lightly on the elbow and whispered, "Aunt Sophie, in Poland they shoot without question people who challenge their authority."

"That's absurd," my aunt said.

"Please, Aunt Sophie," I pleaded. "It's the truth, and if we don't cooperate, he will arrest or shoot us."

She was about to say something but caught herself as she turned and apparently noticed the fear in my eyes as I nodded toward a family in the distance being led away at gunpoint, all, including the three small children, with arms up, fingers laced behind their heads.

She reached into her handbag and produced her identification papers. "Let's do as he asks, Vincent, so that we can be on our way."

Anger reddened my uncle's face as he handed the guard his documents. I gave him mine and noticed Karina's hand tremble as she retrieved her forged papers. I took her papers and held them out to the guard, hoping he wouldn't notice her nervousness. The guard glanced at the papers of my uncle and his family and returned them. He looked at mine a little longer and then said in German, "Your residence is Warsaw. Why are you here?"

"I don't understand," I responded in Italian, pretending not to understand German.

"Why Italy?" he asked in his heavy accent.

"I'm visiting my uncle," I replied in Italian. It was apparent he didn't understand.

"You Jew?" My heart skipped a beat, and I hoped he didn't notice me flinch. Unlike Karina, I didn't look the least bit Jewish with my sandy hair and blue eyes.

"Cattolico," I uttered, attempting to stifle the quiver in my voice as his threatening gaze tried to frighten me into a confession. "Katholisch," I said again with what I hoped was a poor German accent.

To assert his superiority, he flung my papers to the ground, forcing me to bend over to pick them up.

That left him studying Karina's documents. His gaze shifted from the papers, to Karina, to my uncle, back to Karina, then to my aunt, then to Karina again. Sweat dripped from under my arm and trickled down my side, and my heart thundered in my chest. The guard's partner, who had just checked the identifications of another group of worshipers, called out to him in German, "Hurry up, Oskar. It's time for lunch."

"Coming, coming," the guard sighed as he returned Karina's papers and marched off after his hungry partner.

My stomach churned, and Karina trembled as she fumbled with her fabricated documents. I looked up at the puffy clouds and said a silent thank-you to the Polish artist who unknowingly had just saved Karina's life. I was also thankful that my uncle had not read Karina's papers, which identified her as his son. I have no doubt his explosive anger would have been our downfall.

"I've never been so humiliated in all of my life," my aunt ranted as we boarded the boat for the trip back up the canal to my uncle's mansion. "Of all the nerve! Who do they think they are, stopping us after Mass like that?"

I wanted to tell my aunt not only who they thought they were but what they were and that she was lucky that there were not more dire consequences for our defiant behavior.

My uncle's rigid jaw and unusual silence was unnerving as he navigated his craft up the Grand Canal, and I expected that the new occupiers had been disrupting his business, not unlike they did to my father's.

Did that mean he would not be able to secure passage for us to America?

CHAPTER 39

Another two tedious weeks had passed when my uncle summoned me to his library after supper and said he had arranged transport for us. "I have a ship heading for America. New York."

It took every ounce of restraint I had not to jump up and cheer. "When does it leave?"

"Day after tomorrow. It's not a free ride. The ship's cook . . . the imbecile," he added under his breath, "can't seem to keep an assistant. Each new one disappears whenever the ship docks. You and your friend are his new assistants. I hope you know how to cook."

"We're fast learners."

"You better be. There will be a few stops along the way. Remember what I told you before. British, American, German, and Italian warships and U-boats are patrolling the waters of the Mediterranean as well as the Atlantic shipping lanes. There will not be an escort until you reach Morocco. Even that is not a guarantee the ship will not be attacked."

"I understand." I brushed off the warning.

"One more thing." My uncle stood from behind his polished ebony desk. "I got you on the ship. But I cannot arrange for a visa to get you into America."

"What exactly does that mean?"

"It means you do not have permission to enter the country."

"Oh."

I was so excited, the following two days passed in a blur. Karina, however, grew melancholy, as this leg of our journey would take us off the continent and a world away from Warsaw and the hope of reuniting with her family. I had every intention of keeping my promise to find them after the war was over, and I tried to convince myself that they would somehow survive.

For our voyage, Aunt Sophie bought us each two traveling outfits. I told her that they were too nice to wear on a merchant ship, especially in a greasy kitchen, but thanked her anyway and packed them in the small valise she'd bought for us as well. I stuffed my knapsack with the dead German's pistol and Edward's bullets in the travel case when she was out of the room. Later she took Karina aside and had a "women's" talk, the subject of which neither would share.

At dawn the morning of our departure, my uncle shuttled us across the lagoon in his boat to the port in Marghera. "This is the *Venus Star*," he said as we approached the massive freight liner moored at the pier. "Before the war it was the *Venice Star*, but prudence dictated a name change."

I'd watched the distant ships drift in and out of the lagoon as a child, but I was amazed at the monstrous size of the vessel towering over us as we walked along the pier. Close up the ship looked old and in disrepair, like it was ready for the scrap heap rather than to embark on a long journey across the Atlantic. The faded green paint revealed a stained and rusted hull. The water line, visible well above the surface, indicated that the cargo holds were empty, hence the required stops before crossing the vast ocean. Dockworkers hoisted strapped pallets and wooden crates onto the ship's deck, which were then lowered into the cargo holds below. Knowing my uncle, I suspected that much of the contents were not approved for export by the Italian—or was it now German?—authorities.

We followed my uncle to the dock house, where we met the captain, who was busy shouting orders to workers hustling up and down the pier. When my uncle approached, he snubbed out his cigarette, stood straighter, and called him "sir" as they shook hands.

The captain was a stout man with a slight paunch, which he tried to suck in while greeting his powerful employer. His weather-beaten face and graying beard were an eerie reminder of the captain from our trip up the Vistula out of Krakow. However, this skipper sported a clean shirt, pressed trousers, polished boots, and, thankfully, a mouth full of graying cigarette-stained teeth.

My uncle explained to the commander that we were the kitchen help, and the captain reached for his radio and summoned someone to escort us to the galley. For appearance's sake, I was sure, my uncle shook our hands and said goodbye. I picked up the suitcase, and Karina and I followed the escort up the gangplank and into the nucleus of the massive liner.

The guide led us down three flights of narrow metal ladder stairs and through a maze of dim, smoke-stained gray hallways to our quarters. "Not the Waldorf-Astoria," he commented as he opened a steel door to a room not much larger than a closet. The space was furnished with a metal bunk bed with thin mattresses and frayed blankets and two metal footlockers. "The head's at the end of the hall." He pointed. "You can leave your bag here, and I'll take you to the galley."

The mess hall consisted of two long gray metal tables lined with gray metal benches bolted to the gray metal floor. "Cookie, your help is here," the escort shouted.

A head poked through a pass-through on the far wall from the kitchen. The escort looked at us. "Sorry. I didn't catch your names."

"I'm Michal, and he's Karl."

"Well, don't jus' stand there. Get ta work," the cook growled as ashes dripped from the cigarette dangling between his thin lips.

Without a word, the guide slipped away and left us alone with the grumpy cook. The chef's tall, lean frame was swallowed by a stained and stretched-out undershirt, and his ghostly complexion and stooped shoulders suggested a man who'd spent his years belowdecks hunched over a hot stove and a sink full of dirty pots and pans.

"Ah, what would you like us to do?" I asked.

"Those supplies need unpacked and stored," he grumbled, lifting his elbow toward a pile of crates stacked in the corner. "The cabinets and closets are labeled. Make sure everything is tightly secured."

Karina and I spent the next several hours unloading supplies—sacks of flour, rice, beans, canned meat, salt, dehydrated potatoes, powdered milk, and coffee. Crates of eggs went into a walk-in refrigerator, and a limited supply, the cook complained, of frozen beef and poultry were stored in a small industrial freezer.

The lights flickered, and a loud shriek followed by the hum of engine noise indicated the ship was loaded and ready to begin the long voyage to America. I got so turned around in the maze of hallways following the escort to the galley, I didn't know which direction the bow was. The churning engine noise permeated throughout the ship. A loud whistle squealed from overhead, and the vessel jarred as it was pulled from the dock by an overburdened tugboat.

We were finally on our way to America.

The cook noticed my daydreaming, and his bark startled me back to my chores. "First shift for supper is in a little over an hour, so get your butts over here an' get ta work."

"Uh, sorry. What do you want us to do next?"

"Dice the potatoes, carrots, and onions for the stew. We eat the fresh food first before it goes bad."

I searched for a pair of knives, handed one to Karina, fetched the vegetables, and began chopping. I was barely into my first carrot when the cook snarled at me, "Yer gonna lose a finger doin' it that way. Ain't ya ever worked in a kitchen before?"

"Uh, no, we haven't. But we'll learn quick."

"Darn right you will. Here, gimme that knife and I'll show ya how it's done. Sailors don't like finger parts in their stew. Can't have 'em complainin' 'bout the tough meat. Only gonna show ya once, so pay 'tention."

We watched the cook's swift knife work as he diced a carrot and then a potato. I gripped the knife and tried to imitate his motions, but my inexperience resulted in lopsided vegetable chunks.

"Takes some practice. Importan' thing's to keep yer fingertips curled so the sharp blade don't slice 'em off. Gets a little trickier on the high seas."

The stew wasn't quite ready when a dozen burly seamen filed into the dining hall, each wearing a crumpled plaid shirt, scuffed boots, gray cap, and grizzled beard. The sailors retrieved their tin trays, silverware, and tin cups from a holder. Cookie poured a ladleful of stew into each bowl, which I transferred to each sailor's tray, which Karina topped off with a wedge of black bread. The sailors filled their own cups with thick black coffee and sat hunched over the metal tables to consume their meals.

After the process was repeated with the next shift of sailors, we spent the following two hours washing dishes, wiping tables, and mopping floors. I was so exhausted when I crawled into the top bunk of the metal bed in our closet room, I expected to succumb to a deep sleep. Instead, my tired eyes stared into the darkness. For the first time on our journey, I realized my destiny had been sealed. There was no going back. The thin mattress sagged between the bunk's hard metal crossbars, and I thought of the soft, luxurious bed and feather pillows from my uncle's mansion. My ears tuned to the constant humming of the engines, and I felt its vibrations rise through the floor and up through the metal bed frame and seep into my weary bones. My mind's ear heard the melody of the Brahms sonata in the rhythmic humming, and I fingered the notes over imaginary strings as the ship carved through the waters of the Adriatic Sea on its way to the Mediterranean Sea and ultimately the great Atlantic Ocean.

Banging on the metal door of our cozy cabin jarred me from my slumber. It was pitch black. "Get your lazy asses out of bed and into the galley. Pronto!" Cookie shouted through the door.

"Wha . . . What?" I was groggy and confused. The swaying and the humming engine reminded me where I was.

"It can't be morning yet. Can it?" Karina moaned from the lower bunk.

I reached into the darkness and tugged the chain, which illuminated the dull lightbulb that dangled from the ceiling. "No way can it be morning." Of course, wherever we were deep in the bowels of the ship, there were no windows, no sense of night or day, wind or calm, rain or shine, dawn or dusk. Neither one of us had a timepiece. If we had, it would have been traded for a few morsels of bread some time ago.

"Yer late!" Cookie snapped when we dragged ourselves into the galley.

"Sorry," I apologized. "What time is it anyway?"

"Breakfast time! Get started on the biscuits. Bag of flour, liter of water, spoonful of baking soda, cup of egg powder. Bowls are over there." He tipped his white chef's hat toward the metal cabinets of supplies against the far wall.

By the time the crew had rotated in and out for the morning meal, I was exhausted. My hands were sore and arms tired from stirring the lumpy biscuit batter. While they were baking, we reconstituted and fried dehydrated eggs and potatoes. My face was flush from the heat and sweat trickled from my neckline down the back of my shirt. I was preparing for a rest when the instructions came to clean the dishes, followed by prep work for the next meal. I now had a new appreciation for our family cook back in Warsaw.

"Whoa!" I cried as the floor suddenly shifted underfoot and the load of trays I was carrying flew from my hands. My legs jelled, and I felt like a drunken old man trying to stand upright on a sea of ping-pong balls. I didn't know if we had reached the Mediterranean or plowed headlong into a fierce storm.

Unconcerned, Cookie grinned. "Haven't got yer sea legs yet, I see." It was the first time I had seen him smile, and I knew it was going to be a long voyage across the Atlantic, which we hadn't yet reached.

Karina threw up into the nearby sink. I was able to hold the churning contents of my rumbling stomach until I reached the head, as I wasn't about to puke in Cookie's presence. I was afraid to sleep that night, even if I could with all the jostling, because I feared falling from my bunk and splitting my head open like a cantaloupe on the hard steel floor.

We reached Morocco five days later, the last stop to load additional cargo and crew members before heading into the vast Atlantic. It was the first time that Karina and I were able to escape the dullness of the ship's core and go topside, as the sailors called the ship's deck and upper quarters. I squinted when the piercing rays of the bright midday sun scorched my sensitive eyes, which hadn't seen sunlight in days.

The same sailor who escorted us to the galley days ago gave us the grand tour of the deck and the upper levels. "What are cannons doing on a merchant ship?" I asked of the bank of high-powered artillery guns mounted on circular platforms lining the deck.

"In case we're attacked. Though these measly guns would be no match against nimble enemy bombers or U-boat torpedoes. At least it makes us feel like we're defending ourselves."

"Has this ship been attacked?" I asked.

"Not that I'm aware of. But it could happen. That is why we will be sailing in a convoy with several other merchant ships and a navy frigate on each flank. If there is an attack, at least some of us should make it through."

My uncle's warning that I had brushed off suddenly burned like a bed of glowing red coals sizzling in my gut.

CHAPTER 40

It happened moments before the break of dawn only days before we were to reach America. It had been a harrowing night. A fierce storm hurled the ship through the angry sea, like a shriveled pea in boiling water. Karina and I were rising for another gloomy day in the confines of the stifling gray galley when the sirens blared. I opened our cabin door as Cookie rushed by shouting, "Topside, topside. All hands-on deck!"

We darted after the lanky cook. Suddenly there was a loud bang and the ship listed, flinging us like sacks of potatoes to the steel floor. As we helped Cookie to his feet, another explosion blasted from behind us and thrust us back to the deck. Blood poured from Cookie's forehead, and he was dazed when we struggled to prop him up. I was reminded of the navigator as Karina and I each wrapped one of his wiry arms around our necks, stumbling and grunting as we dragged him through the tight hallway. When we reached the narrow metal stairway, Karina shouted, "How are we going to get him up the ladder?"

Just then two other crewmembers rushed up on their way topside, one still in his long johns, and the four of us heaved Cookie up to the next deck. As we reached the landing, another deafening blast erupted from beneath us, and despite our best efforts to keep him upright, Cookie tumbled backward down the ladder. I started after him, when one of the other sailors grabbed my elbow and jerked me back. I watched, horrified, as a foamy torrent of seawater littered with pots, linens, and foodstuffs swooshed beneath me and swept the gangly cook away.

"Cookie!" I shouted as the sailor held me in a bear hug and tugged me away from the landing.

"Let him go," he shouted. "There is nothing we can do. Get topside. Hurry!"

Torrents of rain whipped away the tears that streamed down my cheeks when we reached the main deck. Commands shouted by sailors swirled in the gale as they prepped and lowered lifeboats to the furious waters below the doomed vessel. We followed the long-johned sailor to one of the dinghies just as another explosion rocked the ship, slamming us to the deck. As I struggled to my feet against the pelting rain, blistering wind, and listing ship, I spied a sailor tumble backward over the bulwark. Karina screamed, and I spun around to see her sliding on her stomach, feet first, as if lassoed by the vicious sea that was devouring the ship's splintered stern.

"Karina!" I dove after her and clasped my hands around her wrist. Stretched on my belly, I held on for dear life as the slick deck became a slide hurling us closer to the menacing waters. Karina's frantic screams pieced through the thunderous roar. The driving rain and salty seawater acted like lubricating oil, causing my tenuous hold on her slick wrist to wrestle from my grasp, but I somehow latched on to her outstretched hand. Our downward pace accelerated as the sea's noose tugged us to within a thread of the churning sea. My flailing foot banged against a solid metal object, and I wedged it between a gap in the base of one of the machine-gun platforms—a lot of good my uncle's powerful artillery were today.

I arched my foot and forced it deeper into the crevice to slow our plunge, but my clutch on Karina's palm was loosening. "Hold on! Hold on!" I shouted as Karina's limp fingers slid farther from my weakening grip.

"NO!" I cried as the ship jolted and my wedged foot dislodged from the platform crevice. A wave crashed over us, and when the ebb cleared, I was horrified to see Karina partly submerged in the churning surf. Suddenly, a strong hand clenched my ankle and our downward motion slowed. Another hand grabbed my other ankle, and I heard someone shout, "Hold on!" I willed myself to fight the blistering gale and blinding rain and not let go. Not now. Not after we had come so far.

The rugged hands that dragged us up the wayward deck shoved me into a lifeboat, which jostled over the raging waters and away from the thick black smoke billowing from the *Venus Star*. "Karina!" I shouted when I realized she was not in the boat with me. Alarmed, I rose to find her, but a sailor pushed me down and slipped a life jacket over my head. I had no sooner buckled the bulky vest with my trembling fingers when a massive wave smashed into the side of the boat, flipping it upside down, spilling us into the frigid ocean.

Panicked, I thrashed in the ferocious swells, gasping and choking on the icy seawater. My flailing hand slammed against an oar, and I grasped for the paddle, only to watch it drift from my outstretched fingers. Another sinister wave crashed over my head and thrust me under the surface, and I flailed my weakened extremities, disoriented and unable to breathe.

"Karina!" I gurgled as my oxygen-starved lungs sucked

in the foamy saltwater. My exhausted body became numb and limp, and as hard as I tried to fight, the heavy water immobilized my weary limbs as if they were strapped in a straitjacket. A surreal stillness overcame me, and as if viewing a slow-motion horror film, the ghostly images of all the people I had disappointed stood before me, arms crossed, faces stern—my mother for my running away, my father for wrecking his car, Pani Maria for not saving her beloved son, the navigator for deserting him at the doctor's doorstep, my uncle for crossing him, and in front of them all, Karina's father, ashen tears dampening his wispy beard. And just beyond their transparent silhouettes, the bow of the *Venus Star*, with all her precious cargo, was swallowed into the depths of the unforgiving sea.

CHAPTER 41

Jodi and Juan lay prostrate on their backs on the brittle grass under the dim streetlight near the basketball hoop outside their apartment building gazing at the night sky. Darkness came earlier now, and the last embers of the late summer sunset were sinking into the western horizon. A full moon dangled in the eastern sky, and a whiff of the approaching autumn dusted the tepid desert night air.

Jodi tossed the ball in the air while they lay there killing time, neither wanting to go home to their dank apartments. Juan reached over and intercepted the ball as Jodi was about to catch it. He flung it skyward and asked, "So how's your mother dealing with Tom's arrest?"

"Not very well," she responded. "At first, she was convinced that it was all a huge mistake and that it would sort itself out. When it became apparent that he was guilty, she grew angry and lashed out at every little irritation. If she burned the toast, she would get angry. If her uniform wasn't clean, she would get angry. If the coffee was cold, she would get angry. I think whenever I took a breath, she would get angry." Jodi retrieved the ball from Juan's toss and lobbed it skyward. "Then she went through a quiet period where she didn't talk to me for a couple of days. Now she claims that he's just a selfish, egocentric, good-for-nothing scumbag and wonders what she ever saw in the guy in the first place." After a short pause she added, "Pretty much like all her other breakups."

"Sorry."

"It'll blow over. Just remind me never to get involved with anyone, because as far as I can tell, all men are cheating scoundrels, and I don't want to have anything to do with them."

"Hey! I take offense to that."

"Sorry. Just don't grow up to be like them and you can be the lone exception. Every girl in the county will be clambering over each other to get to you since you'll be the only decent male alive."

"Can't wait! What about you? Who will you be chasing after? Matt?"

"Are you kidding? No way am I going to attach myself to anyone. After watching my mother's string of ex-boyfriends come and go, I'm going to make it on my own."

"You'll be an awesome doctor."

"Ya think?"

"Yeah, awesome, but lonely."

"I'll be too busy healing the sick and wounded to be lonely." After a short pause she added, "But I'll have a fantastic art collection because of a talented artist friend. Assuming that is you don't squander all your masterpieces on all those clambering women."

Juan responded with a friendly punch to the arm. "Speaking of, I have something for you."

"You have something for me?"

"Don't move. I'll be right back." Juan leapt to his feet and darted toward his apartment. He returned with large manila envelope. "Here." He handed her the envelope with a sheepish grin.

Jodi sat up and took the packet but continued to stare up at him.

"Well, open it." He plopped down on the dead grass next to her.

Jodi lifted the tab and slid out a picture that was mounted in a cardboard frame. She stared at it, gaping.

"You don't like it," he said.

"This is awesome! You drew this?" Jodi admired the black-and-white charcoal drawing replicating the photograph of her and Mr. K posing in front of his freshly painted house. "I will cherish this forever."

Juan relaxed in relief. "I didn't have enough money to buy a decent frame."

"The frame is perfect. The drawing is perfect. And you know what else? This summer wasn't exactly perfect, but it was better than any I've had in a long time. I'm dreading going back to school."

"Yeah, me too."

CHAPTER 42

"This corn is so high, someone could hide in here and not be found until spring," Jodi said as she and Mr. K snapped tasseled ears off the towering stalks. "What are you going to do with all this corn?"

"Most will go in the freezer, the rest to the food pantry. Be sure to take some home for yourself. There's nothing like fresh-picked corn on the cob."

"You said that about the peas."

"Nothing like them either."

"They really like you at the food pantry. I guess I never really thought about it before, all the hungry people around here, especially the kids, until you took me down there that day."

"If I recall, you took me there," he teased.

"You know what I mean. I mean, my mom and I don't have much, but at least we have something to eat every day."

"I never thought about it before the war either. Hate to admit it, but I was ignorant that hunger even existed and never could have imagined what it really meant until I experienced it firsthand."

"Is that why you grow this garden every year, because of the war and your time with Pani Maria?"

"So many people helped us on our journey to America. Some, like Pani Maria, even risking their lives. There's no way we could ever repay them, so this is our one small way of honoring them, by helping others."

"So, I still have one more burning question. Of all the places you could have settled, why Idaho?"

"Well, I have to admit"—he chuckled—"I had never even heard of Idaho until we accidently wound up here."

***

It was a glorious but frigid December afternoon when the merchant ship that rescued us from the doomed *Venus Star* docked across the Hudson River from New York in Newark, New Jersey. The swirling sleet, fueled by a howling wind, stung our sensitive faces, which hadn't seen daylight for weeks. But we didn't care. Our feet had finally stepped onto the safety of American soil. I clasped Karina's hand as we disembarked the vessel and inhaled the sweet taste of freedom. Freedom. Sumptuous but scary. We made it. But now what?

Two days after the disastrous sinking of the *Venus Star*, I had regained consciousness under a pile of blankets on a cot in another steel-gray cabin. I had opened my eyes to the most beautiful sight in the world—Karina's chocolate eyes glaring down at me.

Before I could utter a word, she had started yelling, "How dare you go off and almost die on me like that and leave me stranded! How was I supposed to find my way around America by myself? You promised my father you would keep me safe. How can you do that if your stupid dead body is at the bottom of the ocean?"

I had smiled and gently wiped the tear that trickled down her cheek with my clammy finger while she ranted.

Although we didn't have proper papers, no one questioned us when we exited the shipyard with a swell of dockworkers at the end of their shift. One of our crewmates introduced us to a widow who ran a boardinghouse, where we were able to rent a small room. Since all the able-bodied young men were either off to war or preparing to enlist, I had no trouble finding a job at the port. Karina also found work at a garment factory, sewing uniforms for the American soldiers. We struggled to learn English, but the other residents of the boardinghouse helped us as we listened to war reports or President Roosevelt's fireside chats on the radio each evening. We were disappointed that most of the war news focused on the conflicts in the Pacific and later the Allies' invasion of Normandy and the battles in western Europe. There was very little news of Poland.

I was also heartbroken to discover that the roots of prejudice were burrowed deep in American culture. Clusters of ethnic groups colored the poor immigrant neighborhoods, each relegated to a rung on the privilege pyramid, Poles and Jews landing near the bottom. But the undercurrents of bigotry weren't going to get us shot. We were alive and we were together. If we worked hard and did all the right things, we could have a comfortable and fulfilling, and most important, a safe life.

Late one sunny Friday afternoon, fourteen months after our arrival in Newark, I was walking home from my dockworker job. Friday meant payday, and although exhausted from a punishing week of moving heavy crates, I had a fresh wad of cash burning a hole in my pocket and a big night planned. I was going to surprise Karina with a rare night out, the latest Gary Cooper picture show—she had a soft spot for the dashing star—followed by an ice cream soda at the local malt shop. Her favorite was strawberry, and I was partial to vanilla, treats we never could have imagined in Poland. I could almost taste the sweet shake as I whistled a Glen Miller tune and boogeyed down the littered street.

When I rounded the corner to our building, I froze when I heard a blood-curdling scream. "Karina!" I yelled and sprinted for the alley next to our apartment, where I found her pinned against the brick wall by one of the Irish thugs who ruled the neighborhood.

Several years older than I, he towered over me in height and had the frame of a heavyweight boxer, his bulging muscles flexing under his tight gangster tee. Knowing he would crack my skull with one swing if I tried to fight him, I scooped up a metal pipe from the debris that littered the alley and clobbered him in the back of the head with every ounce of strength I had, and then some. Before he even hit the ground, I grabbed Karina by the wrist, and we dashed around the corner.

Once in our room, I slammed and locked the door and leaned against it, as if my slight frame would keep an angry intruder out. Karina sank into the tattered chair in the corner, wrapped herself into a ball, forehead on knees, and wept. I rushed over to the closet and jerked out a battered suitcase that the previous deceased tenant had left behind, flung it onto the bed, and tossed in the few possessions that we had—a few changes of clothes, some toiletries, and the dead German's pistol, the only item that survived my unplanned dip in the Atlantic that horrific day a torpedo doomed the *Venus Star*.

Karina lifted her head, watched me for a moment, and between sobs asked, "What are you doing?"

"Packing."

"Why?"

"We can't stay here. It's just a matter of time before that brute and all his gangster friends will be pounding our door down. He'll kill me before daybreak, and who knows what he'll do with you." I slammed the suitcase closed and hoisted it off the bed, thankful that we didn't have much more to fill it now than when we first stepped onto American soil all those months ago. "Come on," I ordered as I peered into the hallway to make sure it was clear of giant Irish thugs brandishing sticks and clubs.

"Where are we going?" she asked after we had fled out the back door into the opposite alley and well out of sight of our building.

"To the train station."

"And then where?"

"Portland. Seattle. I don't care. As far from here as we can get. Word around the dock is that with the war full on in the Pacific, dockworkers are in high demand on the West Coast ports."

"We can't keep running like this. It's like Poland all over again."

I stopped and spun her toward me and glared into her bloodshot eyes. "Karina, this is not like Poland. The Nazis are not trying to kill us. Our city is not being bombed. People aren't being hauled away to their deaths in overstuffed trains. We're not starving. The war is not here. He is one bad brute, and I've seen how his gang rules the neighborhood. I hit him pretty hard, and he will come after me." I picked up the suitcase and resumed walking. "And I've noticed him leering at you before."

I only had enough money for tickets to Denver. We managed to elude the conductor until we got to Sage Grove, where we were kicked off the train in the middle of the night.

***

"And you stayed?" Jodi asked, incredulous.

"That was not the plan. The next morning, we found a diner, the Sage Stop Grille."

"Hey," Jodi interrupted, "that's where my mom works. Only it's the Sage Grove Café now."

"Well, the owners at that time were an elderly couple, Bob and Mary, and they were having quite a time trying to keep up with business that day. Noticing that they were short on help, we offered our services for a free meal. All that time slaving in the galley of the *Venus Star* paid off. By the end of the day, we were hired."

"But why would you stay in this crummy little town?"

"They were such a nice couple. They welcomed us, as did the customers. Of course, the customers were just happy with the improved service. We were saving to continue our journey west, but months later Bob became ill. Mary couldn't care for him and run the diner by herself, so for the price of only one dollar, she transferred the title over to us. I don't think she had the heart to sell it, because the banker across the street wanted to turn it into a tavern. She was a God-fearing woman, and the thought of her beloved diner becoming a drinking establishment didn't sit too well with her."

"Did you ever find Karina's family?"

Mr. K closed his eyes and didn't speak. Jodi wished she could withdraw the question, as she feared this intrusion crossed a sacred boundary to a painful memory that shouldn't, or couldn't, be unlocked.

With his eyes still closed and in a shaky whisper he responded, "They did not survive."

Jodi stained to hear.

"Upon arriving at Treblinka, her mother and little brother were sent straight to the gas chambers, as they were not deemed suited for hard labor by the screening guards.

Her father was assigned to a prison work crew. He later joined the camp's underground Jewish resistance organization, which plotted to take over the camp and escape. When rumors reached the camp that the Russians were closing in and the remaining prisoners were going to be killed, they revolted against the better-armed guards before they were adequately prepared. He was gunned down in the escape attempt." Mr. K lowered his head, and a tear seeped from beneath his wrinkled eyelid and trickled down his creviced cheek.

CHAPTER 43

The dreaded first morning of the new school year was pleasantly boring. Ms. Cavendish had assigned Jodi to the advanced math class. It was a small class comprised of the school's intellectual elite, which excluded Kristen and her friends. At the end of PE, Mrs. Wilson pulled Jodi aside and mentioned how excited she was that Jodi was joining the basketball team this year. Jodi didn't mention the activity fee, but she had a feeling Mrs. Wilson would somehow get her way. She was known to be persuasive.

At lunchtime Jodi sat alone at a round table in the far corner of the cafeteria, with an open textbook. She used to feel self-conscience about sitting alone while the other kids clustered in groups, joking and laughing and making fun of and criticizing various teachers and other groups of clustered students. Now she realized that she preferred to be alone with her thoughts and her books. She found most of the other kids immature and shallow and didn't have much in common with them to have a meaningful conversation.

Perhaps she was different from other kids her age and didn't fit in with their social groups. But one thing she learned from Mr. K and his remarkable story was that there was a vast world beyond the confines of this small school and isolated town, and whatever challenges might seem overwhelming now, were insignificant over a lifetime. Kristen, Jodi's giant gorilla this past year, would continue to be an agonizing thorn in her side, Jodi expected, and she would always need to be on her guard. But Mr. K was right in that the name calling and silly pranks couldn't hurt her if she didn't let them. Trivial annoyances compared to the nightmares he and Karina endured at her age.

As if on cue, Kristen, sporting her new blue-and-white cheerleading outfit, made her grand entrance, with all the popular kids flocking around her, vying for her attention.

Jodi took a bite of her sandwich and returned to her book.

"Hey, Jodi." Jodi looked up as Julie approached her table.

"Oh, hi, Julie. Kristen's over there." She nodded toward the door where Kristen was still greeting her groupies.

"Actually," Julie said, "she's not my friend anymore."

"I swear I didn't tell her."

"I know. She found out anyway. Seems like the whole town knows now that we lost the house."

"I'm sorry."

"You were right. She wasn't a true friend anyway."

"So how come you're not wearing your cheer outfit for the pep assembly this afternoon?"

"I dropped cheer this year. The outfit is kind of expensive."

"Oh well. I guess I'll see you later at orchestra class."

"I dropped orchestra also. I sold my violin. I didn't really like orchestra all that much anyway. I was just taking it because Kristen was, and she's only doing it because her parents are making her. I'm taking debate for my elective this year."

"Debate, huh. That should be interesting." Although Jodi couldn't fathom why anyone would want to expose themselves enough to argue a position in front of a judge.

After an awkward silence, Julie said, "I do have one thing I want to ask. Kind of a favor."

"What kind of favor?"

"Your friend Marco."

"What about him?"

"He's kind of cute. Could you maybe introduce me to him sometime?"

"Uh, sure. I suppose I could do that, although I haven't really seen him much since the tournament."

Julie's face brightened. "Oh, thank you so much. Oh, there's Sarah. I've been looking for her all morning. See ya around."

Alone again, Jodi watched Kristen work the room, flirting with the boys on the football team and one-upping all the other girls. Jodi put her elbows on the table and rested her chin in her hands as she studied Kristen. She realized her nemesis didn't look so intimidating anymore, almost a little vulnerable, and behind that facade, maybe even a little afraid, like she was hiding behind her cheer outfit, puffy hair and makeup, and phony smile.

Jodi stuffed the last bite of sandwich into her mouth and returned to her book. She lifted her head at the sound of laughter and cringed as she eyed Kristen weaving though the tables toward her.

"Hey, look, guys." The class bully shouted louder than necessary. "It's poor, lonely B-flat, sitting all by herself reading a dreadful book because no one will be her friend. What happened to your scrawny boyfriend? Were you like too ugly and boring for him too?"

Jodi's gaze locked in with Kristen's green eyes. She felt her pulse race and a trickle of sweat slip down her side. "Good afternoon, Kristen," Jodi said, trying to mask her nervousness. "I assume you had a good summer."

"Except for the Frappuccino and new outfit you owe me, it was fabulous. For sure not like your horribly embarrassing summer, sweating in front of all those jocks and causing Matt's team to lose the tournament."

"I had a fantastic summer, thank you for asking. Now if you'll excuse me, I would like to get back to my interesting book."

Glimpsing Kristen's hand twitch, Jodi whisked her half-empty can of Dr Pepper away just in front of Kristen's swooping grasp. "Nice try, Kristen, but I think I'll drink this soda instead of wearing it."

Jodi let out a silent sigh of relief as Kristen stomped off for the food line, her entourage in tow, two of the straggler girls giggling behind her back.

Jodi managed to avoid Kristen during the afternoon periods of social studies and biology. She took a deep breath, counted to four, then released it upon entering orchestra class and spying Kristen sitting in the concert leader position, tuning her expensive violin.

Jodi slipped into the back row and retrieved her scuffed-up loaner instrument and swiped a rosin block along the bow hairs.

As the second hand touched the hour mark, Mr. Johnston, in his trademark sweater vest, entered, carrying his baton, and took his squeaky raised seat on the podium. "Welcome back students," he said, his chair squeaking as he adjusted his position.

Not one for unnecessary conversation, he jumped right to the agenda, "As I mentioned at the end of last year, today we are going to audition for chairs." *Squeak.* "We'll start with the violin section." He turned *squeak* to Kristen.

"Kristen, I'm sure you've been practicing hard this summer. What are you going to play for us?"

"Good afternoon, Mr. Johnston," Kristen said in her usual pompous tone. "I am going to play the 'Bach Gavotte I.'" She snugged the violin under her chin, grasped the bow, and began to play. Jodi cringed at the raspy sound, uneven rhythm, and poor intonation as Kristen plowed through the piece, seemingly unaware of the shortcomings.

"Very nice, Kristen," Mr. Johnston said with a polite nod when she lowered her instrument, the chair quacking, as he faced the next student. "Next."

The other seven fledgling violinists struggled through much easier pieces. Finally, it was Jodi's turn.

"Okay, Jodi." He sounded bored. "What do you have for us?"

Jodi bit her lower lip, looked him in the eye, and said, "I am going to play the opening of the Brahms's 'Violin Sonata Number 1 in G Major.'"

Mr. Johnston raised an eyebrow, as if to suggest she was crazy to even consider such a feat. Like the students before her, she snugged the violin under her chin, caressed the bow between her fingertips, and with shoulders and wrist relaxed, took a deep, calming breath and began to play the sonata's sweet melody.

Mr. Johnston rested the baton on his music stand and sat a little straighter while she played. When she was finished, only the hum from the air conditioner disturbed the still room.

"That was lovely, Jodi," he finally said. "Why don't you move up here and take the concert leader position this year."

***

Jodi was so excited, she dashed to Mr. K's house after the final bell to tell him the news. She rounded the corner to his street and was startled by a flurry of activity in front of his home. A black sedan and two police cars with red and blue flashing lights were parked erratically in the street. She arrived at Mr. K's gleaming gate just as two men wearing dark suits led the old man down the walk toward her. Matt's father, dressed in his blue police uniform, stepped forward and said, "Hold on, Jodi."

"What's going on?" she cried.

"Are you Jodi Evans?" one of the men escorting Mr. K by the elbow asked.

Jodi started to panic. "What's going on? Who are you? Where are you taking him?"

"It's okay, Jodi," Mr. K said in his calm, grizzled voice. "Do you remember when I told you that I hit a man in the head with a pipe all those years ago?"

"The man who was attacking Karina?"

"Well, I must have hit him harder than I thought. These gentlemen are telling me that he died."

The man holding on to Mr. K's elbow said, "We have you to thank, young lady. If it weren't for the article in the local paper about Paint the Town, we probably never would have found him. His name automatically cross referenced with the police's database of unsolved cases."

"But he was . . ."

"Jodi," Mr. K. interrupted her. "It's going to be okay. I am an old man, and I don't have much time left. The truth will come out, but these men have a job to do." He pursed his shriveled lips and said, "I have finished with your violin. It is in the corner of the living room. It plays lovely. I know that you will take excellent care of it."

Nodding toward the battered case in her hand, he added, "You can return that one to your school."

Jodi squinted at him.

"Gentlemen"—Mr. K. turned his head toward the agent clutching his elbow—"will you please allow this young lady to retrieve her violin from my home?"

"I'll get it for her," Matt's father said and turned toward the house.

Matt's father emerged moments later with Mr. K's precious instrument, protected in a faded black case, as Jodi, tears raining down her cheeks, watched the stern detectives escort the stooped, shuffling, wrinkled old man to the idling sedan.

CHAPTER 44

Jodi was still so upset about Mr. K's arrest the previous afternoon that she didn't go to school. She called her mother and told her she had an upset stomach and needed to stay home, which was the truth, as the knot strangling her gut ever since she watched the black sedan, with Mr. K a prisoner in the backseat, disappear around the corner made her physically ill.

She sat cross-legged on her unmade bed staring at Mr. K's unopened violin case, oblivious to the ticking clock, chirping birds, and angry baby. Minutes passed. Then an hour. Then another. Finally, just like the force that drew her through that rickety gate all those months ago, her hand reached for the case and her fingers fumbled with the latch. Trembling, she lifted the precious instrument from its enclosure. A faded yellow envelope rested at the bottom of the case. She removed the letter and returned the violin. It was addressed to "Sig. Michal Kaszubinski," and the return address was Venice, Italy.

Wishing she had a smartphone so that she could translate the letter on the spot, she rummaged through her backpack for a spiral notebook and pencil. Carefully, so as not to tear the fragile yellowed paper, she removed the letter from the envelope and copied the words into her notebook. She slipped into her school clothes, ran a comb through her tangled hair, covered her head with a baseball cap, shoved the notebook into her backpack, and raced to the library.

Once back home, again crossed-legged on her bed, she reread her hand-printed copy of the translated letter.

September 17, 1945

Dearest Nephew,

It is with the deepest sadness that I must inform you of the death of your family. Your dear mother and father both perished in the Warsaw Uprising last fall when German bombs and artillery destroyed every block of the city. This violin is one of the few items recovered from the debris. I know they loved you very much and were terribly distraught by your disappearance. I hope they received my letter informing them you were well and on your way to America so they can at least rest in peace knowing that you are safe.

Your brother, Jakub, somehow survived the uprising while fighting on the side of the Germans against his own countrymen, the AK. However, he was killed when the Russians, who waited only kilometers away as the city was demolished, swept in and defeated the Germans. You can have confidence that he fought valiantly.

Michal, we will never understand why you fled your homeland with that Jewish girl. Yes, I immediately knew that she was a Jew, and I will never forgive you for putting my family in danger. But you are family, and you survived, and for that I am thankful.

Your uncle will be furious when he learns that I have sent you this violin. He has forbidden me to contact you, so I must request that you do not send a return post. I hope that you are happy with your life in America and with the choices that you have made. This violin is all that remains of your past, so cherish it and play it beautifully.

Yours,

Aunt Sophia

EPILOGUE
Future

Deep in the jungle of Central America near the border of Guatemala and El Salvador, Jodi lay on an army cot in a forest-green tent staring into the darkness, deep in thought, as the driving rain hammered the canvas ceiling.

After fierce guerrilla wars fueled by drug gangs and corrupt government officials ravaged the area in the early part of the century, the two countries had remained peaceful over the previous decade. That was until the current dictator and self-proclaimed Supreme Presidente, General Jose Francisco Neito Morales, led a military coup that overthrew the previous regime, which had implemented economic reforms that had improved the lives of many in this impoverished region. Presidente Supremo, as the dictator liked to be called, was now using the military to raid villages on both sides of the border, slaughtering the men and boys who refused to join his ruthless army and kidnapping and enslaving the women and girls. Those who managed to escape his wrath had banded together with military defectors to form their own underground army and had endured mass suffering in the fierce battles they had waged with the dictator's forces.

A soft knock sounded on the tent's wooden doorframe. Jodi clicked on the dim light, sat up in her cot, and said, "Come in."

A young man in his early twenties, wearing green scrubs and wire-rimmed glasses, poked his head through the flap. "I'm sorry to have to disturb your badly needed rest, Doctor, but another ambulance is on the way. Some are pretty young and in bad shape."

"It seems like they get younger every day," Jodi replied to the orderly with a sigh. "On my way."

The attendant disappeared, and Jodi reached for a framed picture displayed on the dented metal filing cabinet that doubled as a bedside table. She sighed as she gazed at the charcoal sketch of her and Mr. K that Juan had presented to her all those years ago. It was her most prized possession, along with Mr. K's violin, and it held a prominent place on her bedside table wherever she was located. She examined the young girl staring back from the drawing, hardly recognizing the scared, lonely, homely kid. In fact, there was a certain confidence radiating from those bright eyes and an attractiveness she was unaware of, at the time, in the proud face smiling back at her. She studied the stooped old man's sparkling eyes and wrinkled features and smiled at the memory of their summer together. She had read in the paper that the charges against him had been dropped due to lack of witnesses, but he never returned to Sage Grove, and she never saw him again.

She took another deep breath and said out loud to the picture, "Mr. K, when are we going to learn not to hate anymore?" She returned the drawing to the table, slipped into her raincoat, pulled her Portland Trailblazers cap low over her eyes, and darted into the driving rain.

An Impossible Promise

ABOUT THE AUTHOR

T. Lynne Jackson holds a BS in Accounting from Central Washington University and an MBA from San Jose State University. When not crunching numbers or writing, she can be found running and hiking the trails near her home in the Pacific Northwest with her dogs.

Contact T. Lynne at:
tlynnejackson.author@gmail.com
Facebook\tlynnejackson.author\